BEND
IN
THE
RIVER

BEND IN THE RIVER

A NOVEL

MICHAEL BANKS

First paperback edition September 2025

Book design by Damonza

Ebook: 979-8-9997868-0-7
Paperback: 979-8-9997868-1-4
Hardcover: 979-8-9997868-2-1

www.authormichaelbanks.com

For Mom, who told me I had a story within me.

And Danette, who believed in me. And loved me.

PROLOGUE

EARLY IN THE morning, on the day Christ was born, grey fog clung thick to the brown syrup that is the Ohio River.

Gravel crunched beneath the wheels of the pickup and the trailer carrying the john boat squeaked as it bounced over a pothole at the top of the secluded and empty boat ramp. The two men inside the cab were alone.

Far off, there was the screech of a hawk on the hunt in a field of broken and shattered stalks and field mice scattered, some innate sense in their tiny minds telling them that death came from above and it would be the slowest who suffered the most.

"It's cold," said the older of the two.

"The best time to hunt," said his companion.

The sun would not rise for another hour yet and it would sit snug behind the thick cloud bank that enveloped the Ohio River Valley this day. This fertile land sprouts fields of unending green after the farmers plant seed and the spring rains fall, but in the dregs of winter, the landscape is as barren and unforgiving as some of the hearts of those who call it home. It's a painting without color, there being only subtle shifts of gray, from the fog bank that remains, pushed by the winds from the north, its droplets clinging to the sides of the grey Ford, to the camouflage of the two hunters who stared out the windshield at the river and watched a thick, black hunk of driftwood pass, the remains of a hickory fallen upriver.

The thermos in his hand was red and the older of the men sipped, embracing the warmth of the coffee, black and strong. The red reminded him of candy canes, those thumb-thick blocks of sugar that by now had slowly started to melt in the stockings left there by the hearth where a log still burned and gifts were unopened. The man, a dentist, thought not only of candy and children and grandchildren, but also of cleanings and cavities and fillings and an appointment book filled through Halloween, when the process would begin anew.

Hours earlier, he'd lain in bed and listened to the quiet of their home. There'd not been the excited pitter-patter of tiny bare feet of grandchildren upon their wooden floors nor the sound of laughter and conversation from sons and daughters from afar who'd come to gather around the tree.

No, it was just the two of them — he and Virginia. Nearly 16 years now. Sure, they'd tried when they'd first married. He chuckled. Oh, how many times they tried and in oh so many places and positions. He sipped more of the coffee though the taste brought him no great pleasure. He was a man of science and they had studied books and read colorful pamphlets and there were appointments, but neither they nor the doctors nor shamans could deliver what they so desired. And so they continued on.

And life became routine, and anniversaries and birthdays came and went. They became older, he now 54, and eventually they quit trying and they talked of children no more. They'd discuss great literature and he'd read her passages of Hemingway and she'd smile politely and say "that's nice, darling" and stare out their front window across the yard to the street where the neighborhood kids rode their bikes.

Virginia had not stirred when he slipped from beneath the warm covers that morning. He'd paused and watched her in her sleep — for a minute, maybe two — then he'd closed the door and ventured out into the pre-dawn darkness and to the river where he now sat.

"Cold as a witch's tit," the dentist said and sipped again from his thermos.

"I'm glad you're here."

"Where else would I be? Warm in bed?"

The hunter grinned and gripped the steering wheel. He had no great need of coffee. Adrenaline pumped through his body and his fingers tapped the wheel, a rhythmic tap, tap… tap, tap, tap. Tap, tap… tap, tap, tap. Tap, tap… tap, tap, tap.

"It's nice. Just the two of us," said the hunter. He nodded. "More ducks for us, right?"

"Yes," the man said. "More ducks for us."

The man had not hesitated when the hunter phoned earlier in the week. In fact, the invite brought him great joy. It was early in the season and ducks would be on the move with the cold weather pushing from the north. His mind had already shifted from work to the sloughs and the river bottoms and the mallards and geese who came there for a brief respite on their travels south.

The fact it was Christmas morning was no matter. He'd spent the afternoon of Christmas Eve reading "The Short, Happy Life of Francis McComber" and that evening he'd told Virginia of his plans and she said, "that's nice, darling" and she'd sipped her gin and carefully wound a red ribbon around his gift till it tightened into a neat, tidy bow.

"I'm really glad it's just us," the hunter said.

"Duly noted."

"You think the ducks will come?"

"They'll come."

"I hope so," said the hunter. "Fresh duck on the table. That will be a feast."

The man smiled and placed the cap on his thermos. "Well, we'll not kill them from here, will we?"

They climbed from the truck and stepped into waders and put on stocking caps and slipped their hands into thick gloves. The man leaned back, his hand upon his hip and turned his face to the sky. The sharp morning wind sliced between the opening of his top collar and he winced when his bare skin was exposed.

"That wind," he said. "It's cold."

"Wait till we're on the water," said the hunter. "Then, you'll feel what cold really is."

They slid the jon boat off the trailer and into the water and the man held the line while the hunter parked the truck beneath a tall sycamore, its branches barren and reaching upwards into the sky softening with the coming morning light.

The man's breath hung in the air, frozen, and he smelled the dampness of the river. He watched the hunter walk down the ramp and toward him, in his arms the guns that would hopefully bring death later that morn. The hunter was big and muscled. The bulky layers of camouflage failing to hide his thick shoulders and long arms. Being a lawman, the hunter knew his way around weapons and those with guilty inclinations.

The two had fostered a friendship over beers at the Coon Club and they'd hunted grouse, doves and turkeys. The hunter had told him he was a good shot and the feeling was mutual. They rarely talked when together in the fields, each comfortable with the other's silence and they both preferred it that way.

Today was their first time on the water together.

"Age before beauty," said the hunter and he handed the man the guns. Then he pushed the boat from the ramp and it slid along the gravel till it cleared, rocking only as the hunter lifted himself up and over the man and into the back of the boat. He pulled once, then twice, the motor firing and the keel turned and pointed upriver.

In the bow, the man held the guns and he took comfort in that, their weight secure against his arms. He bent his head and tucked, twisting his upper body to look back at the hunter, his body upright, cheeks red from the whip of the wind, and the slight uptick of a grin, the stubble on his jaw not quite hidden by the fog.

"Let the hunt begin," the hunter shouted against the wind.

And the man turned and he looked upriver and he gripped the guns and he thought of ducks and he thought of love and deceit. And his finger felt the trigger, hard steel, unforgiving and uncaring, and he caressed the trigger's rough edges, saying to himself, "Yes, let the hunt begin."

And the fog moved swiftly to cover their wake and envelop them in a blanket of wet gray, the sound of the outboard slowly fading, and there was no sight of shore, just two men in a small boat, alone against the Ohio's cold current formed long before them and long before others before them.

And the fog took them.

And they were not seen alive again.

CHAPTER ONE

TOM CRUTCHFIELD WAS certain he'd been here before. It was one of those feelings that sit in the back of the mind and appear at the most unexpected of times. Sort of like a sparrow pecking at a window pane, its own reflection a threat.

He tapped his fingers against the front panel of his Ford Fairlane, the car's aqua green a splash of mint below the orange Gulf sign perched above the gas station.

Tom wished he'd not given up smoking at his mother's request. As he'd packed his bags last summer and prepared to leave for another year's learning in Lexington, she had stood in the doorway and said, "It's a nasty habit, Tom. And it will bring you nothing but trouble in later years."

And so he'd quit. But, at this instance, he craved a Chesterfield. So, instead of a long pull, he drummed his fingers against the metal.

An icy wind gusted suddenly from the north, down what appeared to be a deserted Main Street, the wind's path funneled between the Ford and gas pumps. Tom pulled the collar of his field coat tighter against his neck and hunched his shoulders and wondered why he'd left his gloves there on the front seat, the leather fingers splayed and in stark contrast to the opened white envelope on which they lay.

He'd gotten out of the car to stretch his legs, but now wondered if that had been a mistake to leave the warmth of the car. In fact, Tom was starting to have seconds thoughts as to whether he'd acted in haste when he'd silently pulled shut the front door just before dawn and driven three hours to this seemingly forgotten piece of western Kentucky.

"Bitter cold," said the man, closing the hood of the Fairlane and wiping his large hands on a dirty shop rag. "Oil looks good. This here's a fine vehicle."

Tom nodded. The Meadowvale Green two-door sedan with its quick-as-a-cat V8, half-moon-shaped tail lamps and smooth tail fins had been a gift from his father upon his high school graduation four years earlier. His father had handed him the keys and tuition at Transylvania, along with the unsaid expectation of a business degree four years later and a return home to Valley Station and a small office at Crutchfield Construction, two doors down from dad. Not too close, but not too far either.

"Don't see many of these round these parts," said the man, topping off the fuel and placing the hose back on the pump with a clank. Tom knew the man had already glanced at his license plate and was wondering what brought this young man and this sharp, clean piece of machinery to this small town that seemed to have sprouted up from the flat fields that surrounded it.

Tom anticipated the question before the fuel jockey asked. He considered knowing what another person was going to ask before the thought ever entered their mind, well, that was one special gift.

"Where about you from?" the man asked on cue, cocking

his hairless head, the hands and rag a constant motion. Tom knew the next query would have to do with what brought him here to this fine city.

Time to clip this interview.

"Points north," Tom answered.

"Ah, yes," the man said, stuffing the rag in the back pocket of his work pants. The stuffing of the dirty rag a truce.

"Damn bitter cold," the man said.

"How much?"

"Ten will do it."

As Tom pulled two fives from his wallet, the sound of a siren filled the frigid air. He and the attendant watched a sheriff's car, its blue lights flashing, speed down Main and head to the hills that rose in the northwest. Soon after, three pickup trucks also sped north, blue smoke spitting from their tailpipes as their drivers punched the pedal.

"How 'bout that," the man said, leaning around Tom to watch as the convoy raced out of town.

"Guessing that doesn't happen too often?"

"No, sir. Not much happens here in Morgan's Gap."

Tom had already figured as much. He'd left Crutchfield manor just before 6 a.m. and the two-lane state highway had been mostly deserted, its yellow lines and his aqua green Fairlane the only spot of color in a dismal grey world. He'd passed the Newton County line and, soon after, the entrance to Camp Winchester, the old military post looking largely deserted, the exception being the outline of a lone sentry seated in a guard house at the front gate.

Along the road, hungry, sharp-eyed hawks had sat perched on power lines, looking for brave field mice, as the Fairlane passed beneath and Tom gripped his steering wheel just a little tighter. It was only when he passed the "Welcome to Morgan's Gap" sign at the city limits did his grip loosen, welcomed by the ornamental green wreaths and red candy canes attached to sides of power poles, their lights blinking like fireflies trapped in a jar.

The town was eerily quiet, even if it was the day after Christmas, and most folks were slow to stir this Saturday morning, seemingly content with their coffee and the fire in their stoves.

Maybe that's why the sound of sirens was so jarring. If it had been a warm spring day, there would have been mothers and daughters picking over Easter outfits at the Tot Shop and fathers and sons at the Western Auto, dad looking for a new mower, the boy asking for a new baseball glove. Maybe then, Tom would not have heard the sirens.

But it wasn't spring. It was December 26, 1964. And the mothers and daughters and fathers and sons were not there on the streets. Just the man at the gas pump who had cleaned the Fairlane's windshield, checked its oil and made a quick note of Tom, who himself had been described by his mother as having "never-ending curiosity about things."

That curiosity had led him as a boy to take a scalpel and cut open a bullfrog he'd pulled from the creek that ran behind their home and pull out the frog's innards to see how it functioned. That quest for information had fostered a friendship with the matronly Valley Station librarian, who introduced him to Faulkner and Wolfe and Fitzgerald and sparked his yearning for places far and ideas new. That idea to take the path less chosen led him away from stupor-inducing business and accounting courses at Transylvania across town to the University of Kentucky and its student newspaper, the *Kernel*, where he sought stories and asked questions and wrote words that he believed made a difference.

He glanced to his front seat and, once again, saw the white envelope postmarked 10 days earlier with the seal of the Morgan's Gap Post Office. Slanted letters in black ink, like the feet of crows scavenging a snowy crest, spelled his name and address in Valley Station. If he'd known the words inside and the betrayal and mystery that accompanied them, perhaps he would have never opened the envelope, rather, tossed it into the open flame that burned in the hearth of the Crutchfield's great room.

But he'd not done so.

Again, he was a curious sort.

And, again, he heard the sirens, the pitch of their peal dimming with distance.

"What's to the north?" Tom asked.

"That be the river," said the man.

"And what's there?"

"Must be something if they're running that fast."

The man squinted and he seemed to sniff the morning air as though he wished to join the hunt.

"Seems like we're all chasing something," he said. "Don't you think?"

Tom didn't answer, but opened his door and started his Fairlane. And he steered his car to the north, to the hills, the bottom lands and cold, brown waters of the Ohio.

CHAPTER TWO

THE MULE, STANDING there alone in the middle of the gravel road, should have served as fair warning this day would be far from ordinary.

Earlier, Tom had pressed his foot to the accelerator and tried to keep pace with the sheriff's car and the trucks that fled Morgan's Gap, but he soon lost sight of the caravan when his car descended into a valley covered by a thick, rolling fog. He turned on his headlights, quick enough to catch a weathered sign reading Taylor's Ferry before the words were lost in the grey.

The Fairlane slowed and he turned right at a four-way intersection and soon found himself on a road of potholes, one so jarring he feared it would bend his tire rim and he dropped his speed even more. Whitewashed frame houses were shadowy figures on his periphery, and he was in the midst of looking for a street sign or any semblance of human interaction when the mule suddenly appeared out of the mist.

Tom hit his brakes hard and his back wheels grabbed at the crumbling gravel before skidding to a stop, a few feet from the mule's back haunches. The mule didn't bolt, but rather turned its head to stare through the windshield at Tom. A two-foot length of black rope, torn and tattered at its end, hung from the mule's halter and a swath of brown mud clung to the hide along its back rump.

"Crazy ass mule," Tom muttered. He hit the horn and the mule didn't budge. Instead, it turned its head and stared back out into the fog. Tom hit the horn again, this time pressing a little longer, and still the mule held his position.

"Jesus," Tom said and he thought of backing up and going down another side street. *Only to get even more lost. Plus, it's just a damn stubborn mule. You going to let a mule dictate the day?*

He unrolled his window, stuck his head out and whistled at the mule, mute as a statue. "Hey mule, get on now." The mule only stamped his hoof, splashing the water that lingered in one of the potholes.

Tom had just started to open his door when a woman appeared out of the mist, moving fast.

"Git," said her voice, low and menacing, almost a growl.

A pointed finger attached to a skinny arm, emerged from a red-and-black tartan coat that seemed to swallow the woman whole. Eyes blue as cobalt the only color in her weathered face, framed by thin, long hair that moved with the wind. She stood at the edge of the street and her eyes darted from left to right. Her lips moved in constant motion, matching her fingers that opened and closed.

"I'm just…," Tom started.

"Git," she repeated.

The woman moved fast and her feet made no sound and soon she had grasped the rope hanging from the halter.

"Fool," she said and Tom didn't know whether the words were for him or the mule.

Her hand caressed the mule's haunches and the animal

stood still and Tom watched in amazement as the woman threw a bare leg over its back and climbed on top. Her long hair hung over the mule's neck as she whispered in its ear and grabbed ahold its ears and the mule began to walk and, soon, both slid into the whiteness of nothing and Tom was left alone.

His hands gripped the steering wheel and he again felt the warmth of the heater and wondered at what he had just witnessed. Tom had left home not really certain of what he would find or who exactly he was seeking.

They'd had duck for their Christmas meal and Tom had thought of telling them then that he was leaving school. That he'd not go back at the beginning of the new year. Maybe in the fall he'd return, if he found the answers he sought. But Tom knew his parents would not understand and as his mother spooned cherry cobbler into bowls for him and his father, he'd stayed silent and silently vowed that before dawn he'd head west.

The motor hummed and the Fairlane moved forward and Tom could smell and taste the mist that entered through his open window. He hoped the river was close and, after the mule and the mystery woman, he'd not been as surprised when a boy appeared ahead of him, his hand slapping a red ball in a steady whap, whap, whap as it bounced on the road.

"You lost, mister?" the boy asked when the Fairlane pulled alongside.

"You can say that," Tom said with a smile.

The boy's hand reached out to touch the green paint, wet with dew, but pulled his hand back when he saw Tom's eyes. He held the red ball tight against his hip.

"What you looking for?"

"There was a woman and a mule."

"Don't know about that," said the boy and he began to

bounce the ball again. The steady whap, whap, whap keeping time with the Fairlane's eight cylinders.

"There was a police car, sirens and all that."

"Saw that," the boy said. "They likely headed to the river."

"Any chance you tell me how I go about finding the river?"

The bounce of the ball stopped and the boy looked past where Tom had come.

"River ain't hard to find," he said, then looked back at Tom. "A lot of times it'll find you."

Tom reached into his pocket and held the coins out the window.

"Two quarters, all I got. That help me find the river?"

The boy took the money and put the coins in his pocket.

"You turn around, go back the way you came. Stop at the main road, the one that ain't got no potholes. Turn right and then turn left when you see them three big silos. Go on out past the flood gate and you'll find the river."

Tom nodded his head and went to roll up his window, but paused. "You sure you haven't seen a woman and a mule?"

The boy shook his head. He then looked left and to his right and came close and put his hand on the edge of the half-closed window.

"You come looking for them two men on the river? That's what them sirens are after."

"How you know that?" Tom asked.

"I hear things."

The boy smiled and sticky chocolate clung to his teeth.

"You know what else? They ain't gonna find 'em. They like that woman and that mule. You all just chasing ghosts."

The boy turned and Tom heard his words and raised his eyes to the mirror and watched the bounce of the ball, the spot of red a steady up and down until it was no more and there was nothing but the whiteness of the fog. He turned the Fairlane and aimed toward the river.

CHAPTER THREE

THE BOY HAD not lied. The river had been easy to find once his car cleared the flood gates and left Taylor's Ferry behind. The fog had lifted just enough for Tom to see the blue lights off in the distance. He followed and turned onto a gravel road that led to a parking area filling with vehicles.

They were mainly pickups and the men who jumped out from them quickly formed circles. Nearly all the men wore hats, a few nice fedoras, but mostly caps handed out by seed companies. Some wore suits, but most were in coveralls to fend off the chill left by the morning mist.

Tom found an open space beneath a bare sycamore and shut off his engine. He noticed a few men who turned to look at the spotless Ford Fairlane before they shrugged and rejoined their circle. Two police cars were parked near the ramp that led down to the river's edge. Standing beside them were two lawmen and Tom figured the larger of the two was the man in charge as he stood with folded arms, listening to the other who gestured toward the river and then to the other side of the parking lot where a truck sat with an empty boat trailer behind it.

"What year's that Fairlane?"

The voice surprised Tom and he turned to see two boys

had come up behind him from the willows that bordered the parking lot. It was the heavier of the two who had spoken and he nodded back toward the car.

"I'm guessing it's a '61, looking at them taillights."

Tom glanced down at the mud that clung to the boy's boots and the blue jeans he'd stuffed inside them. He reached into his pocket for a cigarette, forgetting again he'd quit the habit.

"Close enough," Tom said. "It's a '60. You notice those taillights are half-moons. The '61 has got a round light, looks like a jet engine."

"Told you, Robbie," the boy said as he slapped the shoulder of his friend, who stood taller and was more reserved. Robbie wore a navy sock hat pulled low over his ears so just his eyebrows and brown eyes peered out. The boy looked as though he wanted to say something, but stayed silent, digging his hands farther into his two front pockets.

"What's under that hood? A V-8? I'm betting she'll hit 100 won't she?"

Tom chuckled. "Haven't pushed it that hard. She's fast enough. Gets me where I need to be."

He nodded to the two lawmen, who had walked down the ramp and were staring out at the river.

"What's going on there?"

"That's the sheriff and Stick."

"Stick?"

"Yeah, he's the deputy. He's the one got here first. They're looking for them two men."

"Two men?"

"Dr. Webb and Dutch. People say they went out duck hunting Christmas morning. Haven't been seen since." The heavier boy nodded to the nearby truck and trailer. "That's Dutch's truck."

Tom watched as the sheriff and his deputy walked up the ramp. He saw the sheriff scan the crowd and linger on his Fairlane parked beneath the sycamore. He stared for a moment at Tom and the two boys before turning to talk again to his deputy.

"You're not from around here, are you?" the heavier boy asked. "I mean most folks know Stick."

Tom reached into his front pocket and pulled out a notebook and pencil. "It's been a while," Tom said. "Why they call him Stick?"

"Well, you see him don't you? Skinny as a rail. But my daddy says he got the name because he's got about just as many brains as a cord of wood."

The boy's eyes widened when he saw Tom begin to write. The taller one started to fidget and he stole a glance at the circle of men nearby who were taking in the newcomer and his two new friends.

"You said the one's a doctor?" Tom asked.

"Nah, he's a dentist. Over in Morgan's Gap. Every time I go, he tells me I got more cavities and I need to brush and floss more. A big pain."

"And the other guy... Dutch? He's like his fishing buddy?"

The heavy boy laughed. "You sure aren't from around here. You not going fishing in December. Heck, they were crazy to go out on the river looking for ducks. Most people knew there was a bad storm coming in. You'd think Dutch would know better. He's spent most of his life on the river, him being a game warden and all that."

Tom wrote and the heavy boy leaned closer to try and get a look at what was on his pad.

"You like a cop or something?" the boy asked.

Tom wrote some more. "Just call me curious."

The sound of a trailer hitting a pothole caught their attention and the three of them turned to watch as a pickup pulled into the parking area with a large boat on the trailer. On its side, written in bold red letters, were the words River Rescue #1. Following close behind were two state police cruisers and three more pickups. The sheriff walked over and leaned into the window of the lead truck and, soon after, the pickup turned and backed the trailer into the water. Two troopers wearing wide-brimmed hats and dark windbreakers exited their cars and gathered with the sheriff as the various circles of men edged closer to the action.

"State boys," said the heavier boy. "Don't see them much, unless it's like a killing or something."

He leaned in close to Tom. "You think there's been a killing?"

Tom stopped writing.

"Shug!"

The boy stepped back and a frown flashed quick across his face. The voice had come from a circle of men nearby. One of them stepped forward, in his hand a black, steel-tipped cane. He wore a pinstriped suit, the four buttons of the vest latched tight. He was one of sharp angles, his jawline coming to a point and elbows that jutted out from his reed-like body. A black mustache lay over thin, pursed lips. And there was no mud upon his black leather boots.

"Come here, son."

Shug glanced up at Tom as if he was ready to say something else.

"Now!"

And the boy turned and walked toward his father, who grabbed onto his shoulder, spoke into his ear and then pulled him into the group of men who stood near. The man turned and eyed Tom for a good few seconds and then joined the crowd as it moved toward the top of the boat ramp.

Tom turned to ask a question of Shug's friend, *Robbie, wasn't it?*, but the tall, silent boy had slunk back into the reeds near the willows — disappearing just as easily as he'd suddenly emerged from the cane break a few minutes earlier.

By the time Tom had gathered at the fringe of the gathering, the sheriff had climbed into the bed of a pickup and was asking for volunteers, men who had boats. Three or four left and the rest gathered close to hear the sheriff over a cold wind that was starting to blow stronger from the northwest.

"What you hoping to find, sheriff?" one yelled out.

"Well, Dutch and Dr. Webb, of course."

"They were fools to go out."

"That might be, but —"

"The river was running rough yesterday. Waves two to three feet. Damn fools."

The sheriff spread his hands. "Fools or not, we're going to find those men."

Some of the crowd looked down at the ground, shaking their heads, whispering to each other.

"I'll need volunteers to walk the banks," the sheriff continued. "You'll be looking for cushions, oars, things like that from the boat."

Tom noticed the sheriff failed to mention bodies. He wondered how long a man could stand being submerged in freezing water in late December. He pulled his coat tighter around his neck and stuffed his hands in his pockets, wishing again he'd remembered to grab the leather gloves on his front seat.

"Now, the state police are going to be helping out and they tell me Fish and Wildlife will be sending help, especially with Dutch being one of their own. So, we got to coordinate. The rescue boat's heading out and everybody else will need to check in with Stick. He'll get you sorted and we'll start searching the bank."

The sheriff paused.

"Now, both families know. In fact, it was Mrs. Webb who called early this morning and said Doc didn't come home last night. But remember, this is still a rescue. Those men could be holed up on one of those sandbars, wet and cold, waiting for us to find them. And each minute we spend here thinking the worst is a minute more they're out there in the cold. So, let's get to it."

The crowd dispersed and Tom lingered, watching as the sheriff spoke once more to the state troopers. He pulled the notebook from his pocket and started to write, noting the men who started to walk the river bank as two more boats were backed into the river. A stray brown pup, its fur matted, darted in and out along the edges of the parking lot, looking for a scrap from a group of men passing around a thermos.

"Help you?"

The deep voice came from down within the barrel of the man's chest. That was the first thing Tom noticed. It was one of those bass voices you'd hear in church on Sundays when the choir broke into "Swing Low, Sweet Chariot." The man smelled of peppermints and Tom heard the crunch of one being mashed by the big jaws that protruded and flexed from below the flat brim of his hat. The sheriff's eyes, like dark pebbles, sat deep in the folds of skin. The sheriff nodded toward the green Fairlane parked beneath the sycamore.

"That yours?"

Tom nodded, the notebook and pencil still in his hands.

"Fayette County plates," the sheriff said, jaws flexing as he crunched the mint. "That's a ways from here."

Tom figured it was more a statement than a question. *What's it your business anyways,* he wanted to answer. Instead, he shrugged and looked over at the edge of the cane break where the mutt sat, its rib bones showing through the fur. The dog looked hungry, like it needed a home.

He looked back at the sheriff and held his gaze.

"Noticed you didn't say anything about bodies."

The crunching stopped and the sheriff looked down at the writing pad.

"You a reporter or something?"

Tom considered the question. If his father had his way, then he'd be finishing up his engineering degree — ready to write contracts to build roads and bridges in small towns and boondocks like this. Two years earlier, his father had shrugged and walked off when Tom told his parents he was transferring to the University of Kentucky to study journalism. His mother had risen from her chair and gone into the kitchen. Tom had stood alone in the parlor listening as she had begun to put up dishes. He'd entered when he heard a saucer hit the floor. "Mistakes," she'd said and left the room, leaving Tom to pick up the scattered pieces.

So, was he a reporter?

"I guess you can say so," Tom answered. "And you're Sheriff...."

"Sturgill."

Tom began to write. "That's S-T-..."

"I've got nothing for the press."

"It looks like you've got two missing men."

Sturgill resumed chewing his peppermint. "I'm thinking we'll find them soon enough."

"And the two missing, they are..."

"We're not releasing any names quite yet."

"But, it's the doc and, let's see, uh, Dutch, right?"

"I said, 'We're not releasing any names.'"

Tom looked out at the river as a boat turned over its engine and pulled away, three men in its bow and another behind the wheel.

"You suspect foul play, sheriff?"

Sturgill reached up and with the back of his hand wiped a bead of snot from the tip of his nose. He sniffed once, then twice.

"What paper you with, anyhow?" he asked as he looked over Tom's hair that stretched past the collar of his flannel shirt, and down to his brown corduroy slacks and loafers. "You don't look like anybody J.C. would hire for that rag of his."

Tom had wrapped up work on the final edition for the student newspaper, *The Kernel*, earlier that month. It'd be another four weeks before students would return to campus. He'd not be among them. The letter and his parents' response had seen to that.

"I guess I'm between jobs, right now."

"Well, I guess I'm out of answers, then. You take care, Mister.... "

"Crutchfield. Tom Crutchfield."

The sheriff nodded, then turned and walked back down the ramp to the water's edge.

As more people gathered, Tom remembered his camera. He pulled the Pentax from the trunk of his car and began to shoot a roll of film. He saw the boy Shug, his hands crossed in front of him, standing behind his father, who was leaning forward, both hands upon his cane, talking to a group of men. Across the parking lot, a group of women had gathered and Tom smelled coffee as they handed paper cups to those who walked the shoreline and boarded boats. He searched for the mutt, but the dog had disappeared. And with his final frame, he zoomed in to capture the flow of a wake left behind by a boat that faded from view.

The photos were good. That he knew. And he had the makings of a good story. Two hunters go missing on the Ohio River on Christmas Day. One a dentist, the other a game warden. No sign of their boat nor them.

He'd not had a story like this while at the *Kernel*. He'd written of parking problems on campus, raids at fraternity beer parties and a review of "Ivan the Terrible." His father had not been impressed when Tom had showed him the review, saying, "I'm paying tuition for you to watch movies now?" His mother had said, "That's nice, Tom" and then asked if he'd thought there was too much salt in the potatoes.

That had been then. This was now.

CHAPTER FOUR

"SOME SAY A single powerful photo can convey much more than a thousand words."

Tom turned and regarded the man who had quietly walked up on him. He wore a plaid wool coat and a navy bucket hat pulled low to where it sat just above a pair of bushy white eyebrows. The man shrugged as he pulled a white handkerchief from inside his coat and wiped at the condensation that had gathered on the lens of his wire-framed glasses.

"Me? I'd argue one could take whatever meaning they will from a photo. Whereas, if done correctly, carefully considered words can paint a scene and give meaning and much more."

The man slid the glasses back upon the perch of his nose and offered Tom his hand. "JC Wheeler. Pleased to meet your acquaintance."

Tom was surprised at the strength of the grip that came from one who stood not more than five foot, five inches. He answered, "Thomas Crutchfield, sir."

The man turned and regarded the ramp where another boat was backing into the water and another had started to make a slow circle in the brown waters of the Ohio.

"What do you make of this all hubbub, Mr. Crutchfield?"

Tom considered the man who stood beside him, his hands sunk into his pockets, head cocked as he watched the men and women along the river.

"Appears to be a search of some kind."

A smile slowly formed at the corners of his mouth. "Quite astute, Mr. Crutchfield."

He nodded at the camera and the corner of the reporter's notebook that stuck out from the top of Tom's coat pocket. "That's all the intel you gathered during your short conversation with our high sheriff?"

Tom reached down and folded his coat pocket over the notebook, away from prying eyes. "What'd you say your name was again?"

"Junious Caliphate Wheeler. My acquaintances call me JC, easier on the tongue and the old memory bank. Others, well, they may opt for various breeds of certain four-letter words and their vulgar off-shoots. Those variations often follow news articles in *The Register* that do not shine quite the positive light upon said individual and his doings."

"*The Register?*"

"My handiwork, my mistress, Mr. Crutchfield. *The Newton County Register.* Your most reliable source for the unvarnished news of this here county."

Tom slowly unwound the film in his camera, popped open the back and held the cartridge between his fingers.

"I've got a roll of film here and a notebook full of quotes."

"That you do."

JC reached into his wool coat and pulled out his own note-book. A man with a rope in hand and the other carrying a cup of coffee grunted as he passed by. The newspaper editor nodded and turned back to Tom.

"Crutchfield is not a name we hear in Newton County."

"I'd reckon not."

"And what brings a visitor to the river's edge on a winter's day?"

"Just a visit."

"How long a visit?"

Tom remembered the white envelope that still sat there on his front seat, the letters scrawled in black.

"Not sure yet."

JC leaned back and took a deep draw of the brisk morning air. "And I take it that fine green vehicle parked beneath the sycamore is your's, Mr. Crutchfield?"

Tom grinned. "Quite astute, Mr. Wheeler."

JC nodded at the film canister in Tom's hand. "And that?"

"I'd say it's your front page this week."

JC leaned forward. "A lovely Christmas cantata by the First Baptist choir is my front page this week, Mr. Crutchfield."

"I'd say this is better than that."

JC shook his head and turned his eyes upward toward a darkening western sky. "Walk with me, Mr. Crutchfield?"

Tom nodded and the two of them walked down the ramp toward where the bulk of Sheriff Sturgill stood by the water, arms crossed, his deputy Stick standing sentry beside him.

"Sheriff Sturgill wasn't the most forthcoming," Tom said as a warning.

"That's not a surprise," JC said. "I endorsed his challenger in the last election a couple years back. Cullen, he's not one to let bygones be bygones."

They made their way to the river where the two lawmen stood.

"Mr. Wheeler," said the deputy.

"Stick," answered JC.

Sturgill's head turned and he glanced at JC then Tom and back to JC. "He with you?"

JC paused for a moment, looked over at Tom and answered, "At the moment."

The sheriff chewed his peppermint and looked back out at the river.

"Any sign of Doc or Dutch?" JC asked.

Sturgill shook his head.

"Found the boat?"

The sheriff pulled his hat lower and a slight stream of water tipped from the bill.

"That boy Shug Lincoln did find that styrofoam cooler washed up," Stick said.

"Oh yeah?" JC asked with a quick turn to the deputy.

Sturgill's eyes cast a hard glance at the junior lawman and Stick went silent. The four of them stood and looked out at the river. A smudge could be seen through the thickening mist as a small boat made a zig-zag pattern, trying to stay on path despite the push of a northwest wind and the swift current. Tom shivered as he felt the wetness strike the back of his neck.

"So," JC said, "I figure I'll just ask around, see what people are saying."

He and Tom turned and were a few steps away when they heard Sturgill's voice. "Stay out of my way, Junious. You and the boy."

JC turned as if to answer with a wise retort, apparently thought better of it and pointed his head toward two men leaned against a pickup, one holding an umbrella, the other a jug he brought to his lips. The two nodded when JC and Tom walked up and offered the jug when JC pulled a half-pint of whiskey from the front pocket of his coat.

"Something to fight the chill," JC said.

They murmured and passed the bottle and Tom felt the sharp bite of the whiskey when it hit the back of his throat and then the soothing warmth as it spread across his chest and filled his belly.

"Heard anything, Wayne?" JC asked, taking another sip and passing the bottle to the bigger of the two men. Wayne held the bottle to his lips, paused and then took a long pull. He passed it to his friend and wiped the back of his hand across his lips.

"Nobody's back yet," he said. "Figure they not gonna find anything out on that river. Damn mess it is. About as bad as that storm that came through late yesterday. River's running rough."

"Think they could hole up on one of those sandbars if the boat did get swamped?"

Wayne shook his head. "You're not starting a fire in this."

JC turned to Tom and told him how he'd written a story that previous summer on the 35-pound catfish Wayne pulled from the river not far from here. He'd used chicken livers and he'd fought the cat for about 15 minutes before pulling him from the bottom where the big fish like to feed.

"Wayne's been fishing on this river his whole life," JC said. "Ain't that right, Wayne?"

The big man looked down and kicked his foot out at piece of gravel that landed in an ever-growing puddle of dark water. "You say so, Mr. Wheeler."

A gust of wind came stronger and nearly knocked the umbrella from the man's hand. Rain hit Tom's face and he felt the clock ticking as the light started to fade. *We're wasting time talking about catfish and chicken livers.* He stood silent as JC went on and on about how Wayne's mom had called the paper, bragging on her son's accomplishment as if the big catfish was a medical school diploma.

There was a story here and JC was missing it.

"What about Doctor Webb?" Tom asked. "He a fisherman? You see him down here often?"

Wayne looked up at Tom and then glanced at JC, who nodded his head.

"Nah, sir. I don't know that man. But Dutch, he's down here all the time."

Wayne pointed to JC. "Soon as you did that story, the next week I'm down there past the grain dock, fishing like I always was, looking for them cats that like to feed off that spilled corn and beans, and Dutch rolls up, asking me if I got my license. He was always busting my chops. Shit, man didn't even have a real badge. Play police all he is."

Tom raised his eyebrows. "Are you saying Dutch roughed you up?"

Wayne gave Tom a hard glance. "Who is this guy, Mr. Wheeler?"

Tom felt JC reach over and touch his arm. "He's still learning, Wayne." Tom took the bottle that was offered and, embarrassed at JC's remark, he angrily took a swig. He felt the warmth spread quicker this time.

"You weren't down here, yesterday, Wayne?" JC asked.

"No, sir. There's a lot of times I like to come down here and just sit. You know, watch the river, how the current pulls that driftwood, the tugs pushing them barges, all headed somewhere else. Other days I fish. But yesterday, being Christmas and all, me and momma walked down to my aunt's."

"Christmas dinner?"

"Yes, sir. Ham, greens, sweet potatoes. Hell, Mr. Wheeler, I helped myself to two helpings of peach cobbler while listening to that wind and rain blow outside. There was nowhere else to be. Sure as hell not down by the river."

Hearing Wayne talk of ham and cobbler, Tom's stomach churned, the whiskey sitting hard on his empty stomach. He thought of his mother and how she took delight in feeding him when he'd come home from college. She'd found new recipes in her *Better Homes and Garden* and the beef stroganoff was good, but he still favored her barbecued pork chops and macaroni. He felt a pang of guilt at not waking her and telling her goodbye when he'd left earlier that morning, which now seemed days ago.

The four of them turned as they heard the sound of an outboard motor in the distance and watched as three boats made their way to the ramp. They shuffled with the others to the river's edge and watched as mooring lines were tossed to those on the bank. Sheriff Sturgill waded into the river, the cold water to his upper thighs, and held onto the edge of the nearest boat, talking with one of the soaked searchers. The man shook his head and the sheriff's head bowed for a moment before he raised his arms and motioned for the searchers to come ashore.

Sturgill turned and the crowd parted as he made his way up the ramp. "Sheriff," JC called out. Sturgill paused and the group circled the lawman.

"We're losing light and another storm's moving in," Sturgill said, pausing to look around at the wet, defeated faces. "We run the risk of losing more men out there in the dark. Go home," he said, his gaze lingering on Tom and JC. "All of you."

A younger man, hatless and layered in black, stepped forward and Tom noticed the collar of white around his neck and the rosary beads he held in his wet fist. "Perhaps, it's best," he said, "if we ask now for the Lord's guidance and offer prayers for the safe return of our brothers."

While most lowered their heads and closed their eyes in prayer, Tom watched Sturgill stride from the group and head toward his cruiser. He figured the sheriff was on his way to tell the families of the two men that they'd not yet been found. And he wondered if that night, after Sturgill had removed all his wet clothes and sat on the edge of his bed, if he'd turn his eyes upward and ask for the Lord's guidance as well. Or if the sheriff figured he knew best in most matters.

CHAPTER FIVE

"Do you consider yourself a religious man, Mr. Crutchfield?" JC asked as he leaned against a back wall of the *Register* office, steam rising from the cup of coffee he offered the younger man.

Tom considered the question as he sat on a stack of past issues, cradling the warmth from the coffee. Parts of him were still wet from the river so he had gladly accepted JC's invite to follow him back to the newspaper office in Morgan's Gap.

"I consider myself a learned man," JC continued, "If I see a wooly worm, I'm not thinking of a beautiful butterfly. I'm thinking that's a prickly caterpillar that hugs the earth. And if I see boats coming off the river with no bodies nor personal effects, then I'm betting it's a search and no longer a rescue.

"Maybe I'm a pragmatic sort," JC paused and he rocked the cup in his hand, watching the black swirls before he turned his gaze back to Tom. "Reason I ask, I saw you look away as the others around you went to prayer down by the river. You don't strike me, Mr. Crutchfield, as a man who puts much weight in a higher being."

Tom considered the question as he took his last bite of a ham sandwich.

The Crutchfields were pillars of the First Baptist Church

of Valley Station, his grandfather on his mother's side even a deacon in the church. There were Sunday school lessons and summer days in Vacation Bible School. He knew of the burning bush and of Cain and Abel and as a 10-year-old boy he carried a slingshot and became David, slaying the mighty giant. But to be truthful, Tom had always questioned the story of Lazarus and if it was truly possible to raise a man from the dead.

And isn't that what they were attempting to do down on the river? Not just one man, but two.

As he'd gotten older and gone off to college, Tom had spent less time in church. Sure, he still sat beside his mother on Easter Sunday and they sang the gospel hymns, but he found himself straying further from faith as professors talked of Darwin and theories of evolution.

And then, 10 days before Christmas, the plain white envelope postmarked Morgan's Gap had arrived in the mail.

"I'm not really sure what I believe any more," Tom answered.

And that was true.

That mid-December afternoon, a few days after he'd returned home from college, standing there in the foyer of his parents' grand home, Tom opened the mailer addressed to him. The card inside showed a small home blanketed by snow, a wisp of black smoke rising from a chimney, and a green wreath upon the door. The words written in red, Merry Christmas.

Opening the card, letters in black ink.

Dearest,

I'm pleased with the man you've become. I hope one day you'll know the love I have for you and perhaps forgive me for what I done.

Love,

Mother

Tom had felt his chest tighten and he closed the card. Yet, the words remained: Love, Mother.

Tom opened the card again and studied the curves of each letter, searching for similarity with his own handwriting. He brought the paper to his nose, hoping for a whiff of a person or a scent of a place he'd not known. He went to his father's study and pulled an atlas from the shelf and used his finger to trace a western route to Morgan's Gap, a small, nondescript town bordered by the Ohio River and the coal fields to the south and east. It was as mysterious a land as the frozen frontier Jack London wrote of.

That night at dinner, his mother had prepared beef stroganoff and, after his father gave a short prayer, Tom slid the envelope containing the Christmas card across the polished table.

"What's this?" his father asked, a noodle perched on his fork.

"I was hoping you'd tell me."

His father glanced at the return address and then sat his fork down. Tom watched his eyes as he scanned the card once, then twice, before he placed the card back in the envelope and sat it on the table. He picked up his fork, stabbed a hunk of beef and noodles, and stared forward as he ate.

"What is it, dear?" his mother asked, her gaze flitting between Tom and her husband.

Tom's father sighed, pushed his plate forward, and said nothing. Tom reached over, handed the card to his mother and watched as she read. There was a slight tremble of her lower lip and she put the card back in the envelope and placed both hands over it. She looked down at her hands and avoided Tom's gaze.

"Is it true?" he asked the only two people he'd ever known as his parents.

"We should have told him," his father said.

Tom's mother shook her head, yet stayed silent.

"The boy should have known."

Tom felt a hollow emptiness in his stomach, and he stared at the mass of noodles and meat swimming on his plate.

"You were God's blessing," his mother said, reaching across to place her hand atop his. "We had given up hope."

Tom yanked his hand away. "What are you saying? Are you telling me you're not my mother? My true mom?"

"No, Tom," she said. "We never told you anything that wasn't true."

"We should have told him," his father repeated.

His mother's eyes darted across the table. "There was nothing to tell, Owen."

"Who is she?" Tom asked.

His mother reached again and held his hand. "We don't know."

"What? How do you not know?"

"It was part of the arrangement," said his father.

"Arrangement?"

"There were issues that prevented us from having a child

of our own. Genetics, the doctor said. We tried the different methods they proposed, but.... your mother, well, we were not getting any younger and there were not a lot of acceptable babies available for adoption. The pool was limited, Tom."

Tom felt his stomach lurch as his father told of how one of his business associates in western Kentucky, knowing of the Crutchfields' inability to have a child, had reached out and offered a solution. There were babies available, but there was a price.

"How much?" Tom asked.

"Tom...," his mother pleaded.

"How much?" he asked forcefully.

"Inconsequential," said his father, who looked across the table. "I'd buy the moon to bring your mother happiness."

"You didn't answer the question!"

"It's been many years, Tom. And lower your voice. You'll do well to remember that I'm your father and you'll respect that."

"I'm not sure what I know."

"You are our child, Tom," his mother said, holding his hand tighter.

Tom pulled his hand back and sprung from the table. "Am I? I mean, really. Who is even my father? Do you know that?"

Tom's father shook his head.

"Thomas, please," his mother said, again reaching out her hand.

"No," and he paused, noting that he omitted the word mother. He saw how it pained her and for a second he felt remorse. But then he remembered the 21 years of silence, of not telling, and he let the sting rest with her. With both of them.

"Thomas, sit down," said his father, his voice rising.

"Not happening!"

"Thomas, please," said his mother again.

He spun and left the room, up the grand staircase and into his bedroom, where he closed the door. He lay upon his bed and looked around him, the room the same as it had always been. There was the Cincinnati Reds pennant that hung along the wall and the trophy he'd won at the junior high science fair.

He went to his mirror and stared at the face before him. If he'd looked closer, he would have noticed how much different he was physically than the people claiming to be his parents. While he went shirtless in the summer and his skin quickly bronzed in the afternoon sun, his mother was often under wraps, her skin fair and quick to burn. His shoulders were broader than his father's and he was already taller than the old man.

The physical differences were there, if only he'd had reason to look.

Instead, he had been happy to play his role. Tom had never wanted. He'd had his own room and there were always new clothes and new shoes to fill his closets. He'd wanted a guppie and his parents bought him two gold fish swimming in a crystal bowl. A set of barbells, another want, now sat in the corner, gathering dust.

But now, the items all seemed like props, simple things needed to fill space in the role of good son that the Crutchfields had set out for him. And, for that, Tom now felt a fool. A rube. If they'd kept from him the story of his birth, then what other lies had been told?

There was a slight knock at the door, then his mother's voice. "Thomas."

He didn't answer, instead, going back to his bed, where he lie, arms crossed across his chest.

"Thomas. Can I come in?"

He sighed. "It's your house."

She seemed smaller than before, her shoulders hunched. She gave him the briefest of a smile and paused, glancing around his room. She walked over to a chest of drawers and grasped a framed photo.

"This was a good day," she said with a glance over her shoulder.

It was a photo of the three of them. His father standing rigid, a fishing pole in his right hand, cigar clamped between his lips. His mother, a turquoise scarf around cinnamon-tinted locks, and her hands upon his shoulders. Tom, in the middle, no more than 10 or 11 years old. In his hand he held tight a stringer with a largemouth bass dangling.

"Nearly bent my pole in half, that one," he said.

They'd spent the weekend in a cabin at Lake Cumberland and had fished for three days. It was in the final hour of the last day that Tom had pulled the giant bass from the waters. Another fisherman had snapped the photo and just before he pressed the shutter, he'd called out to Tom's father, "That's a fine fish. Chip off the old block, eh?"

There had been a grimace from his father and a tightened grip by his mother.

"Why not tell me?" he asked her.

She replaced the photo and came and sat on the end of his bed, hands in her lap.

"It was never our intention to deceive you."

She paused, her fingers picking at a loose string on her dress.

"In fact, we thought of telling you that very weekend. But I thought you were still too young. And then, junior high came and high school. And, before we knew it, you were off to college and your whole life was ahead of you. Why bring up something from the past?"

She swiped at a tear that fell across her cheek. Tom handed her a cloth.

"You know nothing about her? Or him? Why they did it?"

She shook her head and wiped at her eyes.

"It was hot that day. Unbearably," she said. "The call had come the night before. We'd been to see the fireworks down by the river. Your father said there was a baby boy and our prayers had been answered."

She paused and Tom watched her eyes, as she searched and relived the past that had changed his future.

"There was a tall man in a blue suit and he placed in my arms the sweetest, most beautiful baby I could have ever wished for. It was the only time I've ever been to that town. And I'll not go back. I believe there was a part of me that thought if I told you of where and how you came to us, you'd go searching and you'd never return."

And for the next 10 days, Tom walked the woods that bordered their back yard, stood before the line of family photos that lined the long hallway and tossed and turned in his bed sheets as sleep evaded him.

And on Christmas Day, after the presents had been opened and the Crutchfields sat before the burning hearth in the great room, Tom stood and told his parents he would go to Morgan's Gap and find the woman who had given up on him. And the three of them looked into the fire and watched it burn.

⤳

"You think they'll find them?" Tom asked the newspaper publisher.

JC placed his empty coffee cup on the printing press. "I no longer think it's a rescue mission."

"I want to write the story."

"There are many things we want, Mr. Crutchfield. But often our wants and desires are outdone by the toil and tasks needed to acquire these things," JC said, bending to run his hands over a metal arm of the press, his eyes going from bolt to rivet to seal. Satisfied, he straightened and wiped his hands with an ink-stained rag.

"Me? I thought by now I'd be a correspondent for the London Times, covering the war in the Ardenne or following the bulls in Pamplona. Instead," he said, with a wave of his arm, "here I am. In the land time forgot."

Tom glanced around him. The smell of ink was heavy in the air and dust lingered on the tops of shelves. Along one wall was a stand of vertical tables where the paper was mocked up. In the center of the room, not far from the front counter, were two wooden desks. Each had a typewriter and a lamp. Papers were scattered across the top of one, while the other was nearly spotless.

JC walked over and sat in a chair behind the desk covered in papers and motioned for Tom to have a seat in the one of the two chairs across from him.

"What exactly is it you want, Mr. Crutchfield?"

Tom considered the question. He'd come to Morgan's Gap in search of his birth parents. But now, in his coat pocket he carried a roll of black-and-white film, three pages of handwritten notes, and a story of two men who had seemingly vanished on the Ohio. It seemed the more time he spent in Newton

County, the more he accumulated. And, right now, there was a whole lot of empty that needed to be filled. And getting those answers was going to take time and a place to sleep and money for food and gas.

"I need a job, Mr. Wheeler. And it appears to me that you could use some help around here."

"Who says?"

Tom pointed to the adjacent desk with two of its drawers half-opened and three empty boxes nearby. "Looks as though someone left in a hurry."

JC chuckled. "My previous employ, Mr. Garrett, found that the hours of newspapering interfered with his courting of the home extension agent across the river over in Saline County. He didn't even provide me the courtesy of a two-week notice. Coincidentally, in my estimation, the expected length of that romantic entanglement."

JC looked across the desk, an ink-stained finger tapping at his stubbled chin.

"That was pretty perceptive, Mr. Crutchfield."

"My professor thinks so. I've spent the last two years writing at the *Kernel* in Lexington."

JC raised his eyebrows. "Bobby Ausenbaugh still there?"

"He taught me everything I know about editing. Showed me where I'd find deeds in the courthouse, where I'd find the autopsy photos at the coroner's office. He'll vouch for me."

JC leaned back and laced his hands behind his head.

"He's a good man. We spent years together at the *Courier-Journal*. He worked the courthouse, I worked the cops. We owned that front page. Junious Wheeler and Robert Ausenbaugh. Those were the bylines you saw. Those were fine newspaper days."

JC closed his eyes. "Times change, Mr. Crutchfield. The Binghams sold out and we got new editors and new edicts. And one fine spring day, I walked into a book store down on Bardstown Road and met this pretty red-headed co-ed from some frontier town called Morgan's Gap. And, well, Bobby? He got tired of digging through people's trash, I guess, and took a university job."

He opened his eyes and turned his gaze to Tom.

"I treasured my time here with my wife, Carol. I did. But I wouldn't be an honest man, Mr. Crutchfield, if I said there weren't days when I wish I was back there at the CJ. Me and Bobby Ausenbaugh. Chasing big stories. Ones that people will talk about and remember long after I'm gone from this earth."

JC paused and looked once more around the silent room. It was as though he was searching for someone.

"It's not an easy occupation, Mr. Crutchfield. I'm an old man now and I've grown weary. It's going to require diligence."

"I can do it."

"I ask for commitment."

"I can give you that."

"There will be work. Other stories. Church bazaars, business openings, city council meetings, water board sessions."

"I'll be your man about town."

"Pay's not great."

"I'm just asking for a chance."

JC rose slowly and motioned for Tom to follow him to a side room. Inside was a cot with a blanket and pillow. An empty plate and whiskey bottle sat on a wooden table alongside a small reading lamp.

"There are nights," JC said, "when sleep comes easier here."

He picked up handwritten notes scattered across the floor

and a Bible that appeared to have been flung into a corner. "You can bunk here tonight and tomorrow. There's a sink and toilet back near the dark room. Come Monday, you can find a place more suitable for a bachelor."

"What makes you think I need a place to stay?" Tom asked.

"I'm perceptive as well, Mr. Crutchfield."

Tom sat upon the cot and tested its firmness. There was a slight dip, enough to confirm his guess that JC had spent many nights here on this cot. Tom had not given much thought that morning as to what he'd find when he drove into Morgan's Gap, much less where he'd spend the night.

"Thank you," he said.

JC ran his hands through his hair and paused at the door. "I'll leave you to it then."

Tom smiled. "Your wife, Carol…"

JC's silhouette was framed in the door, his figure stooped as though the man was carrying a heavy burden upon his shoulders. There was a deep sigh and JC reached to close the door.

"Good night, Mr. Crutchfield. Tomorrow is another day."

CHAPTER SIX

SUNDAY BROKE COLD and those gathered at the river's edge built bonfires under heavy gray skies that kept the chill close. Tom shivered and wrapped a scarf he'd found at the newspaper office that morning tighter around his neck. He'd remembered his gloves this time and while they provided warmth, the thick cloth made taking notes cumbersome as he took in the scene.

Men, paired in five groups of three, slid the boats from where shards of brown ice clung to the shore and began to drag the river. As one manned the steering wheel and kept the runabout at a steady two knots, another fed a drag line to another, the tender, who held the line in his hands. Beneath the water, hooks crept along the bottom with hopes of snagging a body.

However, since the searchers were uncertain where the boat may have capsized, the search area was resembling more of a hunt for a needle in a field full of haystacks.

Tom saw Stick walking up the ramp where he had helped push another boat load of searchers out into the icy water. The deputy glanced at a piece of paper and made his way over to another group of men huddled around one of the fires, faces hidden under sock caps and scarves wound tight, loosening only to sip from tin cups. Tom caught up with him as he made his way from the group.

"Deputy, Tom Crutchfield with the *Register*."

Stick stopped when he heard his name. He looked around and, not seeing the sheriff nearby, he nodded.

"Can you tell me if they've found anything yet this morning?"

Stick shifted his eyes to the ground, but stayed in place.

"I'm not supposed to talk to you, Mr. Crutchfield."

"Call me Tom."

Stick raised his eyes and Tom noticed how they hugged the slope of his nose as though they'd been pinched by his maker.

"He said you'd be asking questions and nosing around. He told me to keep my trap shut."

"I'm guessing we're talking of Sheriff Sturgill?"

Stick shrugged and the collar of his thick jacket shifted from one shoulder to the other.

"He'd never know we talked. I protect my sources, deputy."

Stick glanced at the men huddled nearby, their eyes on the two of them. The deputy raised his voice, "I told you, reporter, there's nothing to tell. Now, off with you!"

"But deputy—"

"I warned you!"

"Stick—"

The deputy reached out and gripped Tom's arm and started to walk him up the ramp and past the men slyly keeping watch.

"You keep interfering, reporter," the deputy said. "Now, walk with me."

Stick's hold on his arm was firm, but not enough to leave a bruise, and he guided Tom past the onlookers and to the edge of the parking lot where the deputy's car was parked. He opened the door to the back seat and Tom hesitated.

"Is this really necessary?"

"Get in."

Tom slid into the back seat. It was the first time he'd ever sat in the back of a police car and he looked ahead to the deputy, who slid his thin frame into the front seat and pulled the door closed. Stick started the car and the two of them felt the warmth of the heater. Tom could see his eyes in the rearview mirror.

"It's colder than yesterday," said the deputy.

Tom pulled off his gloves and flexed his fingers, feeling the blood begin to circulate. Stick took a thermos from the floorboard and sipped from it. He offered the thermos to Tom, who shook his head no. Stick shrugged and took another drink.

"The state police was supposed to bring a plane, help with the search," Stick said, bending his head to look up at the thick canopy. "That cloud cover's probably going to keep that from happening."

Tom opened his notepad and began to write, which Stick noticed.

"Officially, I'm not saying anything, right?"

Tom met his eyes in the mirror and nodded.

"We're just two… uh, two passers-by, trying to ward off the chill, right?" the deputy asked.

"Right."

Stick took another drink from his thermos.

"Sheriff may come off as a bit of a hard ass, but he's treated me right."

"How long you been a deputy?"

"About three years now."

"Ever seen anything like this?"

"Not really. Worst I've seen was that boy who drove too fast down Palmer Curve and hit that big oak. Damn mess."

Stick's gaze held steady. "You ever seen a dead man, Tom?"

"Well, there was my grandfather... " He paused, unsure of his familial relations in the wake of the Christmas card surprise. "Well, a man in a casket at a funeral home. But no. Just autopsy photos and stuff."

Stick snorted. "Photos? That doesn't capture what you see, what you hear, what you smell when you're the first one on a scene like that. Trust me. You never get over the smell of blood and oil and burnt tires. I tell you, it's a damn mess."

"Why do you do it then?"

"That's a fine question." Stick paused and took a mouthful from his thermos. "I imagine it's what's expected of me."

"I don't understand."

"Well, my daddy was the chief of police over there in Taylor's Ferry," the deputy said, pointing a long finger toward the woods and the levee that rose behind it. "His daddy before that was a deputy sheriff. Same as me. Some people farm. Some dig coal. We Nelsons carry badges and guns."

"You ever think about doing something different?"

He chuckled and shook his head.

"What about you, reporter? This your end-all and be-all?"

Tom didn't reply. Instead, he looked out the window where a trio of boats continued to drag the river.

"Plenty expected of me, too," he told Stick. "My father has his way, next summer I'll be along some highway in Eastern Kentucky, telling a road grader where to cut through a bunch of wood and lay blacktop."

"Yet, here you are."

"Here I am."

Stick again offered his thermos to Tom, who took it and

drank. The coffee was warm, slightly sweet and a deep roast remained on his tongue.

"That's good coffee," he said.

"Made it myself," Stick said as he took the thermos and screwed the lid back on. "You know I'm a damn fine cook. I'd say my cherry cobbler's better than most."

"Why not pursue that? A chef?"

"I don't know, flipping burgers," Stick said with a wave of his hand, "that's not paying the bills. Especially now with it being just me and my momma."

"Ah."

"Several years back, one June morning they found my daddy slumped over the front wheel of his cruiser, parked down there by the KC Hall. Doc said it was a heart attack. He was dead when the ambulance got there. I was 15 years old. Another damn mess."

The two of them sat there in Stick's patrol car, listening to the low hum of the motor and feeling the warm air that came from the vents. The fog from their breathing clouded the windows, making them invisible from those who gathered at the river.

"Did they find a body this morning?" Tom asked.

Stick shook his head. "No, but one of the first boats this morning came back with a pair of hip waders."

"Where at?"

"Couple miles downstream. Washed up on the Illinois side of the river."

Tom weighed the new information.

"Could have been anybody's, I guess?"

"Could have been."

"How cold's the river water?"

"I heard somebody say 43 degrees."

Tom recalled the shock he'd felt when he had slipped into an icy creek one late fall afternoon in the woods that ran behind the Crutchfield home in Valley Station. He'd been wearing boots and heavy socks and it sure as hell hadn't been 43 degrees. If the boat carrying the two men had overturned? Despite the warmth of the patrol car, Tom shivered.

"Those boats out there now. They're dragging for bodies, right?"

Stick nodded. "They've got a pattern they're running. But that current's running fast. And when the water's cold like it is... could be two weeks or more before a body will float to the surface. Probably wishful hoping they're going to find anything. We're at the mercy of the river."

There was a sudden knock on the window, the fogged windows preventing the two of them from seeing outside. Stick unrolled his window and the face of Sheriff Sturgill appeared. He took a long look at Tom sitting in the back seat and turned his gaze back to his deputy.

"Problem?" he asked.

"No, sir," Stick answered. "I was just informing Mr. Crutchfield here of our operating procedures and how things work."

"That right?"

"Yes, sir."

Tom watched as the sheriff's jaws flexed and a cold blast of air filled the interior. The sheriff looked out at the river and back to his deputy.

"Come along. Another boat's due in."

"What about him?" Stick asked, nodding at the back seat.

The sheriff looked at Tom and his teeth crunched again at the peppermint.

"Figure you can stay out of our way?" Sturgill asked.

Tom nodded and he and Stick joined the sheriff and others as they walked to the river's edge. There was a scrape of metal as a hull struck the ramp and one of the searchers leaped out. His cheeks were red and scarred and he walked stiffly up the ramp to where the sheriff stood.

"We found some things," he said, raising his voice to be heard over the wind.

Tom and the onlookers edged closer to the boat. He saw another of the searchers lift an oar from the bottom. Next was a gasoline tank, duck decoy and a seat-type life preserver.

"You find Dutch?" someone shouted.

The searcher shook his head no.

Tom heard other voices.

"That boat done overturned."

"I'm betting you a barge hit them. Didn't see them when that storm came up fast."

"Can you imagine how cold that water was? They wouldn't last a quick minute."

The main searcher turned to the sheriff. "We found most of that down below Bell Island. Not far from Old Shawnee."

The sheriff turned to Stick.

"We'll need to shift our search maybe another mile downstream, focus on that channel nearer the Illinois side. I'll ring the sheriff over in Gallatin County, see if maybe they can help walk that shoreline."

"What about the families?" Stick asked. "Tell them what we found?"

"Not yet. I'd like to get something a little more definite."

The sheriff glanced at Tom, watching his pencil move fast across his pad.

"We don't want to create any misgivings or misinformation," Sturgill said. "There'll be plenty of time for innuendo later on. Our focus here is still on finding those men …"

Tom spoke out, "Alive, sheriff?"

Sturgill scowled.

The sheriff moved off and some followed while others went back to their groups and huddled around the fires. Stick gathered the next group of searchers and they looked over a map of the river, plotting a new grid. Tom pulled out his camera and began to take photos. He captured the launch of new searchers and the wake they left behind as the motor caught and churned downriver. He shot photos of those huddled on the shore, the fires burning.

Near the back of the parking lot, where willows grew, Tom noticed JC talking with a group of men. As he got closer, he recognized one of them as Wayne, the fisherman they'd spoken to the day before. JC met him halfway.

"Wayne tells me they're not going to find those bodies today. The current, the wind. There's no way to predict where that boat overturned, if it did."

"That's pretty much what Stick said."

JC raised his eyebrows.

"We had a conversation."

"Good."

JC motioned toward two men who had emerged from a car, one of them carrying a camera bag, and the other in a long trench coat and black fedora.

"The big boys have arrived. Must be a story now."

"What do you mean?"

"That's the *Courier-Journal* correspondent who covers this

part of the state. A prickly piss ant. He's damn good and he knows it."

Tom watched as the man looked over at the two of them and nodded and said something to his photographer, pointing toward the river.

"You got your notes?" JC asked.

"I do."

"Good. Photos?"

"Shot about a roll."

"Good. You'll need to start writing tonight. Get in the dark room, develop that film."

JC pointed to the two CJ newsmen.

"Being a daily, they're going to be out on the street about a day before our paper prints. And the others are going to be here soon. Evansville, Paducah, Metropolis. We're going to need to be better, have more."

He looked at Tom. "You up for it?"

"Yes, sir."

"How was the cot?"

"Comfortable."

"You eat?"

"Biscuits and gravy at the diner."

JC reached into his back pocket and pulled out a weathered leather wallet. He removed a $5 bill and handed it to Tom.

"Head on back. Brew up some coffee. Grab a sandwich. I'll stick around here, see if anything pops up. Doubt it, though. Wayne usually knows what he's talking about."

Tom turned and made his way to his car. He started the engine and sat, letting the engine warm before he turned on the heat. He saw JC walk over to the reporter from the *Louisville Courier-Journal* and slap him on the back. His boss smiled wide and nodded as the correspondent spoke, the two of them comfortable with each other, probably sharing stories about working on the biggest newspaper in the state, one of the most respected in the country.

Tom's mouth ran dry as he realized his work would be compared to that of the more experienced newsman, a reporter with more resources and the guile to mine these poor country folk for even more, secrets they held close to the chest. Hell, what was he thinking? He was just a reporter at a student newspaper, writing about sorority balls and the rising costs of textbooks.

After he returned to the newspaper office and developed his film, Tom settled at the empty desk beside JC's and slid a fresh sheet into the typewriter. There was something satisfying about hearing the snap of the rollers holding the paper in place, waiting for his words. But they did not come.

Instead, he sat, hands resting light on the keys. His fingers did not move. Tom rose from his seat, walked the perimeter of the office, poured the last cup of coffee and then sat back down. The words still did not appear. He remained there for another 30 minutes, scratching on a pad, reviewing his notes, but the page remained clean. He reached over and picked up the black-handled phone.

"It's me," he said.

"Oh, Tom," his mother replied.

There was quiet and he picked at the river mud that clung to one of his loafers.

"Where are you?" she asked.

"Here. Morgan's Gap."

"Have you eaten?"

"I'm fine."

"Did you bring your sweater? The one from last Christmas?"

"I'm fine."

The mud clung to the sole and he used a pencil to wedge it free. The clump landed with a thud near a metal trash can.

"Dad there?" he asked.

He heard his mother take the phone from her shoulder and then muffled voices before her voice returned.

"You know Dad. He's knee deep in the numbers for that new parkway, the Cumberland," she said. He heard his father's voice in the background, then her hand over the handset and another muffled reply. He looked again at the empty page.

"How long do you think you'll be, Tom?"

"I don't know."

She paused and he thought of how she would wind the cord around her finger when in thought, the cord getting tighter and tighter until her fingertip nearly turned white. It was then when she'd release the cord before starting the process anew.

"Have you... found her?" she asked.

Tom thought of the hours he'd spent at the river and how his thoughts had only been of two missing hunters. Not of the woman who had given him up.

"Something's come up," he said.

"Oh."

"I think I've got a job."

"What?"

"There were these missing hunters. Down at the river. The sheriff. The cold."

"I don't understand."

Tom ran his hand through his hair. "It's like this story found me."

"I don't — "

"I've taken a job at the newspaper here. The editor is a guy who seems to know what he's doing. He's given me a shot, Mom." He paused. "I'm finally doing something I felt that I was meant to do. It's like I'm finally somewhere I was meant to be."

There was more silence and he thought of her white fingertips and the stretch of a phone cord.

"Tom," she said. "Oh, Tom."

And they said goodbye and he turned again to the white blank page.

CHAPTER SEVEN

IT DIDN'T TAKE long for Tom to realize Monday was a busy and long day at the *Register*. He was still lying on the cot in the back room when he heard the ring of the front door bell. As he rubbed sleep from his eyes, he caught a glimpse of JC shuffling past and smelled coffee brewing. The hands of his wristwatch showed 7 a.m.

"Burning daylight, Mr. Crutchfield," Tom heard as he slid into his rumpled pair of khakis and buttoned his dress shirt. He'd not thought to bring a tie, but he did pull a sweater from his bag and, as he did, Tom caught a whiff of the detergent his mother used. He remembered the call home from the night before and the quiver in his mother's voice when she said goodbye.

As he settled at his desk, the paper remained blank, crisp and white. There'd been no magical sprinkle of reporter fairy dust and a hard-hitting, 10-inch story had not suddenly appeared. He felt JC's presence as his boss walked behind him, paused briefly and then sat down at his own chair.

Through the front window, there was movement on the downtown streets as people began to stir and Tom heard JC slurping his coffee. JC then inserted a sheet of paper into his typewriter and started to bang away on the keys, the tap, tap, tap and shhhhaaaazzzzoootttt sound of a hard return and another line of copy being written. Tap, tap, tap. Shhhhhaaazzzzoooottttt. Tap, tap, tap. Shhhhaaazzzzoooottttt.

For the fifth time, Tom read over his notes. Soon, he heard the tapping stop and JC ripped the paper from the roll. His editor turned to him.

"A bit of advice, Mr. Crutchfield?"

"Yes, sir."

"You're not Faulkner. You're not writing the next great American novel."

JC took a drink from his coffee cup and placed it back upon his desk.

"Write what you know. And that first step is writing the first word."

He pointed to a large round clock that hung on the wall.

"I'll need your copy by 2. No later. Understood?"

Tom nodded and JC turned and inserted another sheet of paper and began to type.

Tap, tap, tap. Shhhhaaazzzzoooottttt.

Tom closed his eyes and he saw the boats on the river and remembered how the cold rain hit against his neck. He smelled the dampness of earth and a stench of dead fish. He heard the whispers of the men who huddled around the fires. And he typed his first word.

When Tom stopped, he glanced up at the clock and was surprised to see that an hour had passed. JC's desk was empty and Tom made his way to the front where his boss was looking at a ledger while a thin lady in a blue top and cat-eyed glasses stood at the counter, counting out stacks of quarters.

"Thomas Crutchfield, meet Doris. She's our do everything around here."

She rose and extended her hand. Tom caught a whiff of Ivory soap and her hand was cool to the touch. She smiled for the briefest of a second. The bell above the door rang and a postman dropped a bundle of mail upon the front desk.

"Junious. You heard about the doc?" he asked.

"I have, Albert."

"You think they'll find them?"

"I really don't know, Albert."

"A sad, sad story."

"It is."

"What do you know?"

"Now, Albert, if I tell you all that I know, then what's the odds of you plucking down a quarter to get your *Register* tomorrow?"

"Oh, Junious, you devil."

"Good day, Albert."

"Good day."

JC pulled a newspaper, the *Louisville Courier-Journal*, from the stack of mail, glanced at the front for a minute or so and then slid it across the counter to Tom.

"Appears the CJ has your story."

Tom's stomach lurched as he saw the front page. At the top of the page was the headline: "Weather Hinders Search Of Ohio For Duck Hunters" and below it a photo showing one of the search boats being pulled from the river.

"What do you have?" JC asked.

Tom handed him his page of copy and JC began to read, pausing to scratch out a word, replace it with another. As JC proofed his copy, Tom read the story from the *Courier-Journal* correspondent. The article was to the point, easy to read and factual with bits of info on the two missing men that Tom did not have in his notes. JC handed him back his copy. The page was a mish-mash of proofreading marks.

"Work to do, Mr. Crutchfield."

Doris had resumed counting the money, the coins clattering into a tin money box. She did not glance up.

"Take a drive down to the river," JC said. "See if anything else has surfaced. The last thing we want is our front page saying that the search continues and they've pulled the bodies from the water. We need details, Mr. Crutchfield. You've seen the competition. Now, let's do better."

Tom gathered his note pad and camera and headed for the front door.

"Don't dawdle, Mr. Crutchfield," he heard JC shout out. "I'll be needing your final copy by 2."

꿍

There were fewer people at the river when Tom arrived mid-morning. More women were present, the men pulled away by shifts at the coal mine or livestock that needed to be fed. The cold was still bitter, but the sun had broken through the cloud bank. Fires still burned, but there was also a table set up, manned by a covey of women, who served sandwiches and poured coffee.

Boats still made zig-zagging patterns across the river, but they had moved farther downstream, nearly out of eyesight from the ramp. Tom saw Sheriff Sturgill near the edge of the water in his usual place, looking out over the river as pieces of dead wood, caught in the current, moved swiftly past. Out of the corner of his eye, Tom noticed Stick, who signaled with his head toward his patrol car that was parked back out of the way, nearly hidden by a grove of willows. Tom snapped a few photos as he sidled to the grove, pausing for a brief second before opening and sliding into the back seat of the deputy's car.

"Stick."

"Tom."

He waited as Stick shifted in his seat.

"We found something this morning."

Tom waited, remembering the voice of one of his journalism professors. *Let them speak.*

The deputy held up a clear evidence bag. Inside appeared to be a small flotation device attached to a set of keys.

"Dutch's," Stick said.

"You're sure?"

"Yep, the sheriff went to Dutch's truck, inserted them and it started right up."

"Where at?"

"Washed up on the Illinois shore. Down by Bell Island. Near where they found the other things. Gallatin County deputy walking the shoreline came up on it."

"Anything of the doc's?"

Stick shook his head.

"Boat?"

"No sign of it."

"Bodies?"

"No bodies."

Tom looked out through the windshield. He didn't see any sign of the *Courier-Journal* correspondent or any other reporters.

"Why you telling me this?"

Stick shrugged. "Maybe a story like this keeps you off a backhoe building roads. Figure you could use a break."

"Rather than doing what's expected of us, huh?"

"Something like that."

Tom reached up and put his hand on the deputy's shoulder. "Appreciate it."

"Remember. No names."

"No names."

Tom went to open his door.

"There's a joint, other side of the levee by Taylor's Ferry," Stick said. "Serves the coldest Buds. I like to go down there on Tuesdays. Day off. And you being new in town and all that."

Tom nodded. "Figure I can find it."

As Tom made his way from the willows and down the ramp, he saw Sheriff Sturgill coming toward him. The two met about midway down the ramp and Tom noticed the sheriff was still chewing on peppermints.

"Good morning, Sheriff."

"Uh huh."

"Any updates?"

"Nothing new, reporter."

"Nothing new recovered?"

"As I said, nothing new, reporter."

The sheriff looked at the camera hanging from around Tom's neck and the notebook in his hand. Out of the corner of his eye, Tom saw Stick making his way along the outside of the food table and the women huddled around it and down toward the river.

"Where's Junious?" the sheriff asked.

"Back at the office, working on tomorrow's paper."

"You're writing this story?"

"Yes, sir."

The sheriff sneered. Tom opened his notebook and held his pencil.

"Anything new, sheriff?"

"No comment, reporter."

With that, Sturgill walked off toward the women serving sandwiches. Tom snapped a few more photos of the boats on the water, but little had changed from the day before, other than the discovery of the game warden's keys.

However, it was one bit of information that only Tom Crutchfield had in his possession. A scoop. He glanced at his watch and noticed it was near 11 and he had less than three hours to finish his story.

He was near his car, parked at the back of the ramp, when he noticed a woman bundled in a full-length coat of red, leaning against the front of a royal blue Cadillac. Her frosted blonde hair was pulled back and held in place by a black scarf. She was smoking a cigarette and Tom noticed how her red lipstick clung to the filter. Her eyes were dark and they looked out over the river.

"Morning," he said and she tipped her finger and an ash fell to the ground.

Tom paused. She was alone and was nothing like the other women there hunched over in dark coats.

"My mother asked me to quit smoking," he said.

Her head turned to him, paused, and then swiveled back to the river. She pulled a long drag from the cigarette, enough to flame the tip red.

"And did you?" she asked.

"Well, it was my mother."

She reached into her coat pocket and pulled a pack of cigarettes. She offered him one. Tom didn't hesitate. He cupped his hands toward hers, touched his cigarette to the burning tip she offered and sucked in deep, feeling a dizzying rush as the tobacco and nicotine filled his lungs. The two of them smoked and looked at the river.

"That's good," he said.

There was a slight smudge of red at the corner of her lips, her upper lip thinner than the bottom. A streak of black mascara dipped just above her cheekbone. She took another draw from her cigarette and turned to him.

"The things we've been told are not for us. The things that will only bring us harm. Well, that only adds to the allure. Wouldn't you agree?"

Tom shrugged. "Sin is sin."

"Yes," she said, a slight smile at the corner of her mouth. "But isn't it delicious?"

Tom shifted and peered back at the river. "Think they'll find those men?"

"Some things stay hidden."

Tom glanced around the ramp. None of the faces appeared to have noticed the two of them together.

"I'm a reporter with the *Register*. Tom Crutchfield."

She took another drag off her cigarette and flicked away the remaining ash.

"The camera and notepad kind of gave it away, Tommy."

His cheeks flushed. Tom took a longer draw and thought of tossing the half-spent cigarette to the ground and walking off, but something made him linger.

"I'm writing this story."

She said nothing, her gaze still on the boat that crossed

back and forth across the water. Tom pulled his pencil from his pocket and opened his pad.

"What brought you here today, Miss….."

"Webb," she said, her eyes cutting to his. "Virginia Webb. That's my husband they're out there searching for."

Tom paused, the pencil above his paper. "My condolences."

"Condolences? Do I look like a grieving widow?"

Tom looked down and tossed his cigarette to the ground. He snuffed it with the toe of his loafer.

"I'm sorry. I just meant…"

She dismissed him with a wave of her hand. He turned to make his way to his car just as she turned. Their shoulders touched and remained in place.

"Who goes duck hunting on Christmas Day?" she asked in a soft voice and he smelled her perfume, like lilacs on a spring day. "Who leaves their wife all alone on the most family day of all days?"

"Did he say he was meeting Dutch?"

Her eyes narrowed for a second. "He said it was a friend. And that he'd not be gone long. But my husband wasn't always the most forthcoming."

"How well did he and Dutch know each other? They go hunting a lot?"

"I think my husband liked the idea of being around Dutch. Made him feel younger. More virile," she said with a slight smile. "But most of their time was spent talking about that maddening wildlife refuge. It was endless."

Tom made a mental note to learn more about the wildlife area. It was the first he'd heard of it.

"It's been three days now," he said. "Do you think it's possible —"

"What? That he no longer breathes?"

"I can't read you."

She smiled. "Not many can."

"What should I know?"

She laid her gloved hand upon his arm and leaned in close. "Dutch was a friend. I would mourn him."

"And your husband?"

"Oh, Tommy. It is a sin to lie. A delicious sin."

And Tom felt the grip of her hand as it lingered before she turned and walked to the other side of the Cadillac. He watched her open the door and slide behind the wheel and heard the engine stall, then catch, and she drove off with a scattering of gravel.

Tom turned back to the river and watched the boats continue their waltz and wondered what all lurked below the brown waters. And he knew there was more, much more, to write.

CHAPTER EIGHT

THE FINISHED PRODUCT lay on the desk before Tom. His first byline in a bona-fide newspaper. Not only that, but the lead story, right under a bold 60-point headline reading: Hunters Go Missing On the Ohio.

≈

By Tom Crutchfield

Virginia Webb said her husband turned to her Christmas morning and said he planned to hunt ducks and that he'd not be gone long. Four days later, her husband was still missing and police and searchers were dragging the Ohio River downstream from Taylor's Ferry after recovering items from what appeared to be an overturned boat.

Dr. Wesley Webb, a longtime dentist in Morgan's Gap, and James "Dutch" Blackburn, also of Morgan's Gap, apparently met early Friday morning at the Taylor's Ferry boat ramp to hunt ducks. Mrs. Webb indicated that she believed the two were meeting to discuss their plans to spearhead the purchase of some 5,000 acres of surplus military land to establish a wildlife refuge in Newton County. Blackburn, a bachelor, is a game warden with the Kentucky Department of Fish and Wildlife.

However, Webb didn't return home that night and the next morning, Saturday, Dec. 26, Mrs. Webb notified police of her husband's disappearance. The search, led by Newton County Sheriff Cullen Sturgill, commenced immediately, but as of Monday, Dec. 28, the two men had not been found.

A source said that Blackburn's keys to his truck, which was parked at the Taylor's Ferry boat ramp, were attached to a flotation device that was found Monday morning on the Illinois side of the river by a Gallatin County Sheriff's Office deputy.

The keys were found just a bit upstream of Old Shawnee and not far from Bell Island where searchers on Sunday recovered an oar, a seat-type flotation device, gasoline tank and duck decoy. The discovery prompted many of the onlookers gathered at the boat ramp to speculate that the hunters' boat overturned during a winter storm that struck Christmas morning and probably led to the men's demise in the freezing waters of the Ohio.

Sheriff Sturgill offered no comment.

When interviewed by this reporter Monday morning, Mrs. Webb did not appear to be grieving as she watched searchers in boats that crossed back and forth over the Ohio. She also said that Blackburn was a friend and that she would mourn him if he was indeed dead.

The searchers were hampered by poor weather conditions as a bone-chilling rain, whipped by northerly winds, fell all day Saturday and the temperatures plummeted into the single digits on Sunday. There were a great number of onlookers huddled around makeshift fires and women from the community offered food and warm drinks to volunteers, many using their own personal boats to search for the two missing men.

Tom read the story once, then again. A photo he'd taken showed one of the searchers holding aloft the oar they'd found. The black-and-white image ran large on the front page. Inside were two other photographs Tom had taken of the boats on the river and the women handing out warm drinks. JC had found headshots of Dr. Webb and Dutch that had been used in other *Register* stories. It was fine work.

He heard the front bell and looked up to see the postman dropping off the morning mail.

"Quite the story, Doris," Tom heard the postman say. "That's good stuff."

The bell rang several more times and people placed their money on the counter and took a copy from the stack of papers. Doris went to the back room to get more copies.

Tom located a pair of scissors near one of the mock-up tables and carefully began to cut out the article. He planned to place the article in an envelope and mail it to his parents.

Perhaps then they'd see that he could make a living as a newspaper man.

The front door bell continued to ring and more came in and bought papers. Tom watched as their eyes immediately went to his story at the top of the page and they began to read even before they were out the door.

He'd written the story in a little over two hours and had turned the copy in to JC, who was in the midst of mocking up the pages alongside Doris. A pressman had arrived earlier and was readying the machine for the night's run. JC had handed the copy back with more editing marks and Tom wrote again. Again, JC polished the story and Tom handed him the finished copy. Finally, after three rewrites and with the pressman waiting, Tom's story was typeset and placed on the page and it was off to the printers.

Later, he helped JC as they dropped off copies at the post office and then at all the groceries and convenience stores, as well as the *Register* boxes scattered across Morgan's Gap and Taylor's Ferry. Bundles were left for the boys who'd ride their bicycles down the tree-lined streets and toss them on front porches and lawns. All those people reading Tom's words. It was after midnight when he finally fell asleep on the cot.

The front bell had become a constant Tuesday morning so Tom hadn't noticed when the large man had walked in past the counter and appeared before his desk. It was only when a copy of the *Register* slid across the desk, disrupting the fine cut of his scissors did Tom look up. And there, standing before him, was Sheriff Sturgill. He looked down and saw Tom cutting out of a copy of his article and he sneered.

"You're lucky I don't lift you up out of that seat and put you up against that wall, reporter."

"Sheriff—"

"I told you to stay out of my way. And then I got to read this hogwash?"

"I did nothing—"

"Bull shit."

"I only reported—"

"I told you no comment."

"And I mentioned that in the story."

"You running this investigation now?"

"It's an investigation?"

The sheriff leaned forward and placed his rather large hands on Tom's desk.

"You write what I tell you to write."

Tom glanced to the front where he saw Doris' head jerk down, suddenly intent on counting the money, the coins clinking into the tin box.

"Who told you about the keys?"

"I can't—"

"Stick?"

"I really can't—"

"Who told you to talk to Virginia?"

"Virginia?"

"The woman is grieving."

"She didn't appear—"

"You had no right to go barging in. I'll tell you when and if the families want to talk."

Tom saw JC appear from the back of the office, a cup of coffee in his hand. He expected his boss to come up and defend him. Instead, JC leaned against the wall and sipped from his cup.

The sheriff leaned closer.

"You're not from around here. Meddling in our affairs, raising rabble. Only to slink back out of town when the time suits you."

He jabbed his finger at Tom.

"Stay out of my way, reporter. That's your second warning. There'll not be a third."

Sturgill straightened and glanced at JC, who still leaned against the wall, watching.

"Keep your dog on a leash, Junious."

JC showed no expression. "Sheriff."

And as fast as he'd arrived, Sturgill turned and left the office, the door clanging shut behind him.

Tom ran his tongue over his lips and wiped his palms on his pants. JC came over to his desk and sat down. He shuffled through some papers.

"You OK, Mr. Crutchfield?"

"I'm not sure."

"People are not always going to like what you have to say."

"Why didn't you, I don't know, step in? Back me up?"

"I thought you were handling the situation just fine."

"So, just sit there and take it?"

"Was there anything incorrect in what you reported?"

"No, sir."

"Do you feel that what you wrote accurately represented the information of which you gathered and observed?"

"Of course."

"Well, then," JC said. "You've done your job. Congratulations on your first big story."

Tom gathered the clipping he was cutting and placed it in one of his desk drawers.

"Now," JC said. "There's a woman who's going to be showing slides from her recent trip to sub-Saharan Africa to the weekly meeting of the Lions Club at noon. I'll expect you to cover the event and take photos and write up a story."

"But the search—"

"Yes, Mr. Crutchfield. The search will continue and you will also write that story. But for now, it's elephants and wildebeests of which I'm expecting you to write eloquently. Capeesh?"

Tom nodded.

"Good. A new paper begins today. Now, off with you."

Tom gathered his notebook and camera and was about to head out of the office when JC looked up.

"Oh, and Mr. Crutchfield, you should go see Mrs. Tyner over on Waller Street. Big brick house at the end, bunch of overgrown rose bushes around her porch, a rather large evergreen in her front yard. She's expecting you. And I'm needing my cot back."

❧

The one-bedroom apartment above Mrs. Tyner's two-car garage was certainly not the estate of the Crutchfields. There was a small living area with a worn, floral couch. A tiny round table and chair served as the dining area with a mini stove and refrigerator and sink nearby. The bedroom allowed for a single bed and there was a sink and vanity, the toilet and a closet that would hold the contents of Tom's suitcase and little more.

"Now, I'm a church-going lady, Thomas," she said, opening a window to allow a burst of fresh air into the apartment. "I'll not allow games of chance or whoring on my premises. But, I do enjoy my cup of sherry and see no reason to deny a man his drink."

Tom said he would take the apartment and he was grateful. He said payday at the paper was Friday and he'd have his rent money then.

"How is Junious?" she asked. "I worry for him."

Tom shrugged. "Seems fine."

She shook her head. "Just a poor shame with Carol. Such a learned and sweet lady. Did you know we were on the library board together?"

"I'm still kind of finding my way."

She closed the window and handed Tom a key.

"It's just me now. Wednesdays, I cook a roast and it's usually way too large a portion for me. If you're inclined?"

The Christmas dinner of duck had been Tom's last home-cooked meal.

"You're too kind."

"Well, I believe the stimulus of sherry when paired with the roast and vegetables and a side dish of educated conversation makes for a good evening. I read your story, Thomas. There is talent there."

"Well, JC edited quite a bit."

"But it was your eyes that saw and ears that heard. It's lovely to have a writer so near."

She glanced around the living room and bent to straighten one of the cushions on the couch.

"Wednesday it is then."

CHAPTER NINE

LATER THAT DAY, after the wildebeests at the noon Lions Club, Tom made his way to the boat ramp where the search for the missing men continued. There was a smaller crowd, which made it easier to spot the hulking figure of Sheriff Sturgill, who glanced his way when he arrived and then turned back to the river. Tom took a photo of the sheriff, his silhouette dark against the falling afternoon sun.

With the start of another news week, he'd need an updated story, so he decided to get back in his car and drive along River Road No. 2, a gravel lane full of potholes that mimicked the snaking curves of the Ohio. He kept his eye on his odometer and at the two-mile mark, near where the search was concentrating, he pulled his car to the side of the road. The cold remained, but not as bitter as the weekend. Still, he buttoned his coat and lifted his collar. He saw an opening in the brush that lined the road and made his way through brambles and a clump of Devil's Walking Stick until he found the riverbank.

The ground was a mixture of dark mud and sand and some of it clung to his brown loafers. He would need a good pair of boots soon. Out on the water, still dirty from the weekend rain, a pair of boats worked in tandem, steering against the current, trying to maintain a straight line as they dragged for whatever the river had to give up. Tom walked the bank, his eyes near the shore, looking for something for his next story, an item no one else would have. Maybe it would be more duck decoys? Perhaps a heavy winter coat worn by the doctor? He figured the guns would have sunk to the river bottom and they'd never be found, but why hadn't the boat been located? It seemed the John boat, having flipped and losing its passengers, would still rise to the surface and be easy enough to spot by a passing barge. He briefly thought of finding a body and what he'd do. Would it be bloated, filled with gasses, pushed to the surface? Would the eyes be open and full of nothingness? The lips and skin pockmarked where the catfish had begun to feed?

Tom shivered and nearly stumbled over a piece of driftwood, half submerged in the muck of sand and mud. He realized he'd walked nearly a mile and all he'd seen were a few rusted beer cans and the half-eaten remains of a carp, a pair of black vultures scattering when he'd walked up on them. They'd lifted from the dead fish, but remained in the limbs above, watching as Tom nudged the carp with the toe of his shoe. He walked on and knew the vultures would drop and feed again.

Soon after, the sun fell behind the western hills and the cold crept in. Tom turned and found his way back to the river road where he jogged, his loafers scuffling against the dusty gravel, back to his Fairlane, the green no longer as lustrous — a coating of Newton County mud on its rear panels.

He remembered Stick's invitation and turned the car to Taylor's Ferry. As the deputy promised, he found the beer joint, white paint flaking from wooden panels, the structure back off the road, flanked by a stand of willows, whose limbs dipped down to touch the hoods and rusting tops of four pickups. The words Rainbow Tavern painted in red and blue letters above the entrance and the screen door screeched when he pulled it open.

There was little lighting inside, most of it provided by a few beer lights promoting Strohs and Pabst Blue Ribbon. A juke box sat in the corner and Tom heard a country song, the singer telling of a cheating wife and a heavy heart and a shotgun full of shells. Three men sat on stools and their bellies pressed against the wood. Tom had to do a double-take before he noticed Stick at the end of the bar, the deputy nearly invisible without his gun and badge and the brown uniform of the Newton County Sheriff's Office. He lifted his hand and motioned for Tom to join him, the other three men turning back and continuing to talk about a place called Vietnam.

"I wasn't sure you'd show," said the deputy.

"I could use a beer," Tom said. "It's been a week."

Stick nodded and called out, "Mary Diane."

And from the dark behind two swinging doors, she appeared. She wore a red chambray shirt untucked and Tom noticed her eyes, a green hazel, and they lingered on his.

He faintly heard Stick, "What'll you have, Tom?"

And he pointed to the deputy's beer. "Same."

She nodded and turned to walk to a cooler at the other end of the bar. Tom noticed the shirt tail ended right above her rump and he liked the blue of her jeans. She turned and caught his gaze and a scant smile appeared. She used a bottle opener on a PBR and the top hopped and spun on the counter, landing against Tom's fingers.

"Whose your friend, Stick?"

"Tom. He's new in town."

"That so?"

She turned to look at him and Tom thought of a cat, the way her head tilted to the side, taking him in from head to toe.

"We don't get a lot of visitors in Taylor's Ferry."

"Streets are empty," Tom answered.

"If you're Santa, you're late."

Tom chuckled.

"Mary Diane's a pistol," Stick offered. "Watch yourself."

She cut her eyes at the deputy and he lifted his beer and took a long drink. Tom joined him and felt the cold of the beer hit the back of his throat and fill his stomach. He felt a belch coming on, but held it in.

"How long we known each other, Mary Diane?" Stick asked.

"Long enough."

"Tom, this girl. She could outrun any damn one of us. We'd have field day at the elementary school and dang if she didn't win every damn blue ribbon. She could have beaten the boys if they'd let her run."

"A runner," Tom said.

"Stick talks a lot," she said. "A lot of foolishness."

"Now, Mary—"

"I'm hoping that he's told you he's a lawmen. Sworn to protect and serve. One of Newton County's finest. Sitting here on a stool all by his lonesome on a Tuesday night."

"Now, Mary—"

"Tom, you do know you are drinking with the law?"

"We're acquainted," he answered.

"I'm off-duty, Mary. Sheriff Sturgill don't mind if I have a beer with the boys."

"That so," she said, pausing to wipe a cloth across the bar, catching the sweat of a wet beer. The conversation paused and another song talked of love lost and bad choices.

"Anything new from the river?" she asked.

"They're still searching," Stick said.

Tom noticed the worry that lingered on her face.

"Sheriff know you're out drinking on a Tuesday night?" she asked.

Tom noticed a slight creep of red that climbed along the deputy's neck.

"Not his business."

"Well, I thought it was Sheriff Sturgill's business to know everything."

"Change the subject, Mary."

"You brought it up."

One of the three men at the other end of the bar called out to Mary for another round and she left Tom and Stick alone. The deputy motioned for Tom to join him at one of the tables in a corner, away from the light and music coming from the jukebox. They sat across from each other, eyes on the bar and the front door.

"You read the story?"

"I did."

"And?"

"Seemed accurate."

"The sheriff stopped in."

Stick's bottle paused before his lips.

"He wasn't particularly happy with my reporting. Wanted to know where I got my information."

Stick drained his bottle and wiped the back of his hand across his mouth. "What'd you tell him?"

"I told him nothing."

"Good."

"They find anything else yesterday? I went down today, fewer searchers, same boats dragging."

"I was off work, but haven't heard anything."

"Sheriff said to stay out of his way."

"He does that." Stick paused. "Virginia Webb."

"What about her?"

"Careful of that one."

"What do you mean?"

"She's got her tendrils in a little bit of everything."

"She's damn fine looking."

"She is."

"You think she was telling me the truth?"

"I think she was telling you what she wanted you to know."

Tom took a long drink from his beer. "That deal about the wildlife refuge?"

"Uh huh."

"Any ideas?"

"You run across Thadeus Lincoln, yet?"

"Doesn't ring a bell."

"Should. He runs this county."

Tom heard the screech of the front door and saw a group of four men enter. Stick eyed his empty beer and looked at the men, who settled in at a nearby table. They glanced his way and a couple of them nodded. Stick rose from his chair.

"Careful out there, Tom. They are saying another storm's headed our way."

Tom nodded, watched as Stick stopped at the table, said a few words, exchanged a glance with Mary behind the bar and left, the door clanging behind him. Tom drained his beer and thought he'd have another. He caught her eye and raised his empty bottle.

❧

Tom leaned against the stack of empty beer boxes and watched as Mary slid her hand down the front of her jeans. It was just the two of them, back behind the Rainbow, and he could hear the second verse of a country song, the singer's lonesome wail muffled through the concrete walls.

She pulled a pack of Camels from her front pocket and smacked the plastic-wrapped foil against her palm until a pair of cigarettes emerged from the wrinkled pack. She offered and Tom took a cigarette and Mary the other. She pulled a lighter from her pocket and brought the flame to his lips where the cigarette hung. He cupped his hands to shield the wind and again he noticed the hazel in her eyes.

He pulled back and took a deep drag and felt the smoke fill his lungs and the nicotine hit his nerves. Damn, that was good. He watched as she climbed atop a wooden picnic table across from him and take her own hit. He noticed nearby a stack of concrete blocks, five layers high, formed in a square with a blackened, metal grate atop. Four posts held a makeshift roof of tin above the structure.

He sensed her eyes on him and glanced her way, quick enough to catch her gaze before her eyes darted downward.

"They cook the meat there," she said with a nod toward the stack of blocks. "You can fit an entire hog on there. Let it simmer throughout the night, slow and low heat over that hickory wood. It's good eating."

Tom took another drag from his cigarette and let the smoke linger before he released it, a thin line emerging from his lips and drifting upwards toward the bare branches of a huge oak that would be full and green in the spring and summer and shade those who feasted on the grilled hog. He noticed there were just a few nighttime clouds above and the moon was full and its light fell on the two of them.

After Stick had left, Tom had ordered another beer and sat alone at the table and nobody had taken much notice, except for Mary. She'd come from behind the bar and brought him another cold Strohs, told him it was her break and asked if he wanted to see where they cooked the best pulled pork in five counties. And so here they sat.

Mary pulled the collar of her black overcoat up around her neck and leaned forward, one hand in her coat pocket, the other holding the cigarette to her lips. Tom noticed a slight shiver in her hand and he reached into his coat pocket and offered her his gloves. She eyed him for a few seconds and then took the gloves, balancing the cigarette on her lips as she pulled them over her long fingers. He noticed she wore no nail polish.

"Why a hog?" he asked.

Mary leaned back and took another drag and her hazel eyes lingered on his face.

"Easier to get," she said. "They cook a mean mutton, it's actually better in my opinion, but a sheep's harder to come by. But a hog? You can drive down most of any of these backroads and find a pig farmer before your heater's spitting out hot air."

She smiled. "I guess most folks around here will choose the easy way most times."

Tom nodded and took another drag off his cigarette. He released the smoke quicker this time.

"You're not from around here are you?" Mary asked.

Tom shook his head.

"You from across the river?"

"That a bad thing?"

Mary chuckled. "No, but you don't move like a Hoosier. And you're far too pretty to be from Old Shawnee."

Tom grinned.

"Owensboro? Paducah?" she asked.

"Farther east."

"Ah, a big city boy. The golden triangle."

Mary took a drag, this one longer than before and she held it in, eyeing him. She pointed to his feet. "Loafers. I should have guessed. We don't see many of them here at the Rainbow."

Tom crossed his feet and leaned his back straighter against the concrete wall.

"Earlier, you asked Stick about the search. You know those two men?" he asked.

A frown flashed across Mary's face and she snubbed out her cigarette and tossed it to the ground.

"Thing you'll find out if you stay here long enough is that everybody knows everybody. Good and bad." She paused. "So, what brings you to the country, city mouse?"

Tom took one last draw off the cigarette and flicked it to the ground where he used the toe of his shoe to rub the butt into the black dirt. He looked across at Mary and saw how the wind had caught a wisp of her auburn hair and the long curl hid part of her face. Her cheek remained hidden until she raised her gloved hand and tucked the curl back behind her ear.

"I guess I come looking for answers," he said.

"And?"

"And?"

"Have you found them?"

"Still searching."

"You're awfully young to have so many unanswered questions."

"Oh, really?"

"Yes."

"Well, how old do you think I am?"

She looked him up and down and, feeling her gaze, Tom shifted his feet and ran his hand through his hair. She made a clucking sound with her tongue.

"Ohhhhhh, 24."

Tom chuckled. "Not hardly."

"Strange," Mary said. "I can usually pinpoint an age. Call it an occupational hazard."

Tom reached to his back pocket and pulled out his wallet. He fished out his drivers license and handed it to her. He noticed she had glanced at the empty sleeve of photos where guys kept pictures of their girls. Mary brought the license close to her face and she used a gloved finger to rub along the surface. Tom raised an eyebrow.

"Some will try to fool you," she said, handing back his license. "Make out to be somebody they're really not. You see a little bit of everything here."

Tom nodded back to the back door. "Then, why do it?"

Mary reached back into her pocket and pulled out the pack of cigarettes. She smacked the pack against her hand, hesitated, then slid the pack back into her front pocket. She leaned back, extended her arms and gripped the table.

"That's the question, isn't it," she said.

"What's that?"

"Why do the things we don't want to?"

"I'm guessing most people have reasons."

A cloud moved overhead and they were in the dark. Tom

heard Mary rise from the table and he caught a scent of vanilla and cinnamon that floated in the frigid air. When the cloud moved, Mary stood just a few feet away, her auburn hair dark in the moonlight, eyes shaded by shadows.

"How long are you staying?" she asked.

"Till I finish my beer."

"I didn't mean just tonight."

He pushed forward from the wall and stood tall, a good seven inches over her, enough for Mary to raise her eyes toward his and he could see the hazel again. There was a dryness in his mouth and he didn't know if it was from the Camel or the nearness of her body.

"I guess I'm here until I find who or what I'm looking for."

Mary stepped closer.

"Are you that cold?" she asked. "You're shaking."

He pulled the front of his jacket across him. "I'm not sure I fully thought it out. Kind of just grabbed what was nearby."

His fingers, stiff and cold, fumbled with the buttons.

"Tsk, tsk, city mouse," Mary said as she swept away his hand and fastened the three buttons. "There. Much better."

Her hand lingered on his jacket and she brushed dust from the collar. Tom slid his hands into his pockets.

"I should get back inside," she said.

"You should?"

Mary stepped to the side and her shoulder brushed his arm and he smelled more of the cinnamon. She grasped the handle of the back door and paused. She turned and looked at him again. "Will I see more of you, city mouse?"

Tom smiled. "I think my answer to that would be a yes."

"Good," Mary said as she pulled open the door and the

sounds and smells and faded light from indoors fell upon her for an instant before the door shut closed.

Tom was left alone in the dark. There was the faint smell of burned meat from the rack and he brought his chilled hands to his mouth and blew on them. He reached into his pocket for his gloves and they were not there.

He heard the muffled voice of Mary through the closed door followed by a hearty laugh and another song began to play on the jukebox. He'd left his beer inside and knew by now it would be warm, its glass bottom in a puddle, adding another mark to the worn wooden table. He blew upon his hands again and felt the chill of the wind upon the back of his bare neck.

Morning would come soon and there'd be stories to write. He knew he'd return for his gloves.

CHAPTER 10

TOM WOKE WITH the gunshot, the blast so near that he jumped out of bed and pressed his bare belly to the wooden floor. His discarded khakis lay crumbled in a heap near where he had tossed his socks the night before. He slid towards the front window where the sun's first morning rays began to light the room. He had just reached the window, his fingers grasping the wooden sill, when another shot was fired.

What the hell? Tom pressed his back to the front wall.

He recognized the shot as a shotgun blast, its sound filling the space and Tom pressed his hands to his ears just as he'd done when his father hunted quail along a lonesome fence row in Spencer County.

Tom straightened and carefully peered out the window, which showed tufts of green grass and the brick walkway that led from the garage and around the backyard to a patio and Mrs. Tyner's back door. He saw her emerge from the far right of the backyard, the flash of her blue housecoat in stark contrast to the green leaves of the cedar that reached to the ground. She cracked the gun open, two shells spit out and she pulled two more from a front pocket and placed them into the gun. Tom watched as Mrs. Tyner raised the shot gun, pointed it toward the top of the garage and pulled the trigger.

He ducked and the blast was loud, the closest yet, and he heard the sound of numerous sticks and branches falling upon the roof.

She's lost her damn mind.

Tom rose to his feet and carefully opened his door and called out, "Mrs. Tyner!"

"Yes," he heard her say.

Tom stuck his head out from behind the cover of the wall. She peered up at him, the stock of the shotgun open, two more spent shells at her feet.

"Good morning, Thomas."

She bent to pick up the red shells at her feet and placed them in her pocket. Her grey hair was pulled back into a severe bun and her hands were steady as they held the gun. Tom, wearing just his boxers, felt the cold bite of the morning wind as it came through the door and hit his bare chest.

"Mrs. Tyner, can you please stop shooting?"

She peered up at him and then down at the shotgun in her hands and seemed a bit surprised. She pointed the barrel at the ground.

"Did I wake you?"

Tom shut the door and grabbed his pants from the floor and a t-shirt that hung on a bed post. He came out and stood on the small deck at the top of the stairs. Mrs. Tyner still remained below, her thin frame enveloped by the light blue housecoat that nearly stretched to her feet encased in white slippers. Her eyes were on the trees above him.

"Starlings," she said. "Damn pesky birds. They'll take over if you're not careful."

Tom turned and followed her gaze to the tree branches that arced out and above the garage. They were bare except for the white of a few shattered limbs, their wooden chunks scattered across the top of the roof. Tom didn't notice any dead birds.

"Outsiders," she said. "They come in flocks, loud and aggressive, to my feeders and run away my cardinals, the gold finches, my pretty bluebirds. I've no use for them, Thomas. I have little patience for a pushy bird."

Tom ran his hand through his tangled hair and looked up again at the bare limbs. Dark clouds could be seen to the west and he felt the wet in the air. He looked down again to where Mrs. Tyner stood looking up at him.

"But a gun?" he asked. "For a couple of backyard starlings?"

"Well," she said. "Theodore Roosevelt, Teddy, who I consider to be a great president, is known to have said, 'Speak softly and carry a big stick; you will go far.'

"And Thomas," she said, snapping the shotgun's stock back in place, "this is my big stick."

She then turned and started to make her way across the back yard before she stopped midway and called out, "Dinner at six. Don't be tardy. Seize the day, Thomas. Seize the day."

And he watched as she made her way across the yard and patio, the barrel of her shotgun catching on the hem of her housecoat before she gave it a yank and pulled the back door behind her.

᠊ᡈ᠊

Tom spent his morning cleaning up and typing hand-written roundups gathered from JC's stable of "community correspondents" — which consisted of curious, some might say nosy, older ladies writing about the goings-on of their neighbors. Things such as who visited whom over the Christmas holidays, who had been bed-ridden by a bad bout with the flu and whose red velvet cake had been to die-for, served on a plate painted with holly leaves. "There's gold in those stories, Mr. Crutch-field," JC had promised, but they'd done little more than make Tom hungry for lunch.

He spent the first part of the afternoon at a short meeting of the Morgan's Gap Businessmen's Association, who talked of the need for a new awning in front of the drug store and whose Christmas sales had exceeded those of their competitor, and it hadn't taken him long to write the story and turn it in to JC.

Dark clouds from the west had steadily gathered through the day and formed a thick cover when Tom made his way back to the boat ramp. There were fewer searchers and fewer onlookers as a single boat could be seen criss-crossing the river. He saw Stick near the shoreline and nodded. The deputy shook his head and the two did not speak. A light snow began to fall and it increased in intensity as the light fell from the sky. The snow began to stick to the cold earth and when he pulled into Mrs. Tyner's driveway, there was nearly an inch on the ground.

The snow clung to his shoulders as he knocked on her back door, at two minutes before 6, and she answered. The blue housecoat had been shed, as well as the slippers, and she greeted Tom in a green dress and her hair had been loosened and it fell on her shoulders. A simple gold locket was around her neck and her hand was warm when she grasped his and led him into the living room.

"Promptness is a fine virtue for a young man, Thomas," and she took his coat and hung it nearby. "Please, sit."

He sat at the end of a small sofa and she in a plump chair

across from him. On the wall behind her hung a large painting that showed a woman, her hair hidden in a red scarf, standing in a field of yellow daisies, the grey arches of a gothic cathedral prominent in the background. The two sat there and Tom heard the ticking of a nearby clock. It struck six and soft chimes filled the room.

"This is nice," he said.

"I often think of painting the walls in a different color. But, here I sit and the pale tan remains."

Tom could smell the roast cooking and his stomach made a rumbling sound. He shifted in his seat and his pants scratched against the fabric of the white sofa. Near him was a table and lamp and a worn copy of William Faulkner's "The Sound and the Fury." A large stone fireplace dominated the farthest end of the room and even though there was a blackened grate, no fire burned tonight. A television was at the opposite end and Mrs. Tyner made a move as if to turn it on, but then pulled her hand back.

"The weatherman said we could see up to three inches tonight," she said as she glanced out a large bay window to the front yard, partly illuminated by a lone street light, and the snow continued to fall. She crossed her arms and rubbed them. "It's a bitter cold. I should have started a fire."

Tom began to rise from his seat. "I could—"

But Mrs. Tyner shook her head. "Over 12 years now and you'd think it'd be easier, but…"

She rose from her seat and crossed over to her bookshelf. On the fourth row, above the set of Encyclopedia Brittanica, she pulled a glass from the shelf and a glass decanter filled halfway full with brown liquid.

"Something to warm the insides, Thomas?"

"Sure."

She poured and handed him the glass and then served herself a drink. Tom could smell the hint of vanilla and felt the bite of the bourbon as the taste lingered on his tongue and the warmth spread across his chest and filled his stomach. He took another sip.

"Nicholas rarely enjoyed his bourbon on ice. He'd say, 'Elizabeth, we'll not spoil this fine Kentucky bourbon by watering it down. No, no. We'll save the ice for that horrid Tennessee whiskey.'"

She chuckled and took a sip from her glass and they watched the snow fall.

"Nicholas?"

She glanced at him and smiled. "My dear husband."

"I —"

"The war took him in '52. He was a helicopter pilot. And a damned fine one. He was always thinking we could lift ourselves out of the direst of situations."

She took a longer sip from her glass and her free hand went to her lap where she smoothed the green fabric.

"It was a medical evacuation. That's what he did. Rescuing others. You know the soldiers called them 'Angels of Mercy.'"

She shook her head and glanced out the window.

"They were only supposed to make daytime runs. And he was on his way back to the base that day, late afternoon, when a call came that said two soldiers had been hit, but the area was still crawling with Communists. Of course, Nicholas went after them. That's what he did. He was hit on entry and the helo crashed."

She turned back to Tom. "November 6, 1952. Two days later, an airman knocked on my front door and told me my husband died a hero, saving others. He left and I sat alone in this chair for a very long time, Thomas. A very long time."

Tom held the glass in his hand and swirled the liquor that remained.

"I'm sorry to hear that."

She smiled. "They say it gets easier with time. And perhaps that's true, but there are many days and nights when I still wish Nicholas would walk through that door."

She finished her drink and rose from her chair and Tom did the same. They walked to the kitchen and Mrs. Tyner filled his plate with roast and potatoes and carrots and gravy. They drank sweet tea and Tom sliced butter and put it on hot rolls and ate till his stomach was full.

Mrs. Tyner told him of how she'd continued to teach high school English after her husband's death and had only retired when the "penny-pinchers at the school board deemed it was her time to take her leave." She still tutored and was on the Newton County library board and, last fall, she and her sister, who lived in Bardstown, visited Mammoth Cave where they viewed massive stalagmites during the day and drank wine at night.

Tom told her of the stories he wrote for the *Kentucky Kernel* and his first week at the *Register*. He dried the dishes as she handed them to him and then they both sat at the kitchen table as a pot of coffee brewed in a nearby pot. Mrs. Tyner suddenly rose from her seat and asked Tom to follow her. He followed her to a long, dark hallway that stayed dark even when she flipped the switch.

"The bulb's out," she said and pointed to the fixture high above her reach. "Would you be a dear?"

Tom brought a chair from the kitchen and, as Mrs. Tyner

held his legs steady, he began to unwind the small screws that held the light fixture's cover in place. One screw refused to budge and Tom applied extra pressure and his weight shifted, but Mrs. Tyner held a firm grip around his knees.

He was reminded of a Christmas two years past when his mother had held firm to a ladder as Tom reached to place an ornamental star atop their 10-foot Christmas tree. She'd laughed and told him that it had seemed that it had been just a year earlier when he could barely reach the middle branches when he flung the silver tinsel on the evergreen branches. "You're no longer my baby boy," she'd told him and they had both stopped and admired the star atop the tree.

He handed the light fixture to Mrs. Tyner and began to unscrew the spent bulb.

"Nicholas was always one to wait," Mrs. Tyner said as she brought out a cloth and began to wipe the dust from the fixture. "He was a thinker. He would have made a fine analyst, that I do believe. Meticulous in all things. Oh, how it used to drive me mad."

They exchanged bulbs and Tom carefully screwed the bulb, slowing as he waited for the bulb to catch and for light to fill the hallway. When it did, he took the fixture from Mrs. Tyner and placed it over the bulb and tightened the screws. He took her hand as he stepped down and they looked up at the fixture and Tom noticed the numerous photos that lined the hallway. In the dark, he'd not noticed them.

As Mrs. Tyner returned the chair to the kitchen, he walked the hallway and followed along Mr. and Mrs. Tyner's life story. There were grainy black-and-white photos of them as children — Mrs. Tyner holding a fluffy puppy on a dusty road and Nicholas straddling a mule beside a coal mine. There were high

school graduation portraits and a photo of the two of them
with their heads ducked, jubilant faces, as rice fell upon their
shoulders and a church steeple stood tall in the background.
There was a photo of Nicholas in his dress blues, a row of
ribbons across his chest. Another showed Mrs. Tyner in her
classroom surrounded by a group of children. The final photo,
the closest to what Tom guessed was the main bedroom, had
been taken in the front yard of their home, the two of them
bundled in sweaters and with arms around each other, a stack
of near-dead autumn leaves behind them.

"We lived a happy life," she said, her voice surprising Tom
as his attention had been focused on the photos and he'd not
heard her approach. He watched as she brought her fingers to
her mouth and held them against her lips, her eyes on the photo.

"We'd talked of children. Many times," she said with a
smile. "But Nicholas had thought it best to wait. To wait until
he received another promotion, another step in pay. To wait
until the next spring when his tour in Korea would be over. To
wait until life slowed down."

Tom noticed a dampness in her eyes and he looked away.

"Shame on the two of us for not realizing time was simply
waiting on us," she said and he watched as she knelt and brushed
away a stray spider's web from a corner of the remainder of the
wall left vacant, the emptiness of 15 lonely years.

Mrs. Tyner led Tom back to the kitchen and out to her
mud room where she pulled a pair of men's rubber boots from
beneath a bench.

"You must protect your feet, Thomas. And those loafers are
no match for our winters here."

He tried on the boots and they fit his feet well. She reached
back into the closet and pulled out a long navy scarf, a dark

toboggan and a pair of wool gloves. She stepped back and put her hands on her hips as she watched him try on the items. She nodded when he was done and stood for inspection in his rubber boots, the scarf wrapped tight, the toboggan pulled low and his gloved hands holding onto his loafers.

"The winter months can be brutally cold," she said. "If you'll be out, you must be prepared, Thomas."

Mrs. Tyner opened the back door for him and the snow was falling harder than when he'd arrived two hours earlier.

"Thank you," he said.

She stepped forward and gave him a hug, holding him in place for a few seconds. He could feel the strength that remained in her arms and he didn't notice the stray flakes that fell on his face.

"Don't wait for the perfect moment, Thomas," she said. "Take the moment and make it perfect."

He followed the faint path of his footprints from earlier and climbed the wooden stairs to his apartment. Tom shed his clothes and pulled the blankets over him. He could hear the snow as it lightly touched upon the roof and the limbs of the cedars.

He wondered if the snow was falling as hard at Valley Station and he pictured his father adding another log to the fire, sparks jumping and the light falling on his mother's face as she sat silent on the sofa and listened, waiting for the latch of the front door to sound and to hear the thump of his steps on the wooden floor.

Tom remembered seeing the telephone that hung on the wall of Mrs. Tyner's kitchen and he thought of rising from the warm bed, putting back on his clothes and boots and making his way back across the frozen yard — then knocking at Mrs. Tyner's door, asking to make a long distance phone call, to hear his mother's voice, certain that Mrs. Tyner would agree.

But the winter cold remained and he pulled the bed sheets closer. And as sleep came, Tom thought of another woman and wondered if she thought of the baby boy she'd held for just a moment many years ago. Outside, the cold, cold snow fell and the backwaters of the Ohio turned white and froze and those below remained hidden.

CHAPTER 11

As Tom slogged his way through the four inches of snow that had fallen overnight, he was happy for Mrs. Tyner's boots. They kept his feet warm and dry as he walked the six blocks from his apartment to the newspaper office. Two gravel trucks with blades attached worked to clear the downtown streets and Main was mostly cleared, but Tom had opted to keep his car parked.

The cool morning air cleared his head and it was needed as he knew he'd be expected to have another update for that week's paper. There'd been no developments at the river and he'd learned little about the two men. And now it was Thursday and the Monday deadline loomed.

The bell above the front door clattered when he entered the offices of the *Register* just after 7 a.m. Doris wasn't at her desk as she'd said she was taking the day as a holiday. As Tom removed his scarf and jacket, he was about to head for a cup of coffee when he saw Sheriff Sturgill seated in his desk chair. Across from the sheriff, JC was leaned back in his own chair, hands folded across his stomach.

"Sheriff, would you mind repeating what you told me so that my reporter could be caught up to speed?" JC asked.

The sheriff swiveled in the chair and turned to Tom. His

bulk filled the frame of the seat and it was a mass of brown, from the round bill of his hat to the thick jacket down to the laced leather boots that faced Tom. His eyes took in the gun holstered along his hip and the sheriff's hands that hooked into his belt. Sturgill's jaws clenched as he chewed a peppermint and Tom felt the sheriff's eyes take him in, lingering at the rubber boots that were wet from the snow.

"We're calling off the search," the sheriff said.

And, with that, Sturgill swiveled in his chair and rose from his seat.

"But," Tom said, "it's been, what, less than a week?"

The sheriff looked at him, paused and then turned to JC. "I'm letting you know. Save you a trip to the river."

Tom reached for a pencil and notebook on his desk. "Has anything else been recovered? The boat?"

The sheriff continued to look at JC. "Those volunteers have been down there the entire week. We've asked all we can of them."

"Do you think there's any chance you may have missed anything?" Tom asked. "Have you told the families that you've given up hope?"

Sturgill turned suddenly to face Tom and there was a slight snarl at his lip. "We've done all we can."

"Is that what you'll tell Mrs. Webb? The other family members?"

"You leave Mrs. Webb and the families to me, reporter. You've already done enough to upset folks."

"You think those men are dead?"

The sheriff paused. "I think it's no longer a rescue."

Tom thought of his conversation at the river with Virginia Webb.

"What happens now?" he asked. "Do we just go on and accept that it was nothing more than an accident?"

"Accidents happen, reporter."

"Just seems there's a lot of unanswered questions."

Sturgill took a step and Tom was aware of how the sheriff stood a good three inches above him. The smell of peppermints was close and Tom noticed the stubble along the sheriff's chin.

"You know something I don't, reporter?"

Tom glanced at JC, who raised his eyebrows, but remained silent. He wanted to ask the sheriff if he suspected foul play. What was the relationship between the Webbs and Dutch? Who stood to gain if one, or both of the men, disappeared? Instead, he just shook his head.

"That's what I thought," Sturgill said.

Tom heard the squeak of JC's chair and his editor appeared between the two of them.

"We thank you for the update, sheriff. Will there be anything else?"

The sheriff's eyes lingered on Tom until they darted to the side. "That's all."

Sturgill turned and was out the door in five long strides, his exit punctuated by the clatter of the bell. Tom walked over and sat in his chair.

"Unbelievable."

JC shrugged. "They searched longer than normal. You knew they'd not stay out there until the new year."

"Still, there's two men missing. You just give up?"

"Weather's getting worse. River's rising."

"What do we do now?"

"You write the story."

"I have little other than they've now called off the search."

JC leaned back and ran his hand over his chin. Tom noticed the stubble along his jawline and dark circles under his eyes.

"What's all that about unanswered questions?" JC asked.

"I don't know... fishing, I guess. I mean Mrs. Webb was a little evasive about how her husband and Dutch got along."

"Anything to it?"

"Nothing I know about."

Tom paused. "Stick suggested I talk to a Thaddeus Lincoln."

"Why's that?"

"Something about the plans for a wildlife refuge."

JC nodded.

"Yeah, that's been a bit of a mess. Soon after Pearl Harbor, the government came in and claimed a bunch of good farm land and put up Army barracks and an airfield and turned it into Camp Winchester."

Tom started scribbling in his notebook. "I remember seeing that on my way into town."

"Yeah, the military took over this area for a long time and claimed a good amount of crop land. Some farmers weren't too happy about it, but I mean we were at war with the Japs and Germans. Wouldn't have been very patriotic to complain about the price per acre you got."

"I'm guessing Thaddeus Lincoln was among them?"

"The way I understand it, a large portion of the land that the military seized was his. If you haven't already, you'll figure out Thaddeus Lincoln is very involved in this town. He's probably the biggest landowner in the county and he's president of the board at the Bank of Newton. But he usually stays out of the spotlight. Operates more in the shadows."

JC glanced at his wristwatch. "There's a morning coffee crew down at the diner. Thaddeus is usually among them. Head out now and you may be able to catch him on his way to the bank."

Tom grabbed his scarf and coat and was halfway down the block when he saw a tall slim figure emerge from the diner. The man wore a black coat that reached below his knees and a black fedora pulled low, but enough of his profile was revealed that Tom recognized him as the imposing figure he'd seen at the boat landing the day after Christmas.

"Mr. Lincoln," Tom shouted out.

The man stopped and turned Tom's way. With a gloved hand, he pulled a watch from his vest, glanced at it for just a moment and pocketed the timepiece, turning his neck to look up toward the blue, cloudless sky as Tom approached.

"Mr. Lincoln," Tom said again, extending his hand.

Thaddeus Lincoln looked down, frowned and hunched his shoulders forward, driving his arms deeper into his pockets.

"Tom Crutchfield, with the *Register*, sir."

Lincoln nodded slightly and peered over Tom's shoulder to see if anyone followed, but the two were alone.

"I saw you down at the landing the day Dr. Webb and Mr. Blackburn went missing."

Lincoln had a sharp angular nose and it only added to the sharpness of his features. His hair was cut close along the sides and it was only his eyes, a bright shade of indigo, that brought color to his pale face. He pulled the gold timepiece again from his vest, glanced at it again before snapping it shut.

"I've got to be at the bank, Mr. Crutchfield."

"Just a moment of your time, sir."

Lincoln considered him and then motioned with his head for Tom to follow along. His strides were long and Tom worked to keep pace.

"What brought you down to the landing that day, Mr. Lincoln?"

"Curious, as were most folks."

"Did you know them well?"

"Of course, Mr. Crutchfield. It's a small town."

They paused at the end of the block as one of the bladed trucks passed before them.

"Do you think Dr. Webb and Mr. Blackburn are still alive?"

Lincoln's eyes glanced his way and then back to the street.

"I'd say the odds are highly likely that those two men are deceased."

"Odds?"

"Statistical probability, Mr. Crutchfield. In my business, we tend to rely on what the numbers present and we make our decisions based on that likelihood. The items they've recovered, the temperature of the water, the strength of that current. That tells me those men are not going to be found. Happenchance has little bearing in my world."

"They've called off the search."

Lincoln pursed his lips. "Wise. They were only endangering more men. There's no Christmas miracles, Mr. Crutchfield."

His long stride carried him over the ice and snow gathered at the street's edge and Tom followed him to the front steps of the Bank of Lincoln, its three stories of stone rising above the rest of downtown.

"Are you in favor of the new wildlife refuge, Mr. Lincoln? I've heard that it numbers some 5,000 acres and would include a good amount of land that used to be yours."

Lincoln paused.

"I think it is widely known my displeasure with the federal government and their rapacious behavior regarding their agreement we had in place to return those lands back to the original landowners once their military use was complete. That includes my family's land, and I will continue to fight for what is rightly mine."

"I hear that Dr. Webb and Mr. Blackburn were big supporters of the wildlife refuge and were leading the push to turn that land into hunting grounds instead of turning it back over to the farmers. I'm guessing that would have put you all on opposing sides?"

"We had our disagreements."

"Any of those disputes turn violent?"

There was a small twitch at Lincoln's cheek and his eyes grew dark and he stared hard at Tom.

"That query doesn't merit a response, Mr. Crutchfield. Do better."

"I'm just saying you seemed to take more than a passing interest in the fate of Dr. Webb and Mr. Blackburn," Tom said. What he didn't say was the idea that the disappearance of Dutch and the doc would greatly help Lincoln's cause. Maybe, even, increase the odds in his favor.

Lincoln released his hold on the door and took a step down so that he was even with Tom.

"Where is it you're from, Mr. Crutchfield?"

"Well, I was studying at the University— "

"No, Mr. Crutchfield. Tell me where you hail from?"

"Well, my parents live in Valley Station. It's near— "

"I know where Valley Station is, Mr. Crutchfield. Where Louisville's high and mighty flee when they no longer want to live on the same streets as some of the undesirables."

Lincoln raised his hand, covered in fine, rich, black leather, and brushed at a smudge of dirt on the sleeve of Tom's jacket.

"And what of your people, Mr. Crutchfield?"

"My people?"

"Yes. Those who raised you and miserably failed at teaching you proper etiquette. Those who'd I hope would admonish your rudeness and impertinent prodding with these questions and accusations. You see, Mr. Crutchfield, I know full well the stock from which I come and my son now carries that lineage. The Lincoln name and what we stand for is known."

Lincoln finished rubbing at the smudge on Tom's jacket and leaned back, cocking his head to admire his work.

"Family is what makes us, Mr. Crutchfield, and that's why it is important that I reacquire that which was unjustly taken from the Lincolns. That land, that earth, belongs to my people. And I'll not stop till it is mine once again."

Lincoln reached for the door, but paused to ask: "Once again, I ask you: Who are your people, Mr. Crutchfield? And, more importantly, are you willing to fight for them?"

Tom stood silent and thought of the Christmas card surprise. The deception of the two people who claimed to be his parents. The woman who'd thought so little of him that she'd willingly given her blood to complete strangers.

Lincoln's lips formed a thin smile. "Your silence is such a beautiful sound, reporter. Good day, Mr. Crutchfield."

And with that, Lincoln disappeared behind the door and Tom stood atop the steps and looked around him. Cars drove by and people now walked the streets. He smelled exhaust from a city snowplow truck and heard its blade scrape as it dug through the snow. A small girl, bundled in a red snow suit, held tight to her mother's hand as they walked beneath the bare branches of a massive oak at the corner of the courthouse lawn.

Tom still felt smothered by Lincoln's words. The sheer

weight contained in each vowel and consonant. Each probing question that dug at his heart.

The lies. The deception. Who would fight for him? Who did he stand for?

On this street and day as a town came alive, Tom felt alone. More lonely than he'd ever felt in his life. And from the opposite corner of the street, standing in the open door of his cruiser, Sheriff Sturgill stood, having taken in the interaction between Tom and Lincoln. There was the slightest tip of Sturgill's cap as he slid into the front of his car and pulled the door shut.

⚓

When Tom returned to the *Register*, he went to the newspaper's morgue where there were stacks of old issues of the *Register* and bound copies dating back to the newspaper's first publication date.

Tom pulled copies from early 1942 when the military first began to acquire the land it would use to build Camp Winchester, which was named after John C. Winchester, a former senator, vice-president and general of the Confederacy. The newspaper reported that approximately 1,500 families were required to sell their land, much of it for considerably far less than they thought it was worth. The landowners had as little as 10 days to relocate their family, farm equipment and livestock and, with little land to be had on the market, many farmers were forced to choose another line of work.

On the front pages of the *Register* were more and more reports of local boys fighting in far-off lands and work was around the clock on getting Camp Winchester up and running so more troops could be trained. On July 1, 1942, the camp was activated at a cost of more than $39 million. It's 1,800 buildings were meant to be temporary — built on pillars with no insulation. Among the buildings were a 2,000-bed hospital, barracks, mess halls, warehouses, office buildings, chapels, a theater, recreation hall, post exchanges, laundry, incinerator, cold storage plant, motor repair shops, a sewage treatment facility, restaurants, stores and four service clubs.

Over the next three years, some 40,000 infantry troops were trained at Camp Winchester in the use of small arms, hand grenades and mortars with most of them being with the 506th regiment of the 101st Airborne Division. Also, the post served as a prisoner of war camp with more than 3,000 members of the German Army held there.

After the end of World War II, the original plan had been to give the original landowners a chance to buy their property back. But, instead, the Korean War followed and the camp was reactivated for training from 1948-53. It was during the early 1950s, Tom remembered, that Elizabeth Tyner and her husband, Nicholas, moved to Morgan's Gap as he supervised airman training before he was transferred to Korea.

Once the Korean War ended, there was little use for the post and, in the early 1960s, word began to circulate in Newton County that the military had little use for the camp and that's when the landowners, including Thaddeus Lincoln, began to make noise about reacquiring their former land. In 1963, some of the land was turned over to the federally-funded Job Corps for its use, but a large chunk of the 36,000 acres, much of it prime farmland and rolling forested hills, was still at play.

Not only were the property owners wanting the land for growing corn and soybeans, but also for its mineral rights as beneath were large deposits of coal, waiting to be mined, not to mention deep pockets of natural gas and oil. Not just thousands, but millions of dollars were in question, Tom learned. There were rumblings, evidenced by several letters to the editor, that the government was preparing to sell off the mineral rights to Camp Winchester at what some believed would be a profit of more than $35 million. Money that the original property owners thought was theirs.

A year earlier, a contingent of local sportsmen — headed by Dr. Wesley Webb and the game warden for Newton County, Dutch Blackburn — had made a pitch to the federal government that the state of Kentucky's wildlife and forest services division was eager to take some 5,000 of those acres off its hands and turn it into a refuge, a mecca for hunters searching for quail, rabbits, massive bucks and maybe someday wild turkeys.

Much of that acreage was bordered by large tracts of land owned by Thaddeus Lincoln, who had appeared at one of the meetings headed up by Webb and Blackburn during the summer and called their actions "unjust" and accused the two of "pulling money from their neighbors' pockets" before he had stormed out of the meeting. Still, Webb and Blackburn continued their push and a *Register* article in November reported that the push for the public hunting lands was gaining traction.

Tom wondered who would lead the push for the refuge with Webb and Blackburn now missing. It certainly appeared that Lincoln and others stood to gain with the two men silent.

"What'd you learn?" JC asked from the doorway.

"I had no idea the amount of money involved."

"Millions."

"Enough to kill a man?"

JC scoffed. "Many have been shot in cold blood for far less."

"Their disappearance is certainly convenient."

"But it's all just speculation."

"True."

"And we deal in facts, Mr. Crutchfield."

Tom leaned back in his chair. "I've been told that."

JC looked at his wristwatch. "Fact is that it's nearly 5 p.m. on New Year's Eve. And it's time to call it a day."

Tom stood and stretched. He'd been taking notes and deep in the bound copies for more than five hours.

"Plans?" JC asked.

"None really. Maybe a sandwich and soda."

He looked over at his editor and across the office, near the dark room, he could see the inside of the storage room with the cot and blankets. "How about you?"

JC looked down at his feet. "It's been a tough week."

"It has."

"You call your parents, yet?"

"Once. It's been busy. Working this story, getting settled at Mrs. Tyner's."

"Hardly an excuse, Mr. Crutchfield. You should let them know, your mother especially, how you're doing."

Tom remembered the loneliness he'd felt on the street that morning and thought of his mother sitting alone in front of the fire. The sting of betrayal still burned, but its intensity had lessened.

"The holidays are tough," JC said. "Especially when one who has been there all these years is no longer around to celebrate with. Every New Year's Day, Carol would make cornbread and black-eyed peas. A family tradition, she said, passed on from generation to generation. She told me it would bring us great wealth."

He smiled and glanced at the deserted office, the spider webs that clung to the wall above the layout table, the bucket and mop in the corner to catch the water from beneath the back door when the spring rains came. "Great wealth, indeed."

The smile faded. "She also said to stew those black-eyed peas with tomatoes and there'd be the promise of good health."

As JC talked, Tom saw his face transform into that of a man who'd been dealt a face card instead of standing pat at 16. "I'm done with mystics and traditions," JC said.

Tom shrugged. "Why not start our own?"

JC took another glance over at the cot in the corner, the Bible, closed, on the table, and nodded.

"I think that is an excellent idea, Mr. Crutchfield. Perhaps your best one, yet."

CHAPTER 12

WHILE JC EYED the red 3 ball and the blocked side pocket, Tom took a glance toward the bar, hoping to see Mary Diane, but every seat was full and others were standing to shout out their orders at the Rainbow. The New Year's Eve crowd filled the small tavern as the music from the jukebox mixed with the voices of those in search of a good time and more than a few who had already found it.

"Quite a predicament," JC said, straightening his frame and grabbing the blue cube of chalk to cue his stick yet again. "Seems you've got my side pocket blocked quite well with that nuisance of a 14."

Tom leaned against the wall, balancing his cue at his side. This was their third game of eight-ball and it was moving slower than the first two with JC's over analysis of each shot.

"The longer you stare at it, it's not gonna change a thing," Tom said, looking over again at the bar for a glimpse of Mary Diane.

"Quite true, Mr. Crutchfield, quite true. But we must always be on the lookout for other opportunities."

They had climbed into JC's old Ford truck after closing the doors at the *Register* soon after 5. Tom had suggested a trip to Taylor's Ferry and the Rainbow. "Cold beer in bottles," he'd told his boss. He'd left out how he was also interested in continuing his Tuesday night conversation with the good-looking bartender.

The parking lot was nearly full when they pulled up to the tavern and all the tables inside were taken. JC had pointed to the pool table and Tom had agreed and they'd ordered beers from a waitress and Tom was well on his way to a third win. He watched as JC's shot ricocheted off one bunker and then another. Balls scattered, but none dropped into a pocket. He raised an eyebrow and JC saw him.

"Game's a little rusty," JC said.

"That's an understatement."

"Perhaps, I simply need some aiming oil," JC said, motioning for the waitress to bring them two more bottles of beer.

Tom dropped the 14 and then the 12, reversing the cue ball to where he was lined up on the eight ball and the corner pocket and another win.

"Appears you spent more time in the pool hall than the classroom," JC said.

Tom smiled. "My dad. We've got a table in the den. Took more than my fair share of lumps from him, but I learned a few things."

"Possible you'd show a little mercy to your boss?"

Tom leaned over the table and lined up his shot. As he pulled the cue stick back, he looked over at his boss and said, "Not tonight."

With a smooth motion, Tom's stick struck the cue ball true and smacked the eight ball, which hit the back of the pocket with a resounding thunk. Three of JC's solids remained on the felt. Tom grabbed JC's dollar off the rail and stuck it in his front pocket.

"The least you could do is buy the next round," JC said.

Tom nodded and handed the dollar over to the waitress when she brought the cold bottles over to them. "Keep the change," he said and then added quickly, "Mary Diane happening to work tonight?"

The waitress looked him over. "Who's asking?"

"Tell her the city mouse."

The waitress smiled, put the dollar in her pocket and walked over to a nearby table of four men who looked as though they'd started their New Year's Eve party as soon as their shift had ended that afternoon. They wore jeans and flannel shirts, but you could still see the traces of coal dust behind their ears and on the flaps of their dirty boots. Empty bottles filled their table and one of the men spotted Tom eyeing them. He rose from the table and walked over.

"Evening," Tom said.

JC, who was in the midst of gathering the balls and readying them for another game, glanced up but continued to rack the balls.

"Pretty fancy with that stick, ain't ya," said the miner.

"Just a bit of luck," Tom said.

The miner turned around and looked back at the table of his buddies, who were watching the conversation. "Bit of luck he says," and they all shared a laugh with him.

Tom just shrugged.

"Tell you what," the man said. "I got next."

He pulled a dirty dollar bill from his pocket and placed it on the rail. "Break 'em, fancy stick."

JC, who had finished racking the balls, took his beer and

found an empty chair nearby. When Tom glanced his way, he noticed a slight grin on his boss's lips.

Tom's break was clean and the seven ball dropped in a corner pocket. He then pocketed another solid color and banked the two ball off one rail into another pocket.

"Fancy," said his opponent.

Tom's fourth shot was blocked by a pair of striped balls and the ball hit the rail and spun out. The miner grunted and then leaned over the table. He was a big man and his thick fist wrapped around the cue stick, but his stroke was smooth and he soon pocketed two stripes. Tom watched as the miner pointed to the back corner pocket for his next shot, but the cue ball went wayward and struck another stripe, dropping it into the side pocket. The miner looked up at Tom and Tom looked back, seeing if he'd acknowledge that while he had pocketed a stripe, he'd called the wrong pocket, thereby giving the cue ball back to Tom.

"Shit," said the miner. The cue ball was sitting pretty in the center of the table, either one of them could go on a run. The table of buddies was watching, silently, beers to their lips.

"That stripe dropped," Tom said, motioning to the side pocket.

"Well, shit," the miner repeated and then leaned back. "Your shot, fancy stick."

Tom nodded and then proceeded to sink the orange 5 ball and bounced the cue ball off a rail and left it nice and centered where he then finished off a one-four combination, leaving only one solid ball left. Tom sunk the red 3 ball and the cue ball settled, leaving him a one-bank shot with the eight ball. It wasn't an easy shot, but it was one he'd made countless times in the den with his father looking on and one he'd made even earlier that night.

The miner stood across the table, both fists wrapped around his cue stick and his legs spaced wide. Tom guessed he was about six-foot four-inches tall and probably more than 250 pounds. The table of miners were sharing a laugh and Tom guessed it was at the big man's expense. Probably hadn't been that many times when they'd seen the mammoth of a man beaten or embarrassed like this. Even though his face was hidden mostly by a thick, brown beard, Tom was able to see the downturn of a frown, his eyes locked on the mass of striped balls still on the table. Tom was reminded of the look on JC's face when he talked of no more belief in traditions or mystics.

Tom glanced over to his side where his boss watched, his beer nearly empty and the mop of hair atop his head tussled as though he'd just gotten out of bed. His boss gave him a slight shrug. Tom applied a thin slice of blue chalk to his cue and then lined up his shot.

"Eight ball, side pocket," Tom said, motioning across the table to where the miner stood with no reaction.

Tom took a deep breath and slowly released it, just as he'd always done from the day when he'd first picked up a pool cue at the age of nine. The stroke was smooth and the contact good, the cue ball striking the eight, which bounced off the rail and headed straight for the side pocket, where it teetered on the edge and then dropped. The miner blinked twice rapidly and Tom was watching his reaction and failed to keep his eye on the cue ball, which after striking the eight, spun once, then again and bounced off the rail's edge and landed in the corner pocket.

Fucking, scratch.

"Hot damn," said the miner and he slapped the rail and his buddies let out a cheer. "Fancy stick done scratched the eight ball, boys!"

Tom dropped his head and laid his cue stick on the table and pulled a dollar from his pocket and threw it on the felt. He sat in an empty chair beside JC, who handed him a beer. Tom took a long drink from the bottle and watched the miner's face light up, his buddies slapping him on the back and ordering another round of beers.

"Funny," JC said, "I've seen you make that shot without a scratch."

Tom drained the last of his bottle and watched as the miner settled back with his table of friends and was demonstrating how the cue ball had dropped in the back pocket and what he would have done differently if it had been his shot.

"Figured a guy like that could use a win, right?"

JC returned his look and then nodded.

The two of them sat for a moment and Tom was getting ready to go and get another round when he saw her slide around a couple of tables, a couple of beers in her hand and a smile that made him think of strawberry jam smothered on buttered toast. She was wearing jeans and a checkered waiter's towel hung from one of the loops.

"City mouse," she said.

"Mary Diane."

"Becky said some boy was out here by the pool table asking about me. Said he didn't look like he was one of the regulars."

"You had a hunch?"

"Well, I wasn't sure if you'd be back or not. You know, here with us country folk."

"You have my gloves."

"Ha."

She looked over at the table of miners, which were getting

louder as the waitress Becky delivered another round. "See you met Little Jimmy."

Tom glanced over at the miner, who had pulled Tom's dollar out and added it to the pot. "Little, he is not."

"Yeah, we're kind of funny that way with names and such." JC raised a hand. "Miss."

"Oh, you'll be wanting these," she said, handing over the beer to JC and the other to Tom.

"My boss," Tom said, nodding to JC, who took a long drink from his bottle, then said, "Ma'am" with a nod of his head.

"Oh, we all know who Junious is, city mouse. Aint' that right, Junious?"

JC cracked an uneven smile and Tom wondered if his boss wasn't getting drunk.

"I may have set foot in this fine establishment, oh, but a few times," JC said and then tilted the beer back and used the back of his hand to wipe his mouth. "The beer is usually at the proper temperature and the smiles are quite friendly."

"I had no idea it would be this crowded," Tom said.

"It's New Year's Eve, city mouse. Even so, people in Taylor's Ferry don't really need a good reason to get drunk."

"Mary Diane!" Becky yelled as she made her way back to the back with an armful of empty bottles.

"I've got to go," she said.

"Wait," Tom said.

"City mouse, it's a busy night."

"I wanted to see you."

She smiled and he felt her fingers touch his arm. Mary Diane looked around and then leaned close to whisper in Tom's ear. "Two minutes to midnight. Come find me at the back door."

And he felt her squeeze his arm and she was off, Tom losing sight of her in the crowd.

He sat again beside JC.

"Interesting," said his boss. "Mighty interesting, Mr. Crutchfield."

Tom took a drink of his beer and noticed it had warmed. He sat it down and used its wet sweat to carve a figure eight on the wooden table. "What do you know about her," he said, lifting his eyes up to JC.

"Seems to be a smart girl. Better than this place in my opinion, but what do I know?"

Tom thought of taking another drink, but set his beer on the table.

"I'd reckon she's been here three years or so. Maybe more," JC said. "Time kind of sneaks up on you."

"You been here much?"

"On occasion."

Tom watched as JC tilted his beer back and finished it. Tom figured his boss was six or seven beers in, at least two ahead of him. JC held back a belch and motioned toward Becky for another.

"You want another?"

Tom shook his head and looked around at the crowd. A few tables had been pushed to the side and there were about four or five couples dancing to a Buck Owens song on the jukebox. All the other tables were crowded with people laughing and slapping one another on the back or shoulder. It seemed most everyone knew everyone else and even a few had nodded JC's way, but none had came over to say hello as they seemed to give the newspaperman and the out-of-town stranger their space.

Becky arrived a few minutes later with two cold beers.

"I'm fine," Tom said.

She nodded toward the table of miners. "Compliments of Little Jimmy."

Tom took the beer and tilted the bottle toward Jimmy, who offered up a big grin. JC nodded as well and took a long swig and another. Tom noticed some of the beer spilled from the corner of his mouth and dribbled down upon his boss's sweater.

"You alright?" he asked.

JC pointed his bottle at a couple dancing close together. "Carol, she liked Loretta Lynn. I was more Johnny Cash."

Tom watched the couple dance, their fingers interlocked, the woman's head turned, resting upon the man's chest. He stole a glance over at JC, his head nodding along in rhythm, lips moving, but the words silent. He thought of the cot in the newspaper office and how his boss had grimaced when he'd talked about the promise of good health.

"How long ago?" Tom asked.

JC closed his eyes. "Third of September."

"I'm sorry."

JC nodded, still in rhythm with the slow song. His voice was strained when he spoke. "She woke, kissed me on the cheek and said she was going to go pull weeds out of her garden. I woke later, had a coffee, then found her slumped over, half-buried by her Black-Eyed Susans."

Tom noticed a tear that slid from the corner of JC's closed eyes.

"Doctor said it looked like she died sudden. Heart attack, likely caused by the morning heat and exertion. Said it didn't appear that she'd had pain."

JC opened his wet eyes and turned to Tom. "Thing is, she'd asked me a couple days earlier to pull those weeds. That goddamned patch of crabgrass and I'd told her I'd get to it when I'd get to it."

JC scrunched his nose and wiped his fist under his eye. "Fucking crabgrass."

JC downed his beer in two long gulps and slammed the bottle on the table, hard enough that a few nearby faces turned their way. "Let's get the hell out of this dump," JC said as he prepared to stand, but staggered and Tom was quick enough to grab his arm and put him back down in his chair.

"Careful," Tom said. "Why don't you get your bearings and we'll head out soon."

JC's head slumped and he nodded slightly. Tom glanced at his watch and saw it was 10 to midnight. He saw the waitress Kathy nearby and caught her arm. "Coffee for my friend, please."

More couples were gathering and the jukebox played Roy Orbison's "Pretty Woman" and Tom weaved his way through the crowd to the back door. Outside, the temperature had dropped and it was below freezing and he was alone. He'd forgotten his jacket back at the table and blew on his hands to warm them. He climbed up and sat on the picnic table and pulled his legs close for warmth. Inside, he could hear the crowd singing along with Orbison and he hoped the waitress had delivered the coffee.

He'd had no idea of the pain and guilt JC was carrying. One unusually hot, muggy September morning and your whole life could change in an instant. That he could relate to.

The door opened and he saw the dark outline of Mary Diane before the light from the new moon above lit her face with a kind of pale spotlight. She smiled when she saw him there. The door closed and the sounds of laughter and celebration were muffled. She pulled close the lapels of her wool jacket and stepped towards him. The red from her lipstick was made violet by the moon and he watched her tuck a wayward strand of brown curls that had hidden her eyes.

"City mouse," she said.

"On time."

"I see that." She took another step toward him and her hips brushed against his knees.

"I left my jacket inside and it is freezing out here."

"Tsk, tsk."

His legs widened and she slid between them, her body warm and close now, the wool of her jacket against his chest. He reached for her and brought her to him in a hug. And he took all of her in, the smell of cigarette smoke from the bar inside, a splash of gin that spilled on her blouse and the sweet smell of orange blossom and jasmine that lingered on the nape of her neck.

"You are warm," he said.

And she turned her head up to him and the moonlight fell full on her face and he wanted nothing more than to kiss her lips. From behind the concrete walls, he heard the familiar refrain of "Auld Lang Syne" and he pulled her even closer.

"Do we raise a cup?" she asked.

"I have no drink."

"Then we…"

And Tom leaned in and he kissed her lips and felt the fullness of them and her arms came around his neck and they held that kiss until the song played no more and the moon passed into another year. He stood up from the table and they walked backwards, together, until they met the wall and he pressed himself against her and they kissed again, tongues teasing and tasting, and Tom felt his heart race. He breathed in the night air and it was cool, but he was warm, their bodies together.

"Tom," she said.

"Mary."

He felt the thump of bass through the walls and heard clapping and stomping as the jukebox played "I Want to Hold Your Hand."

Tom raised an eyebrow. "Beatles?"

Mary placed a hand on his cheek. "We're full of surprises."

"I want to see more of you. Not just here."

Her hand trailed to his chest and she played with the top button of his shirt. "You're sure?"

"I've never been more certain."

She looked down, but Tom saw her smile. She lifted her face again and her eyes sparkled.

"There's a park near the school. Come Sunday, around 1."

"It's a date."

"Oh, Tom."

"What?"

"Nothing, it's just… "

The back door opened and a man appeared, wiping his hands on an apron. He saw the two of them, wiped his hands some more and shook his head. "Mary, they're lining up in there."

She stepped back from Tom. "Duty calls."

He held her hand. "Kiss me."

"Tom."

"Kiss me."

And she leaned in and he felt her lips again and smelled all of Mary and she lingered until she pushed away with her hands. "Sunday, Tom."

"Sunday."

CHAPTER 13

WHEN MARY WENT inside the Rainbow, Tom followed. The crowd surged forward and the music rang loud and he lost sight of her. He saw JC standing alone by the front door, coats in hand, and he made his way over to his boss.

"It's 1965," JC said.

"It is."

"Ready to go?"

Tom couldn't hide his smile. "It's going to be a good year."

JC tossed his coat to him and the door swung behind them and they went into the frigid, unforgiving night while the party continued at the Rainbow Tavern. The parking lot was still full and there was a thin coating of frost on JC's Ford.

"Get in," he said, heading to the driver's side, keys in his hand.

"You sure about that?"

JC stopped and turned. "Wasn't asking."

Tom paused and looked back toward the front door of the tavern. The party was showing no signs of stopping and he thought again of how Mary's lips had tasted on his.

There was the screech of a cold engine starting and JC's

pickup lurched forward and stopped near Tom. JC reached over and opened the passenger door. "Well?"

Mary was the only person he knew in the tavern and his car was 12 miles away in Morgan's Gap. He looked in the cab at his boss, who gunned the engine once, then twice. Tom climbed into the truck and pulled the door closed and the truck gained a grip on the gravel and spun out of the parking lot.

The two said little as they left Taylor's Ferry and JC shifted into another gear and the truck picked up speed on the two-lane road. They were alone on the highway, surrounded by empty corn fields. The front tire drifted over the center line and Tom shifted in his seat, but JC jerked quick on the wheel and the truck kept moving forward.

"That was a good time tonight," Tom said.

JC just grunted.

Tom reached over to turn down the heater, which was running full blast. JC reached over and turned the lever back to high and the air blew harder. Tom unbuttoned his coat and looked out the window, counting the miles until he could see the lights from Morgan's Gap.

"You going to see her again?" JC asked.

"Sunday."

JC grunted again.

Tom turned his head back to the window. He'd had a damn good time tonight. And, yeah, he was looking forward to seeing Mary again.

"Look," he said, turning back to JC. "That really sucks about your wife. It does and I'm sorry. But damn, it don't mean that you got to carry that weight."

JC's fingers gripped the top of the steering wheel tighter and Tom could see the white of his knuckles.

"It wasn't your fault, man. She could have had a heart attack carrying a load of laundry. I mean, who knows when — "

"Shut your mouth, Tom."

"I'm just —"

"You shut your mouth, now!"

JC glared at him and that's when the front passenger side tire fell off the pavement and hit the slick, wet grass. The back of the Ford fishtailed when JC jerked on the wheel and the tires slid on the pavement and the truck went airborne, its front end clearing a ditch filled with muddy water while the back end landed in mud. The truck came to a jarring stop and JC's chest hit the steering wheel hard. Tom was able to dodge the windshield, but the right of his forehead caught the metal frame atop the door.

"Shit," JC said, his hands feeling over his chest and ribs. He looked over at Tom. "You alright?"

Tom reached up and felt a lump on his forehead, above his eye. There was a little blood on his fingers. He turned to JC so he could see. "Little cut, that's all," he said.

The headlights were still on and when JC turned the key, the truck started up again. He pressed the pedal and there was a little movement, but the back tires spun in the mud. JC looked in the mirror and around them and there was nothing else but the noise of their engine and the trickle of the water in the creek.

"Shit," he said, looking again over at Tom. "Hey, kid."

Tom shook his head, still trying to clear the cobwebs from the hit.

"Hey, Tom."

Tom focused on JC.

"I need you to push us out of this."

Tom looked around. "What?"

"You got muscles. Young guy. Figure you get up there at the front and when I say, 'go', you give us a push, I hit the gas and we're up and out of here and in Morgan's Gap quicker than you can brew a cup of coffee."

"I don't know."

"Come on. I mean, damn, you hadn't been carrying on like that and we'd not be in this mess."

Tom snorted. "What about the half case of beer you drank? I guess that didn't have anything to do with it?"

"Come on. Let's go. We're wasting time."

Tom shook his head, but opened the door and stepped out of the truck. His foot landed on the wet grass and he remembered he'd switched out the rubber boots for his loafers because he wanted to look good for Mary. He walked to the front of the truck and looked around. It was possible they could move the truck and get the back tires out of that mud hole JC was digging each time he hit the gas. Tom placed his hands on the front hood and braced himself.

"Ready," JC yelled out. "One, two, three, go!"

Tom pushed with his shoulders and felt his thigh muscles clench and he heard the wheels spin as JC hit the gas hard. The truck's back end shimmied and the front started to budge just a bit when Tom felt his back foot slide on the wet grass. His hands lost their grip and his feet went out from under him as his head just barely missed the front bumper and he tumbled down into the wet creek.

"Shit, shit, shit," he heard JC yell from the cab of the truck as Tom pulled himself up out of the creek. He climbed up the bank and stood there, looking down at the back tires now sunk even deeper into the mud. He felt the cold water through the wet clothes and mud covered his pants.

He stood on the road and cold water dripped from his coat sleeves and he tried to wipe the mud from his hands. JC stepped out of the truck and walked around to the back end and also looked at the sunken tires. He stood beside Tom and they said nothing for the longest time.

Soon, they heard the approach of a car and turned west toward Taylor's Ferry. JC raised his hands in the air and waved his arms, signaling for the car to stop. And it wasn't only until it was about 50 feet away when its blue lights came on and JC dropped his arms as the Newton County Sheriff's Office patrol car slowly stopped, its headlights illuminating the two newspapermen.

JC looked over at Tom. "1965. Hell of a year so far."

The headlights momentarily blinded both Tom and JC and then they saw the rotation of blue lights stop. They heard a car door open and footsteps on the pavement. A shadow, backlit by the headlights, slowly approached.

"Well, well," said the voice, "look what we have here."

It was when he came closer that Tom saw Stick's wry smile, one hand on his hip, the other gripping a flashlight.

"You boys alright?" he asked.

"Just stuck is all," JC said.

They watched as Stick walked over to the end of the truck, looked at the tires sunk deep and shook his head. "That's a right assessment, Mr. Wheeler. That is so."

The deputy walked closer to where the two of them stood in the middle of the roadway and noticed the water dripping from Tom's sleeves and the mud on his pants. "What about you, reporter?" he asked, the flashlight's beam going from his feet up his torso and stopping in his face, the light lingering on the bruise and cut above his eye.

"Thought I'd push us out."

Stick chuckled. He looked behind them toward the far-off hills of Taylor's Ferry and ahead to the flat, deserted corn fields. They were alone, no headlights from approaching cars.

"Which one of you was driving?"

"I was," Tom answered quickly.

Stick paused, the flashlight's beam on JC's face. "That so, Mr. Wheeler?"

Tom watched as JC chewed on his lower lip. He spoke up again. "Mr. Wheeler had a few in celebration of the new year and I thought it better I drive us home. Just mistimed that curve a bit. Wet road and all that."

"That right?" Stick asked, the flashlight beam switching to Tom's face. "How much you had to drink there, reporter?"

Tom shrugged. "A beer or two. We were playing pool down at the Rainbow."

Stick looked hard at him. "That so? Back at the Rainbow, huh?"

"Somebody told me they had the coldest beer around."

Stick looked at him for a bit more then turned the light on the truck, looking at how deep the tires were sunk. He started back towards his cruiser. "You two hang out here for a moment."

JC whispered, "You shouldn't have done that."

Tom answered under his breath, "Better than you spending the weekend in jail for driving drunk. Stick's alright."

"You better hope so."

A few minutes later, Stick returned and handed over a rag and blanket to Tom. "Called in a wrecker. Should be here in a bit. Have them tow the truck up to the garage, check out the front end. You two hop in the back and I'll get you to town."

About 10 minutes later, the cruiser pulled to the front of the newspaper office and Stick opened the back doors, letting the two of them out. "Be safe," he said and did a u-turn and the cruiser headed back toward Taylor's Ferry.

Tom and JC stood for a minute outside the *Register* and breathed the cold early morning air.

"Well, that's that," Tom said and turned to start his walk home.

"Rather that not become a tradition," JC called out to him.

Tom paused and turned. "Something to remember. You gonna be alright?"

"I'm just tired is all. Feel like I could sleep 100 nights."

JC stood and looked at the newspaper door and then down the street. "I'm going home, Mr. Crutchfield. I'll see you bright and early Monday morning."

Tom watched as his editor turned and made his way down the sidewalk, dodging frozen puddles and humming the words to a Johnny Cash song. Tom turned and made his own way home and he thought of Sunday and a date in the park.

CHAPTER 14

IT WAS THE start of a new year, 1965, and Tom celebrated by sleeping in late and eating an orange at his kitchen table. The beers from the night before lingered in the back of his brain and he had a rather mean-looking lump over his right eye.

Tom put on a jacket, scarf, toboggan and the rubber boots and ventured outside. Smoke rose from Mrs. Tyner's chimney, but he didn't see her. Instead, Tom took several deep, lung-clearing breaths, hoping the chilled air would clear the cobwebs and he began a walk through the neighborhood.

There were few people out this new year's morning and he walked down the middle of the street for several blocks, the cold air freshening his brain and the exercise feeling good in his legs and arms. He'd worked up a fresh pace and so he had nearly missed seeing her when he passed the two-story house that occupied the corner lot.

He heard a tinkling and the sound of a scraping against wood as he turned in time to see the backside of a woman as she attempted to pull a six-foot-tall Christmas tree through a side door. Her hands were gripped around the top of the tree, a star still attached, but the wide base was lodged in the door despite her wrangling it from side to side. Ornaments fell and broke as they hit the ground, while strings of silver tinsel stuck to her arms.

Tom stepped into the yard. "Whoa, whoa, let me help you there."

"Bastard," she said with a grunt and pulled again and again, the limbs thrashing, she stopping only when Tom walked up beside her.

It was when she turned that Tom realized it was none other than Virginia Webb, her cheeks flushed with exertion, her blonde hair no longer pulled back into a severe bun, but rather tousled and hanging to her shoulders.

"It won't budge," she said with another grunt, the branches shaking, but not moving.

"Let me help," Tom said.

He moved to the door and opened it wider, grabbing some of the branches and bending them forward until they cleared the threshold. "Now," he said. "Give it a tug."

And when Virginia pulled and the tree cleared the door in such a rush, she tumbled upon her backside, her tan capri pants landing in a bank of snow. Tom smiled and rushed over to lend her a hand. He pulled her up and she eyed him as she wiped the snow from her green wool sweater.

"The reporter, right?"

Tom nodded. "Tom Crutchfield."

"Ah, yes. Tommy."

He nodded toward the tree. "Done with the holidays?"

She smoothed her sweater and the front of her capris. "Be a doll, Tommy. Would you take that over to the curb for me?"

"The ornaments, lights and all that?"

"All of it."

Tom shrugged and carried the tree over to the curb. She

had tucked her strands of blonde hair behind her ears by the time he was back and he wondered if she'd also pulled a fresh tube of red lipstick from her pocket and applied it during the minute it took him to move the tree.

"Proper thing for me to do would be to offer you a cup of coffee."

"I'll not say no."

She led him to the back door and, once inside, he pulled off his boots, as well as his jacket, scarf and gloves. The house was warm and the back door led to a large kitchen. Just past the kitchen was a large living room with a large brick fireplace where several logs burned. She motioned for him to sit at the table and she poured a cup of coffee black.

"Sugar, cream or a little more daring," she asked.

"Daring?"

She smiled and went to the liquor cabinet and brought out a bottle of Irish whiskey and added a healthy dose to his coffee. She poured herself the same and eased into a chair across from him. He looked at his white cup and wondered if it was one her husband drank from. The letters written in red said "Charter Member of the Coon Club." She smiled at him from across the table.

"Lucky for me you came along," she said.

"Why the rush?"

"I prefer a fresh start. New year and all that."

She pointed to the knot on his head. "What's the other guy look like?"

Tom rubbed his fingers over the lump and shrugged his shoulders. "Just a small bump."

She looked at him as she sipped from her cup and Tom had the sense of being on a witness stand in front of a jury.

He drank his coffee and felt the burn of the Irish whiskey as it spread across his chest. He looked around the kitchen and it was nearly spotless. Almost too clean, he thought. As though it was rarely used.

"I guess you heard about the search being called off?"

She continued to sip from her coffee and her eyes were on his. It was only when she placed her cup in the saucer did she look away. She picked at a speck of red glitter that clung to her sweater. "The sheriff did inform me."

"I'm sorry."

"Sorry?"

"That they've still not found Dr. Webb."

She stretched her arms before her and her hands wrapped around the cup. Tom noticed the flash of her red nail polish and the way her teeth grazed her lower lip before she spoke.

"What do you think, Tommy?"

"What do I think?"

"Yes. Do you believe my husband will be found?"

"I have no idea."

"You're of little use."

Tom frowned and took another sip of the Irish coffee.

"How long have you been married?"

"Long enough."

"I don't understand."

"Nearly 20 years. I wasn't his first."

She reached her hand into the neck of her sweater and pulled free a gold locket attached to a thin gold chain. She held the locket in her fingers and leaned across the table for Tom to see.

"His Christmas gift."

Tom slid forward until just a foot separated them. Her

scent was exotic, a hint of peach and honeysuckle, lingering until she leaned back in her chair and brought the cup back to her lips. Tom heard a snap and pop from a log burning in the hearth in the adjoining room and his fingers traced the lettering written on the cup.

"You said there was another?"

"Carla. She died during childbirth. Both her and the child, a baby boy. Can you believe that?"

Tom took another drink and his eyes roamed the walls. Where there were plenty of photos on Mrs. Tyner's walls showing her and her late husband and the different stages of their life, there were few personal mementoes at the Webb house.

"There was an age difference, then?"

Virginia smiled.

"The man is 54 years old. We married when I was 21. How old are you Tommy?"

"Turned 21 last year."

"Well, nearly the same difference as you and I."

She moved her arms forward and pushed her cup to the middle of the table, nearly touching Tom's hand. "You have a girlfriend, Tommy?"

He thought of the night before and Mary and how he had pressed against her. "I've dated."

She laughed and pushed away from the table. She went to the stove and brought back the pot of coffee. She filled his cup and then hers. She grabbed the bottle of whiskey and raised an eyebrow.

"Sure," he said.

And she filled his cup with a more generous pour than the first and repeated the pour in her own. He noticed the flush in her cheeks remained and that it had spread down her neck and to the top of her chest where the gold locket flashed in the sunlight coming in from the kitchen window.

"How did he and Dutch get along?"

"Well, Dutch is more of a boy."

"What do you mean?"

"He's not much older than you, Tommy. The only thing they had in common was hunting," she said with a nod to the adjoining room. "Have you peeked at all his trophies?"

Tom rose from his kitchen chair and walked into the living room. Alongside one wood-paneled wall three mounted deer heads stared with dead, stone-black eyes. On another wall a mallard was mounted mid-flight and, atop a wooden shelf, a wild turkey glared at him, mounted in a half-strut, its multi-colored feathers fanned behind him.

"Wesley and all his prizes," Virginia said from close behind. Tom turned, unaware she had followed him into the living room. She handed him his cup and motioned to a couch and they sat, just a few feet separating them.

"Do you know Thaddeus Lincoln?" he asked.

"Of course. Everyone knows Thaddeus."

"Your husband get along with him?"

"They had their disagreements."

"Any chance Mr. Lincoln would do anything to harm your husband?"

Virginia sipped from her cup and then placed it upon the table in front of her. "Sounds like quite the conspiracy theory, Tommy."

Sipping the whiskey he felt the tip of his nose turn numb. The liquor combined with the fire was making him sweat. He unbuttoned the top button of his shirt and fluffed the fabric, the air cooling his chest. He turned to Virginia.

"That day at the boat landing you said Dutch was a good friend. You meant to you?"

"Of course. He was always stopping by."

"Always?"

"Enough for people to talk. You know how a small town is, don't you, Tommy?"

"I don't."

"Well, to hear some folks, they'd say we were having a torrid affair behind Wesley's back."

Tom looked into her eyes. "And … were you?"

She leaned in close to Tom and he felt her hand graze his cheek and neck and then into his hair. She bit her lower lip and giggled, pulling her hand back, two strands of silver entwined in her fingers. "Tommy, you've got tinsel in your hair."

"You didn't answer my question."

"Am I on trial?"

"Just curious."

Her hand landed on his thigh. "Curiosity killed the cat, Tommy."

He smelled the whiskey on her breath and saw the lines converge at the corner of her almond eyes, the wrinkles the mascara failed to hide. Her lipstick had smeared at the corner of her mouth and he felt the sharpness of her nails on his thigh.

"I should go," he said.

"But I've not thanked you for saving me this morning."

He pushed up from the couch and stood, woozy for a bit as the whiskey jostled in his empty stomach. "I really need to go," he said, making his way to the kitchen and the door, where he hurriedly pulled on his boots and jacket.

She followed him and handed him his scarf. "Let's do this again?"

He nodded and opened the door.

The whiskey lurched upward and he walked across the lawn fast, 10 steps, then 20, until he was at the street and, when she could no longer see him from the back door, Tom turned and vomited, the whiskey leaving his stomach and covering the evergreen branches of her Christmas tree. He bent over and saw his face reflected in the half-circle of a broken ornament and his stomach lurched again and the vomit came again until he had emptied his stomach.

Tom wiped his mouth and turned, glad to see that neither she nor any of her neighbors had witnessed the purge. He kicked some snow over the pile of vomit and then fled from Virginia Webb and the mounted prizes of her probably dead husband.

⟲

The newspaper office was quiet and Tom was alone. He welcomed the refuge after his encounter with Virginia Webb and his tumble in JC's truck the night before. He sipped water and took two aspirin from a bottle on JC's desk, hoping to quell the headache that lingered.

He placed a fresh sheet of paper in the typewriter, but stared at the empty space. He picked up the past week's paper and read through it again. He'd have to write an update to the search for the missing hunters for the upcoming issue, but he knew there was still more reporting work to be done. There was still little he knew about Dutch and the possibility remained the bodies would surface over the weekend. He re-read his story from the previous week and stared at the byline before him: By Tom Crutchfield.

Earlier, JC had asked that Tom provide some background material as he planned to introduce the *Register* readership to the paper's new reporter with a photograph and front-page article. Tom had been reluctant to divulge the reason he'd come to Morgan's Gap and JC had not pressed him… yet.

Who was Tom Crutchfield? That's what he was here for, right? Thinking back on his life to now, he'd been blessed with comfortable living. But now, he was questioning whose life he had been living? The one that was truly meant for him or the one Owen and Edna Crutchfield concocted from the day they bought him with a bagful of cash.

His stomach rumbled and he remembered the roast Mrs. Tyner had cooked and her hallway of photos. He thought of his encounter with Thaddeus Lincoln the day before and his threatening words about family and knowing one's history. And he recalled JC's revelation and the pain in the man's voice, the guilt of failing to complete as simple a task as pulling the weeds from a flower garden.

He pulled the telephone close and dialed his home number in Valley Station. He heard his father's voice answer and when the operator asked if he'd accept a collect call from a "Tom in Morgan's Gap," there was a pause, then a gruff "guess so" and then the sound of him passing the phone, "It's the boy."

His mother's voice was breathless when she picked up. "Tom."

"Mom."

Her voice wavered. "Oh, Tom."

"I'm fine, Mom."

"Where are you?"

"Morgan's Gap. I told you when I called Monday."

He heard his father's voice in the background and her hand

cover the receiver, but he still heard her say, "Hush, Owen. He's fine."

Her voice returned, clear. "Are you OK, Tom?"

"I'm fine, Mom. Everything's fine."

"But where are you staying? What are you eating? Do you need clothes?"

"I'm fine, Mom. I'm renting a room from Mrs. Tyner. She's a former teacher, a nice lady."

"Do you need money?"

"I'm working, Mom. Remember the job at the newspaper. This week I wrote the front page story. I mailed you a copy the other day."

"I don't understand."

"It's OK, Mom. I'm fine."

There was quiet on the phone and Tom stared at the ceiling tiles above him, one of the corners stained from where water had seeped in from the roof.

"I know I said this before. But I'm truly sorry," she said. "It was wrong for us to not tell you. And putting it off made it even worse."

Tom remained silent.

"Have you found her?"

"I haven't even started to search. I've gotten caught up in this big story I've been covering."

"What will you say to her if you find her?"

"I really have no idea."

"Are you angry at us?"

"I wish you'd told me."

"I'm so sorry, Tom."

"I know Mom."

He heard his father's voice in the background.

"How's Dad?" he asked.

"He doesn't like the uncertainty. He doesn't like being left in the dark."

Tom scoffed. "That's ironic."

"When are you coming home?"

"I don't know, Mom. It could be awhile."

He heard her voice crack and there was a clang as the phone was placed on a table. Tom grimaced as he heard his mother sob and then the sound of his father picking up the receiver.

"What did you say to her?"

"Nothing."

"It was something."

"She asked when I was coming home."

He heard his father turn and place the phone against his chest and there were muffled voices.

"You don't treat your mother like that, Tom."

"I didn't mean to upset her."

"Seems to me you've not thought of her at all. Running off on this fool's errand. You need to get back to school, Tom, instead of chasing whatever it is you think you're going to find."

"I've learned more in this week than I have in two years at the *Kernel*."

There was silence and Tom thought of his father and how he was likely pacing the wooden floor of the den.

"This newspaper thing. How much are they paying you?"

"It's enough. I've got a roof over my head, food in my stomach."

"You know, there's an office waiting for you down at the construction office. Plenty of good men I've not promoted, waiting on you to fill that space."

"I didn't ask you to. Don't put that on me."

"Listen," his father said, his voice rising. "You'll show us respect. We're the ones who have raised you, fed you, clothed you. Bought you a fine car with a nice allowance and there's a career waiting. You remember what we've done for you."

"I know that —"

"And it will best serve you to remember all this when you find the one who gave you up. You remember that, son. This woman, whoever she is, gave you up. And it was me and your mother who took you in and raised you. You remember that."

Tom felt his face flush and his fingers gripped the phone tighter, but he said nothing.

"Next time you call. You call on your own dime."

And then his father hung up and Tom sat at his desk and watched the street lights flicker, the day turning to dusk.

CHAPTER 15

SATURDAY MORNING, A cold drizzle gave way to rain that washed away the snow, leaving puddles and streams of water. When he'd left his apartment, Tom had bundled himself in his jacket and wound the scarf around his neck, but cool drips of water still found their way along his neck and down his back. He tightened the scarf and mentally thanked Mrs. Tyner as his rubber boots sloshed over a creek bed.

He'd come to search for Dutch. Specifically, to learn more about the missing hunter few were mentioning. Most of the meeting of Morgan's Gap businessmen earlier in the week was devoted to Wesley Webb and there'd been numerous calls to the *Register* from people in the surrounding area wanting the latest update on the search for the missing dentist. Few had asked about the game warden.

When Tom had arrived at the newspaper office that morning, he'd found JC at his desk, a cup of coffee nearby and his fingers hammering out copy. He'd nodded a hello and continued to work until the story was complete. Then he sipped from his cup as Tom updated him on where he stood with his stories for the week, the big one, of course, being the missing hunters.

"I plan to focus on the men. I think most people assume

they're dead with the search now being called off," Tom had said. "I've got plenty of information about Dr. Webb. I need more on Dutch."

JC had nodded. "Hell, I've been here more than 10 years and there's little I know about the guy. I've heard he lives out in the woods south of town."

Tom had driven through the rain, stopping when he saw a postman delivering the Saturday mail. He asked where he could find Dutch Blackburn's house. The postman nodded his head toward a one-lane, gravel road and Tom followed it up steep hills until the road ended at a wooden fence.

Tom saw the mailbox perched on a post and a path nearby. He climbed the fence and followed the path for more than a half-mile till he came to a creek, heavy with runoff. After stumbling down the creek bed, he'd found a tree that had fallen and carefully made his way to the other side. He located the path and again climbed another hill, nearly falling when his foot slid in the mud. As he paused to catch his breath, Tom breathed in the smell of cedar burning. And when he crested the hill, he saw smoke coming from a stone chimney at the back of a cabin.

While trees surrounded and hid the cabin from prying eyes from the south, there was an open meadow before it and, off in the distance, Tom could see a large pond nestled among the slope of three wooded hills. Rain fell upon the tin roof and Tom followed the path to a front porch, his boots clomping on the wooden planks. He heard a shuffling from inside the cabin and a voice called out.

"Who's out there?"

Tom paused, thinking that whoever was behind the door likely had a shotgun in their hands, fully loaded with pellets that would tear through his insides.

"Sorry," he said. "Tom Crutchfield. I'm a reporter with the *Register*."

"What do you want?"

"I've been working on the story about the missing hunters, about Dutch."

"Who told you about this place?"

"My editor. Mr. Wheeler."

There was quiet from inside the cabin. Outside, the rain continued to fall on the roof.

"I was just wanting to get an idea about who Dutch is. A lot of people know about Dr. Webb. The way I figure it, Dutch's story is just as important."

Tom shuffled his feet and looked out at the meadow. He thought of how big the bucks that roamed the woods would be and the largemouth bass feeding in the pond. Secluded, the spread was a perfect place for a man like Dutch, a person who seemed to be one with nature.

Hell, it was worth a try.

Tom turned to head back out into the rain, but stopped when he heard the clang of a latch and the door opened. The interior of the cabin was mostly dark and there was a musty smell from within, but a teenage boy's face appeared. There was a smudge of charcoal on his forehead and his dark hair was tangled, spikes shooting upward. He looked Tom up and down and past him and around, dark eyes flitting about.

"You alone?" the boy asked.

"Just me."

The boy stepped into the doorway, cradling a shotgun. Tom had guessed right. The boy noticed Tom looking at the gun and, after a pause, he leaned it up against the logs of the cabin.

"How big are the deer around here?" Tom asked.

The boy looked at him. He shrugged. "Big enough."

"Like six-point? Eight?"

The boy half-smiled. "More like 10 or 12."

"Really?"

"They say there's a monster buck out there. Twenty-pointer. That's what Dutch says."

"You're pulling my leg."

"Believe what you want. I've heard him thrashing about in that cedar thicket before."

"Lay eyes on him?"

"Not yet."

Tom eyed the shotgun against the wall and peered at a window, but all he saw was darkness inside.

"Out here by yourself?"

"Who's asking?"

Tom raised his hands in mock surrender. The two of them stood and looked out at the meadow and listened to the rain hit the roof. A jay called out and Tom saw the flash of blue land on the branch of a sycamore at the meadow's edge.

"It's me and Dutch."

Tom turned. "Dutch, being…"

"He's my brother."

"Mom, dad?"

"Just us."

Tom had found few All-American families here in Newton County: the mom and dad with a boy and a girl, a speckled pup and a white picket fence. The boy spit on the wet dirt.

"We do just fine," the boy said.

"You in school?"

"Just about done. This spring will be my last."

The boy was nearly as tall as Tom, though thinner, at least

what he could tell from the way the camouflage jacket hung loose on his frame. Tom thought back to his walk through the woods, over the creek and hills and then the one-lane gravel road. It had to be a good mile and he'd not seen any other vehicle when he'd parked at the end of the road.

"Dutch gives me a ride. When he can't, I catch the bus down at the end of the road."

The boy seemed to be a step ahead of him, anticipating every question before Tom asked it.

"Sheriff said they were keeping Dutch's truck for a bit. Something to do with the investigation."

"So, you've talked to Sheriff Sturgill?"

"He was here day after Christmas. A few other times."

"Then, you know they're no longer looking?"

The boy's face darkened and he stepped off the porch and walked out into the rain. He went to the edge of the meadow and stood there, the winter grass nearly reaching to his knees. Tom knelt and sat on the edge of the porch. He felt the bite of the wood against his hands and crossed his feet. The rain slowed and then stopped.

When the boy came back, his face was wet and Tom was unsure if tears had fallen. His hair was wet and long and clung to the sides of his head. He sat beside Tom.

"When?" he asked.

"Sheriff told us Thursday morning."

They sat and looked out at the meadow. Tom noticed two more jays had joined the one in the sycamore. Something bigger stirred out in the thicket at the far corner, down near the pond.

"Pretty sure my brother's dead."

Tom nodded his head.

"You know he was tracking deer when he was barely 8 years old. He taught me everything he knew."

"You hear him talk about Dr. Webb any?"

"Said he was always in his ear about going hunting."

"What about Thaddeus Lincoln?"

The boy shook his head.

"Your brother. He have a girlfriend?"

The boy smiled for a second. "Said he didn't, but…"

"You think?"

"Brothers pick up on things."

"What will you do?"

"Dutch said things were changing. He said he wanted more for me. He said things were going to change for us."

"What do you think he meant?"

"Dutch dreamed big, you know. Always after the big bucks."

The boy smiled again, catching the double meaning in his words.

"Said he was going to open a hunting and game store. We'd run it together. The Blackburn Brothers. We'd guide those big money hunters who come from out of town, dress the bucks and does after they kill 'em and Dutch even said he'd pay for me to go to taxidermy school. All we needed was a partner to get started. Somebody with money."

Worrying about cash had never been a big concern for Tom. He remembered his dad's words from the night before and the office waiting for him at Crutchfield Construction. The future was his if he wanted to follow the path his dad had created for him. For this boy, uncertainty was all the future promised and that was harsh.

"You never know," Tom said. "He could be still —"

"Oh, you know," the boy said with certainty. He turned to look at Tom. "You got blood?"

Tom shook his head.

"You'd know. I think I knew when Sheriff Sturgill come up the day after Christmas and stood on this same porch. My brother's not coming back."

"I'm sorry."

The boy stood and held out his hand. "Malachi."

Tom shook it. "Tom."

"What you going to write this week?"

Tom shrugged his shoulders. "They've called off the search. Give some more details about Dr. Webb. And your brother. Maybe some about their plans for the wildlife refuge."

"That'd be nice," Malachi said. "Write that my brother was a good man. He tried to help people."

Tom pulled his reporter's notebook from a pocket inside his jacket and started to write.

"Tell them he's the best hunter in Newton County. There's nobody that comes close. He can track a deer and sneak up and pet its head when it sleeps during the day. And if there's a bear left in Newton County, my brother will track it to its cave where it hides all winter long. Wild hogs. Wild turkey. Don't matter. Dutch Blackburn, the best around."

Tom closed his notebook and stood. There was wood stacked nearby, dry beneath the porch awning. Tom's stomach rumbled.

"You need anything?" he asked.

Malachi shook his head and picked up his shotgun. "Got all I need right here."

"Where will you go?"

"Might stay here. If it gets bad, Dutch said we got an aunt and uncle on the other side of the river down near Golconda."

Tom reached into his pocket and pulled out a couple dollar bills.

Malachi shook his head again. "Blackburns don't take charity."

"Well, if you change your mind."

"I know where to find you." Malachi paused. "You see Sturgill. Tell him I'll be needing that truck. Figure he's due a visit anyhow."

Tom nodded and turned to make his way back down the path when, out past the meadow, there was a rustle and he and Malachi watched in silence as the antlers of a big buck emerged. The deer shook his head a fierce time, then again, and the brambles and branches scattered. The massive deer settled, standing at the edge of the grasses, muscles twitching beneath his hide. He snorted and steam rose from his snout and the buck raised his head, sniffing the breeze that carried from the south.

Tom stood as still as a stone and looked over to see Malachi's fingers twitching, feet slowly inching backwards toward the door and he wondered if the boy had a deer rifle nearby or if it was just the shotgun.

Tom's stomach rumbled and the buck turned its massive head toward the cabin. And, as he'd tell JC later, Tom wasn't sure if it was his stomach or the scent of a city boy out in the country that made the buck suddenly turn and dash back into the dense thicket, its thick antlers tearing at the branches. Two, then three leaps, and gone back into the woods.

"That him?" he asked Malachi.

The boy shrugged. "Only Dutch knows that."

CHAPTER 16

TOM TURNED HIS Fairlane into the gravel parking lot and shut the engine. He glanced at his watch: five minutes early. He had little trouble finding the park as a Catholic church loomed nearby and small houses bordered its three other sides. The park was just where Mary Diane had said it would be.

He stepped from his car and buttoned his jacket. While the sun was shining, there was still a cold wind that blew from the north, and he wrapped the scarf tight around his neck. Tom spotted her sitting on a wooden bench beneath a massive oak, its limbs bare in the dead of winter.

When he shut the car door, she glanced up from a book on her lap, stood and waved to him. Bundled in a tartan plaid coat that ended right above her knees, she was a thing of beauty, her brown hair escaping from a white crocheted hat and falling upon her shoulders. She smiled as he strode toward her and the two stood awkwardly until they embraced in a quick hug and then sat on the bench.

She reached into her coat pocket and pulled out his pair of gloves.

"Your reward," she said.

Smiling, he slid his fingers inside. He placed his hand on

the bench beside hers and watched her own gloved fingers rest on top of his. They were alone in the park except for a little boy in a blue jacket who was swinging near a slide. An older man stood near the boy, keeping watch over him. A pair of red cardinals bounced from limb to limb, chirping, wings fluttering as they picked at the seed from a small garden of dead daisies.

"This is nice," Tom said.

"It is, isn't it?"

"I should have brought something, like flowers."

"Oh, is this a date?"

He smiled. "It's nice to hear your voice and not have to compete with the jukebox."

"Does the city mouse not like our music?" she asked, playfully bumping her shoulder against his.

"I'm getting used to it."

"Such a man of mystery."

"And I know so little about you. Well, other than you were the fastest girl in Taylor's Ferry, according to Stick."

"Fastest?"

Tom chuckled. "Let me restate that. The fastest on two feet running."

She mock frowned. "If Stick is your main source of information, then you are in trouble."

"Oh, he's alright."

Tom then told her of the drive home Friday night and Stick coming to their rescue.

"Were you hurt?" she asked.

He pointed to above his eyebrow. Her hand gently pressed the area and he winced.

"Should I kiss it and make it feel better?"

"I greatly believe in the healing power of your kisses."

"Oh, Tom."

They heard a shriek from the little boy and he called out, "Push me higher, Pappy." And they watched as the old man gave a slight push to the boy whose little legs kicked in the air. Tom felt Mary's hand grasp his and squeeze.

"When I first pulled up, I saw that you were reading."

"You don't miss anything, do you?"

"A curse of my profession."

She reached over and handed him the book. "The Giving Tree" by Shel Silverstein. The hardback featured a green cover and a picture of a little boy catching an apple passed down from a tree.

"A children's book?"

"No, silly. It's much more than that."

He opened the book and skimmed the first several pages. They were well-worn and several had been earmarked. She said, "It's not the first time I've read it."

"I see that."

"It's about a boy who comes to a tree to eat her apples and swing from her branches. And this makes the tree happy. But as the boy gets older, he wants more and more and more from the tree. And the tree gives and gives and gives."

"So what happens?"

Mary turned and looked at him and he was captured by the way the sunlight lit the hazel in her eyes. "To me, it's about a mother's unconditional love, her self-less caring. But I've heard others say it's an example of a boy who just takes and takes and takes."

Tom closed the book and looked out over the park. He heard the screech of the metal ropes of the swing and he took a deep breath, the chill of the air filling inside his chest. He handed the book back to Mary.

"Before, you asked me what brought me here?"

"Yes."

"I'm searching for my birth mother."

He stole a glance at Mary and she raised her hand to her mouth. Her eyes were forward on the boy who swung higher and higher in the air. She listened as he told her of receiving the Christmas card in the mail, his confrontation with his parents and he leaving his home in Valley Station the day after Christmas and driving to Newton County.

"When I arrived that morning, I really had no idea of what I was going to do or where I'd look or who I was searching for. And then the sheriff's car came by with its siren blaring and I followed through the fog and they brought me here to Taylor's Ferry. I made it to the river and there I found my story. And I'd thought of little else until Stick told me to come to the Rainbow and, there, I found you."

Mary leaned over and his arm wrapped around her. He felt the warmth of her body against his and there was the faint trace of cinnamon in her hair. Her hand fingered the second button on his jacket and she asked, "What are you going to do?"

"I'll finish the story."

"Your mother?"

"I'm not sure."

"Do you have any kind of idea or clue of who she is?"

"The note didn't include a name. Just that it was post-marked Morgan's Gap."

Mary lifted her head and looked up at him. "What will you say to her?"

"That's what my mother asked. I really have no idea. My father said I'm a fool."

Mary straightened and her hand caught a wayward strand of hair and pushed it behind her ear. She looked back out at the park.

"How long will you stay?" she asked.

Tom thought for a moment.

"I like working for Mr. Wheeler. I've learned a ton already. This story is all that people are talking about. Each day I'm finding out something new about Dr. Webb and Dutch."

For a moment, the sun disappeared behind a cloud bank and Mary dug her hands in her pockets and shivered as she leaned forward, her back to the breeze. Tom felt dryness on his lips and he ran his tongue over them.

"My parents think I should go back to school in a few weeks and get my degree. My dad especially. They say my life is there with them. Only thing I'll find here will be disappointment."

Mary slowly rocked back and forth, her eyes forward. Tom placed his hand on her back and she stilled and turned her eyes toward him.

"And I've found a reason that I want to spend some more time here," Tom said. "And that's you."

She turned her head and stared again out at the playground. The rhythmic squeak from the swings the only sound.

"Mary."

Silence.

"Mary. Will you say something? Please."

She stood up from the bench and stomped her feet, clad in a pair of cowboy boots. "It's getting cold," she said, looking up at the sky where the sun remained behind the clouds. The wind lifted her hair off her shoulders.

Tom stood and thought of reaching for her, but instead, he placed his hands in his pockets and turned his back to the wind.

"Should I go?" he asked her.

She looked down and stomped her feet. "I don't want you to, but…"

"But?"

Mary took a deep sigh. "I like you, Tom. I do."

He smiled. "And I like you, Mary. And I'd like to see more of you. Next time, I'll bring flowers."

There was a slight smile and she lifted her eyes and gazed back out at the park. The little boy had stopped swinging and the old man was kneeling, buttoning his jacket and he pulled a toboggan from his back pocket and put it atop the boy's head.

"Tom, there are things you need to know."

"It can't be that bad, Mary. Trust me, I know."

"I just don't know if you'd understand."

Tom reached over and held her hand. "You have to give me the chance to try."

The little boy was now running ahead of the man and he had a smile on his face as he ran toward Tom and Mary. Tom felt Mary release his hand.

"Momma, momma," said the boy, "did you see how high I flew? I flew so high."

And the little boy ran and Mary knelt and she wrapped her arms around him. "I'm so proud of you, Joshua. You are so brave."

And as she wrapped her son in her arms, Mary turned her eyes upon him and Tom nodded. The little boy pulled away from Mary and looked up at Tom with a quizzical look. Tom also noticed that the man who had been with the boy had also drawn near. Mary straightened and held her son's hand.

"Joshua, this is my friend, Tom."

And she turned to Tom and said, "And Tom, this is my son, Joshua, and my daddy, Fergus Clanton."

Tom looked at her face and it was one of hope as she bit her bottom lip.

Tom knelt so he was eye to eye with the boy and he noticed his eyes were the same hazel as Mary's. "Hello, Joshua. I'm pleased to meet you." And the boy reached out and shook Tom's outstretched hand.

Tom rose and turned. "And Mr. Clanton, it's my pleasure."

Fergus gave a curt nod, his hands wrapped tightly around a newspaper. He turned to the boy and Mary. "Come now, Joshua. Let's go get some lunch."

Joshua looked up at his mother. "Mom?"

"Yes, love. Go with Pappy. I'll be right there."

She bent and kissed his cheek and Joshua took off toward a house with green shutters. Fergus nodded again at the two of them and followed the boy. They watched them cross the street and enter the house.

"Sorry about Daddy," she said.

"It's Ok."

"Sorry about the surprise."

He turned toward her. "It's Ok, Mary."

She reached over and held his hand. "I didn't know the best way to tell you."

"His daddy?"

She sighed. "It's complicated."

"You're married, separated?"

She shook her head no.

"Is he involved in Joshua's life? Does he see him?"

She shook her head again. "We live with Daddy. My momma died when I was young. It's just the three of us."

"How old is he?"

"He's six. Will be seven this summer."

"Does he ask about his daddy? Does he know who he is?"

There was a frown and a flash of hardness came across her face as though a storm cloud was hurrying in over an open plain. Mary set her jaw and pulled her coat collar tight around her neck.

"He knows his mom loves him very much," she said.

Tom looked at the house with green shutters. It wasn't a large home and Tom could see a wisp of smoke rising from the chimney. There was a battered truck parked in front and a toy tractor turned on its side in the small yard. He turned to Mary and asked, "Can I see you again?"

Her shoulders slumped and she leaned close and he wrapped his arms around her.

"You're sure?" she asked.

"It's about unconditional love, right?" he asked, patting the book in her pocket.

"Oh, Tom."

And they kissed and there was warmth and their bodies blocked the cold winter wind that blew from the north.

After walking Mary to her front door, Tom got back into his car, left the park and passed by the Catholic church, its cross high in the blue sky.

His eyes were focused on the steeple in his rearview mirror and so he nearly struck the woman who was walking alongside the road. Tom recognized the red-and-black checked coat and the thin legs that were swallowed up by a pair of rubber boots and he slowed as the car pulled alongside her. She stopped and he reached over to unroll the passenger-side window.

"Still searching for that mule?" he asked.

Her thin hair covered most of her face and she was silent, shifting her weight from one foot to another. Tom looked out at the vacant street.

"You needing a ride or something?"

Her clear blue eyes darted over and around the car and Tom could see her lips moving, but he heard no words.

"I saw you the day after Christmas. You and your mule. Remember?"

She began to rock back and forth, at a faster pace now, and her thin fingers washed over her hands.

"You live nearby? I'd be glad to give you a lift."

She lowered her head and began to walk. Tom put the car in gear and pulled alongside her.

"You sure?"

She moved faster and suddenly darted off to the right, disappearing in a grove of evergreens. Tom watched the branches sway and waited for her to reappear, the hum of his motor idling in the stillness. Tom shrugged, put the Fairlane in gear and climbed the hill, leaving Taylor's Ferry behind.

CHAPTER 17

MUCH LIKE THOSE who called Newton County home, Tom
fell into a routine once the holidays were over and Christmas
lights were put away. Buckets of coal and armfuls of logs were
brought into homes to ward off the below-freezing temperatures that came with "the hawk" — a strong north wind that
had a way of cutting through all the different layers of clothing
and laying a chill upon the skin of those who ventured out.
Night came early and lasted long and many sat before fireplaces
and snuggled under blankets as "the hawk" screamed outside.

Mondays, Tom wrote feverishly toward deadline and then
helped with the layout and delivering the paper. Tuesdays, he'd
read his stories two times or more, cut out his favorites and
mail them to his parents in Valley Station. Wednesdays through
Fridays, he attended meetings, typed up community correspon-
dence and did what JC directed, whether it was interviewing a
retiring postal worker or writing a preview of the high school's
upcoming production of "Our Town."

Saturdays, he'd find a spot at the end of the bar at the Rainbow and feed quarters into the juke box and sip on long-neck
beers — waiting for when he and Mary could slip away outside
during her breaks. At closing, he'd give her a ride home, taking

the long way, parking at a dead-end among tall cedars, the two of them tumbling into the backseat.

Sundays, they spent together — sometimes just the two of them. He'd taken her to the theatre in Morgan's Gap one afternoon and they'd watched Steve McQueen and Lee Remick in "Baby the Rain Must Fall" and had milkshakes afterwards. Another day, after three inches of snow fell overnight, they'd taken Joshua to the highest hill in Taylor's Ferry and spent the entire day sledding.

Each time Tom stopped by the house, he saw Fergus in a recliner, a newspaper often in his lap. The old man would nod and then turn back to the newspaper. "Daddy," Mary would say, but Tom would just shake his head at her, knowing it was better not to prod Fergus. Joshua was more easy-going and accepting of the newcomer as he loved to ride in Tom's car, especially Sunday afternoons along the roads that led through the river bottoms and climbed into the hills.

Neither Tom nor Mary spoke of Joshua's father. Tom figured Mary would tell him more when and if she wanted to and things were going good between them. Why press my luck, he figured.

He called his mother weekly and she commented on his stories and asked if he was getting enough food and if he was warm. She offered to send money, but Tom said he was doing fine and that he'd call her the same time next week. He hadn't told her of Mary yet and when she asked if he'd found out any more information about "her," Tom answered, "It's been busy, mom."

Wednesday nights he spent at Mrs. Tyner's table. She fed him plates of fried chicken, beef stroganoff and spaghetti. They usually talked about the stories he'd written the past week and what he had planned for the next issue. She spoke of the library board's plans for the upcoming spring festival and if he'd noticed if the starlings had returned.

It was the third week of January and near the end of the evening when Tom told Mrs. Tyner of what first drove him to come to Newton County. They had just enjoyed a meal of beef stroganoff and were standing at the sink, Mrs. Tyner's hands in the soapy water scrubbing a dish while Tom used a towel to dry the plates and forks. She said nothing, but just continued to scrub while Tom told her of the mystery Christmas card and the confrontation with his parents, her attention focused on a sticky bit of brown crust that clung to the side.

"How old are you, Thomas?" she asked.

"Twenty-one," he said, "I'll be 22 in July."

She looked out the window above the sink into the dark night. "July of '43 then, huh?"

Tom nodded, drying a fork and then picking up a knife. "Fourth of July, actually."

"Things had really changed around here by then. The camp was in full operation. New recruits had first started arriving in August '42. I know because that's when Nicholas and I moved here. He'd been assigned to help train soldiers with the 101st Airborne. Wasn't much later until there were about 15,000 men out there at Camp Winchester."

She rinsed the dish and handed it to him.

"I was teaching at the high school, English mostly, and, oh, those teenage girls. All of a sudden, all these young soldiers in and around town. It was hard to keep them on task, Thomas."

She motioned with her head for him to follow her into the front living room. She stood before a wall of shelves crammed with books, her fingers to her lips as she steadily moved down the row before stopping and pulling a book from near the bottom shelf. She handed it to him.

"The 1943 Morganaire?" Tom asked with a quizzical look on his face.

Mrs. Tyner stood with a hand on her hip. "I've got yearbooks from every school I taught, Thomas."

He opened the book and leafed through the pages, stopping at a photo of a younger Mrs. Tyner, holding the sonnets of Shakespeare as she stood before a chalkboard. He smiled, "Shakespeare, huh?"

"There are many lessons we can take from the tales of the Bard, Thomas."

There were photos of football teams and students in chemistry labs. There were large group photos of the pep club and band. There were also class sections with individual black-and-white headshots of sophomores, juniors and seniors. All the students were white, as were the teachers and principal. Most of the boys wore thin ties with bad crewcuts. Nearly all of the girls were in dresses and some wore pearls and others glasses. Some senior boys were already pictured in their military uniform and written underneath was their branch of service and where they'd be stationed. There were several pages devoted to essays and students wrote of their dreams and many talked of war and peace and religion.

Mrs. Tyner sat in a chair and Thomas took a seat opposite on the couch.

"At its peak, there were 55,000 people at Camp Winchester," Mrs. Tyner said, "most of them, young men."

"So?"

"Well, that was a problem. Morgan's Gap, there were maybe 3,000 people here at the time. So, you do the math."

"I don't understand," Thomas said.

"Well, there were four service clubs on the base. Nicholas and I went several times a month, often at the urging of one of his ranking officers. Well at these clubs, there was alcohol, music and a lot of men looking for fun before they were shipped off to Italy or the Pacific. Problem was, there were not a lot of available dance partners."

"I see."

"So, most Monday mornings, I'd overhear idle chatter in the back of my classroom from the more adventurous girls talking of the weekend dances at the camp. And there were always soldiers downtown and walking the streets."

"Ok."

"This is just pure speculation, Thomas. But you said that your parents told you that your birth mother had been forced to give you up. That she could not care for you."

"That's what they said."

"Well, I spent many years teaching teenage girls and there were several, really too many to count, who would suddenly disappear for a semester. Word was they were called to visit an ailing aunt or another relative who lived far away from prying eyes and gossip Betties, but I think most of us knew the real reason for them leaving school. Some would return and there was often a sadness about them. They were not the same girls who'd sat in the back of my room and twirled bubble gum about their fingers and wrote love poems. It was as if life had suddenly turned serious."

Tom looked at the Morganaire in his hands. "So, you're saying they'd gotten pregnant?"

"Yes, Thomas. Birth control was still a new concept and it would be several more years until it became an option here.

Teenage girls, especially pretty and susceptible teenage girls who grew up poor and uneducated, they often became very young mothers."

"Do you remember one of the girls from here suddenly not showing up for school that spring of '43?"

"Not at this instant. But it's believable that a young impressionable girl from Newton County could be easily seduced by the charms of a strong soldier and not take the necessary precautions. And, nine months later, that same girl with a newborn baby in her arms and his father stationed far overseas or, god forbid, dead in a foxhole, may have been forced to make a decision no young girl could rightfully make on her own. And, she chose a different future for herself and her baby. And it's a decision that's weighed on her mind all these years."

Tom turned the pages, his eyes going from one photo to the next, searching for a girl whose nose turned upward at the tip as his did or whose eyebrows were thin and a full bottom lip.

"But it wasn't just the girls of Morgan's Gap, Thomas," Mrs. Tyner said, watching as he studied the pages. "To keep down on the fights among the men at the service clubs, girls were brought in by bus each weekend from the surrounding towns to dance with the soldiers. I can remember sitting at a table with Nicholas and, all of a sudden, there'd be a stream of some 30 to 40 girls walking in, all of them doing their best imitation of Marlene Dietrich or Rita Hayworth. The soldiers called them 'bus girls' and it's possible any one of them could also be your mother, Thomas."

He leaned back in his chair and looked up at the ceiling.

"There's just so many unknowns," he said. "But the card was stamped from the Morgan's Gap post office."

"Has anyone contacted you since you've been here?"

"Not that I'm aware of."

"It's a small town and you're kind of a minor celebrity, a reporter and such. Most people get the *Register* delivered or pick up a copy at the grocery store. So, most of them have seen your name."

He nodded.

"She's apparently kept up with you and is aware of your writing and such. And there is apparently some regret over abandoning you. The Christmas card shows that."

Tom leaned forward and placed the school annual on the coffee table. "When I came here, that was the number one thing on my mind —finding out who she is and why she gave me up for adoption. Now? I don't know if I really want to know."

"You can't mean that, Thomas."

"I really don't know."

"I believe that we all have an innate desire within us to know who we are. And part of that is knowing our origination. Those with whom we share our blood. I just don't think that is something that you can turn on and off as simply as you wish."

"My mind now, it's been mainly about Dutch and Dr. Webb and those left behind. It's like their lives are on hold. Those men's families can't do anything until those bodies are found."

"Thomas, don't you see it's the same?"

"What is?"

Mrs. Tyner leaned forward. "That desire of knowing. It's the answers we seek."

Tom thought of Malachi alone in the woods, the cabin dark and he waiting to hear his brother's steps upon the wooden deck. Or Virginia Webb, she on her couch, the bottle of Irish whiskey nearby, trying to ignore the stares of the dead eyes of her husband's prizes. Or his own mother alone at the kitchen table in Valley Station, waiting for the phone to ring and her son to tell her that he is coming home. And, finally, Mary at the park, her arms wrapped around her son, her hazel eyes looking up at him, searching for an answer, seeking that he'll accept her for who she is no matter her past.

Mrs. Tyner stood and walked over and pulled three more Morganaires from her book shelf. "The '42, '44 and '45 yearbooks," she said, handing them over to Tom. "You're an investigative reporter. Do the work and see if one of those girls in those classes is missing. Maybe it helps narrow the possibilities. Still, there were a lot of families of officers who were moving in and out of the area almost on a year-by-year basis. Wartime was a very fluid time around here."

"So, a needle in a haystack?" Tom asked.

Mrs. Tyner planted both fists on her hips. "At least I'm showing you what haystack to look in."

Tom raised his hands in mock surrender. "You're right. You're right. I appreciate your help."

"Idle hands are nothing but trouble, Thomas."

Tom gathered the yearbooks and the two of them made their way to the kitchen. He stopped at the back door to slide on his boots and button his coat.

"If you'd like, I'll ask around," Mrs. Tyner said. "I know lots of people."

Tom sighed. "Quietly, Mrs. Tyner. I don't want a lot of people knowing my business."

"Discretion is my middle name."

He chuckled and went out in the cold January night, pulling the door shut behind him.

CHAPTER 18

THAT SUNDAY, TOM stood at the edge of a small pool of water, looking down at his reflection that hovered on the ripples. His hair had grown longer, now nearly to his shoulders, and there was a tawny scruff along his chin. He watched as Mary Diane appeared just off his shoulder, her body melting into his.

"They say there are healing powers in that water," she said, her auburn hair tussling in the winter wind. "Long ago, people would come from near and far just to drink from that pool."

Tom cocked his head. "Doesn't look special to me."

She ran her hand over his back and her fingers pressed into his shoulder.

"Maybe that's because you're not looking deep enough. It's full of magnesia and mineral salts. They call it the Healing Springs."

"Healing, huh?"

"Drink enough beer and eat enough hog and you'll be up here soon enough," she said with a smile.

He turned and kissed her on her forehead. "I can think of another reason why I'd come up here with you."

"That so?"

He pulled her close, his body blocking the wind that

whipped around the nearby boulders. They watched as Joshua climbed over a large rock and attempted to scale another, his short legs searching for a foothold.

Tom had not said a thing when Mary had grabbed his hand earlier that day and said, "There's somewhere I want to take you." The three of them had walked past the park and down a gravel road lined with canebrake until Mary and Josh had darted down a dirt path. They had followed the path as it made a steady uphill climb, peaking at the top with the pool of spring water. They'd sat and caught their breath and stared into the water that promised life-giving and healing powers.

"It's our special place," she said with a nod to Josh, who scaled a boulder and was climbing another. "He had a rough time when his teeth came in. Cranky, fussy. When it got to be too much, I'd carry him up this hill and rub that spring water on his gums. He'd quiet down and we'd sit here. Just the two of us. Ever since, it's been our little getaway."

Tom nodded. "It's a good place."

She smiled again and reached to tuck a strand of curls behind her ear.

"Once, way before my daddy's time, there had been plans to build a hotel here besides the spring. A resort. But, plans change…, " she paused and Tom followed her gaze as it looked out over Taylor's Ferry, which was spread below. The Catholic church stood tall with its steeple, gravel streets radiating out as though a spider's web. Rows of compact houses with bare patches waiting for spring vegetables. The storefronts of a small downtown. All of it encompassed by a large grass levee that held back the Ohio when its waters rose.

"Now, most folks have forgot about this spring and this

town. There's just a few of us who remember the Healing Springs and its special powers."

Tom took her hand and held on to it. "I'm glad you brought me here."

She leaned in and he kissed her lips. And when he opened his eyes, she stared into his. And Tom felt very well. There was a quick glance and her eyes widened and he saw concern cross her face.

"Joshua," she said and Tom looked for the boy, who had suddenly disappeared from the boulders behind them. They both stood and Mary called out with more urgency, her hand slipping from his.

"Joshua," she said. "Joshua."

And a rock tumbled off the highest boulder and Tom looked to see the boy's face peer over the edge.

"I'm up here, momma."

Mary stamped her foot and a scattering of loose pebbles splashed into the spring.

"You get down here this instant, young man!"

Joshua's face reddened and Tom saw his lower lip quiver. The boy peered down the wall and shook his head. "I can't get down, momma."

"Well, you found a way to get yourself up there."

Joshua appeared to be on the verge of tears when Tom reached over and touched Mary's arm. "Let me try."

So, with a little effort, Tom climbed the wall of rocks and sat on the ledge beside Joshua. He lifted his arm and called down to Mary. "All's good. Let me catch my breath and we'll be down in just a bit."

Joshua sat cross-legged and there was dirt on the front of his jacket and pants. "Is my momma mad at me?"

Tom shook his head. "No. She's just worried."

He reached over and brushed some of the dirt off Joshua's jacket. "Moms are like that. They're going to be looking out for you. Heck, I'm 21 years old and my momma still wants to know if I'm eating right and wearing my jacket."

Joshua considered this and looked up at Tom. "Where's your momma now?"

Tom paused and he looked out over Taylor's Ferry below him. In the distance, from this height, you could see the curve of the Ohio as it headed south. To the east, was Morgan's Gap. Much farther away was Valley Station.

Tom touched his heart. "She's in here."

Joshua squinted, not understanding.

"It's like even though she's not with me. She's with me. Does that make any sense?"

Joshua shrugged. "My momma tells me I have to be a big boy. And that I have to eat my vegetables."

Tom grinned. "It sounds like she loves you."

Joshua straightened his legs and stood up. He put his hands on his hips. "Want to see what I found?"

"Show me."

Tom stood and followed Joshua, who went around another big rock and a cedar, and when Tom turned the corner, the boy had disappeared again. Tom looked to his left and right and even below, but Joshua was nowhere to be found. For a moment, he thought of the pain that would be on Mary's face when he told her he'd lost her son and how that hurt would stay with him.

So, he jumped when he heard, "Tom Tom."

And when he looked closer, through the thick branches of

the cedar, he saw Joshua's smiling face, his cheeks red from the winter wind. "Come see."

Tom parted the cedar branches and entered into a small cave, its opening hidden by the cedar branches and a large boulder. It was no more than 10 feet deep and maybe five feet in height, so Tom had to bend when he entered. The walls were smooth limestone and the earth was dry. He thought of snakes and bears, but nothing slithered and there were no bones scattered about. When he looked out from the cave, he could see the river below.

Joshua had found a seat on the dirt near the entrance, his back against a wall. Tom sat beside him.

"This is a great place," he said. "I can only imagine river pirates used to stay here."

"River pirates?"

"Yeah, years ago, in the 1700s. Way before you and me, mister."

"Who were they?" Joshua asked.

"I don't know their names, but they'd hide out here in the caves, rob the boats that passed by. Plenty of bad guys probably spent some time here. Maybe even Jesse James."

Joshua's eyes widened and he looked toward the back of the cave and Tom guessed that he was seeing a pack of bandits headed their way. He reached over and touched Joshua's shoulder.

"But that's been a long time ago. The bad guys are long gone by now."

Tom looked around him and smiled. "I'd say this is now Joshua's secret hideout. Can't nobody hurt you if they can't find you, right? And I'd say this is pretty well hidden."

The worry eased from Joshua's face and he reached over and held Tom's hand.

"You won't tell?" he asked.

And Tom pulled him into a hug. "Your secret's safe with me, buddy."

They sat there for a minute or two watching the river and then Tom rose and held Joshua's hand. They made their way down the wall of rocks with little trouble and Mary stood with her arms crossed.

"Joshua Clanton. You'll not do that again."

Joshua lowered his head. "Yes, momma."

She looked at Tom and he nodded. Mary walked over and hugged her son. They reached into the spring water and washed the dirt from their hands and faces and walked down the path toward home. As they turned onto the gravel road lined with canebrake, Mary reached over and held Tom's hand.

"What were you doing all that time?" she asked.

He thought of Joshua and river pirates and hidden caves. "Just guy talk."

"Oh, guy talk," Mary said with raised eyebrows. "Of course."

He pulled her in close. "Don't worry. That boy loves his mother. Just like all boys do."

She smiled and they watched as Joshua walked ahead before them.

"Have you learned anything else?" she asked.

He looked at her quizzically.

"With your birth mother."

"Ah. That."

He told her of Mrs. Tyner's offer to help him in his quest. He told her how he'd taken the yearbooks and looked through them, but had found no one with his features.

"I'm kind of at a dead end," he said.

She was quiet and they held hands as they continued to walk. The end of the road was near and they watched Joshua turn and run into the Clanton backyard.

"And what happens when you find her?" Mary asked.

"What do you mean?"

"Do you just up and leave and head back to college? Back to sorority balls and basketball games and those tramps who linger outside the dance clubs?"

Tom bent and kissed her forehead. "That is not my plan."

"Good," she said, snuggling her head against his shoulder. He felt her lips press against his neck and then whisper in his ear. "I'd miss making out with you, Tom Crutchfield."

They kissed some more and then Tom walked with her to her front door, their feet heavy on the wooden steps. There was a shift in the curtain and Tom thought of Fergus in his chair keeping watch.

On his way back to Morgan's Gap, Tom took a turn and headed over the levee toward the river. He parked his car just above the boat ramp and shut the engine. His was the only vehicle at the landing and when he opened the door, he felt the raw cold. The Ohio River was brown as it was being fed by the runoff from the melting snow upriver and the water was moving fast.

He walked to the front of his car and leaned against the hood, his coat buttoned tight, and he dug his hands into his pockets. He thought of Mary and Joshua and unanswered questions about mothers and the future.

Tom looked downriver and saw two empty barges moored

to steel posts near the river's edge. Unlike the barges, Tom felt untethered. A strong wind blew from the north, across the river, and he shivered and hunched his shoulders. He felt in his pockets for a pack of cigarettes, but he'd not smoked in a week or more.

He heard a car's engine coming over the levee and when he glanced back he saw the grey and brown colors of the Newton County Sheriff's Office. "Just what I need," Tom muttered to himself as he turned his attention back to the river and watched a tug boat pushing an empty barge toward a coal tipple that extended out from the river's edge. He heard the cruiser come to a stop and then the door open. Boots scraped on the pavement and Tom heard the steps come closer. At that moment, he really wished for a cigarette.

"Reporter."

Tom nodded and smiled. "Stick."

The deputy walked up and stood beside him. The two of them watched the tug maneuver the barge below the tipple and coal then began to pour from the tipple in a thick, black stream of chunks, a cloud of dust rising over the barge.

"Thought you were your boss," Tom said.

"Ah. Not often the sheriff is going to work a Sunday."

"What brings you down here?"

Stick leaned back against the hood of Tom's car and crossed his arms. "I could ask you the same."

Tom grinned.

"Mary Diane, huh?" Stick asked.

Tom didn't say anything.

"Well, that appears to be getting pretty serious. What's your intentions with Mary?"

Tom raised his hands in mock surrender. "Easy on the interrogation, deputy."

Stick turned and faced him, his hands at his sides.

"We just look out after our own is all," he said. "I've know Mary Diane since we were kids. I expect her to be treated right."

Tom blew on his hands in an effort to warm them. "If you had a problem with me seeing her, you should have spoken up. It was you who introduced me to her."

Without his hat, the wind caught and tossed Stick's thin, straight hair across his forehead and the deputy reached up and attempted to brush it back. His jacket hung loose on his shoulders and one of his pants legs was stuffed in a side of his boots. Stick followed his gaze and kicked at a loose piece of gravel.

"It's just me and Mary Diane have been friends a good while. That's all."

Tom placed his hands back in his pockets.

"You know Joshua's daddy?"

Stick shook his head, his eyes still looking to the ground where he kicked at the loose rock.

"Plenty of rumors," he said.

"But you don't know?"

He looked up at Tom. "That's something we didn't talk about."

"Yeah. She goes silent the few times I've asked about him."

"I've heard it was a married man."

Tom nodded his head. "Makes sense."

The wind caught Stick's hair and again he reached up to press it close to his head.

"Mary's not easy. Probably because she's not had an easy life. Her momma died when she was young and Fergus is

Fergus. Add in a baby out of wedlock and a dead-end job at the Rainbow. I'm just thinking it'd be nice if she caught a break."

"And you were thinking I could be that break?"

"I just introduced the two of you. Thought maybe the two of you could both use a little bit of a break."

They watched as the last of the coal poured from the tipple and the tug boat ramped up its engines, water bubbling behind the stern, sending a wake out to the river's edge. The water lapped at the boat ramp.

"It's awful cold," Stick said.

"It is."

Talking of the cold made Tom think of the thin woman he'd encountered twice on the streets of Taylor's Ferry, once with her mule and the other time without. He asked Stick if he knew her.

"Creeping Jenny?"

"What's that?"

"That's what everyone calls her. She'll show up out of the blue a lot of times."

Tom told him of how he'd come across her the first day he drove into Taylor's Ferry.

Stick shrugged. "She mostly keeps to herself. Seems she saves most of her words for that mule. She's harmless."

Tom looked back out at the river.

"How long you staying?" the deputy asked.

"A bit longer. I've got nowhere to go."

Stick nodded and they watched as the tug pushed the barge from the tipple and went to moor it downriver. Later, the tug boat captain would cross the river, grab an empty barge and load it, repeating the process until he had a full load that he would push downriver to a Tennessee Valley Authority power plant.

"I'm guessing you'll be at the courthouse tomorrow?"

Tom looked at him with a blank stare. "Tomorrow?"

"Yeah, there's supposed to be a jury and the coroner. They're probably going to rule those two men drowned in the river."

"What?"

"You don't know?" Stick asked.

"First I've heard of it."

"Hmmmmm," Stick said. "Sheriff told me about it Friday. Said I'd probably have to pick up his shift as he and some others were probably going to have to testify."

"They think those two drowned?"

"I'd say so. I mean they found the oar, life preserver, decoys. And there were even Dutch's keys. That storm came up quick, the boat overturned and they fell in the water. They wouldn't have lasted very long in that cold water with that fast current."

"But they haven't recovered either body."

"Apparently, you don't have to have a body. The coroner goes before the jury. They hear witnesses and rule on the cause of death. Supposed to be pretty simple."

Tom shook his head. "I've got the feeling there's nothing simple about this. The longer I'm here and the more I hear people talk, the less I'm certain that it was just a drowning."

"All I know is that I'm covering the sheriff's shift on Monday."

"Sounds like I'll be at the courthouse."

Stick nodded. Tom looked over at him. "We good?"

"We're fine," Stick said.

"Thanks for the heads-up."

"You didn't hear nothing from me."

"I did not."

Stick turned and got into his vehicle. He backed the cruiser and Tom watched the cruiser head up the road and over the levee until he could no longer hear the engine. *Finally, some answers*, Tom thought. And he sat for a while longer at the river, watching the current move fast and he wondered if and when the two missing hunters would ever surface.

CHAPTER 19

WORD SPREAD THROUGHOUT the small community and many had opinions about the fate of Dr. Webb and Dutch Blackburn. Most of the seats in the main court room were filled for the coroner's inquest that Monday. The ceilings were tall and the room was drafty. Tom could hear the radiators along the side grumble as they struggled to heat the space.

On one side of the public gallery was the jury pool, a group of 50 randomly selected Newton County registered voters. They ranged from a farmer in his 60s to a housewife in her 30s to the black mechanic that worked at the Chevrolet dealership.

Questioning each of them was Mr. Sammy Dale Wallace, who ran the only funeral home in Morgan's Gap and served as the county's coroner. Like most rural Kentucky counties, the coroner was the one most comfortable around dead bodies and could usually figure out if somebody had swallowed a bottle of pills or simply died in their sleep.

According to JC, Wallace was a fixture as the county coroner for the past 13 years and usually ran unopposed. He was a Democrat because everybody else in the county was a Democrat. It was such a political stronghold that when the last

Republican won an election in Newton County most of the people had arrived at the polls in a horse and buggy.

Most cases handled by the coroner were pretty simple, but this one was different. There wasn't a body.

"Ladies and gentlemen," Wallace said as he took his place before the jury pool, "you're going to be asked, after hearing testimony, to rule on the fate of these two men, Dr. Wesley Webb and James Blackburn, who have been missing since Christmas Day."

It didn't take Wallace long to weed through the list and come up with six jurors who were not related to either Dr. Webb or Dutch and had only an inkling of the circumstances involving the two men's disappearance.

His first witness was Sheriff Cullen Sturgill. Tom was seated on the second row of the gallery and busy writing notes when he sensed the sheriff stride past him down the aisle separating the two galleries. Sturgill stepped to the witness stand, raised his right hand and swore to tell the truth and then sat, facing the jury.

Wallace opened. "Sheriff Sturgill, if you would, take us through the events of Dec. 26, 1964, please."

Sturgill said he hadn't been in his office long that morning when he received a phone call. The sheriff normally wasn't in the office on Saturdays, but said he stopped in that morning to catch up on some paperwork after the two-day holiday. He said the caller told him that her husband had gone duck hunting on Christmas Day, but hadn't returned. And she was concerned.

"And this caller was who, sheriff?"

"That was Virginia Webb, sir," Sturgill said, with a nod to Mrs. Webb, seated in the second row, directly across the aisle from Tom, looking down at her hands. Tom noticed she was picking at the red polish on her nails, slowly whittling away the glaze.

"And that is Dr. Webb's wife?"

"That's correct."

"And how did Mrs. Webb sound, sheriff? Were there tears? Sobs?"

"No, sir," Sturgill testified, his eyes still on Virginia Webb. "She said she'd awoken that morning and noticed her husband hadn't returned home from hunting and she was concerned. She said Dutch Blackburn had stopped by on Christmas morning and he and her husband had left together in Dutch's truck. I said I would look right into the matter and get back to her."

Tom stole another glance at Virginia Webb, whose focus remained on her nails. Little slivers of red clung to her brown skirt. She glanced up and saw Tom's eyes on her legs. Slowly, she uncrossed them, straightened her skirt, wiped away the slivers of polish from her skirt and crossed them again.

Tom turned his attention back to his notepad and followed along as Sturgill testified. The sheriff said he contacted his deputy and asked that he go to the boat landing at Taylor's Ferry and report back. About 20 minutes later, his deputy radioed and said there was a lone vehicle at the boat ramp — a truck with the seal of the Kentucky Department of Fish and Wildlife on its door and a trailer hitched to its bumper. He said there were no signs of either man.

Sturgill testified, at that point, he called Harlan Pierce, the commander of the rescue squad at Taylor's Ferry and asked that he meet him at the boat ramp and said it was possible that there'd been a drowning. About 15 minutes later, Sturgill met his deputy and Mr. Pierce at the boat ramp.

"What did you find, sheriff?"

"Seeing the situation, I asked that Harlan put in and see if he and his boys could find the boat and the men."

"What were you hoping for, sheriff?" Wallace asked.

"I was hoping we'd find them parked up on a sandbar, huddled around a fire. Instead…," Sturgill paused and flexed his neck. Tom thought he could hear a slight crack as the sheriff turned his head to the left and right and then returned his attention to the jury. "Dr. Webb and Mr. Blackburn are still missing."

At that point, the judge presiding over the inquest asked for a 15-minute recess and Tom walked out to the lobby just outside the courthouse doors. He saw Virginia Webb alone in a corner, her eyes out the window, in her hand a cigarette. Near the opposite corner, along a back wall, beneath a motif of a farmer planting rows of corn, Tom caught a glimpse of Malachi Blackburn with his back pressed to the wall, hands in his jean pockets. The two exchanged glances and Malachi nodded. A crowd of about 20 others, mostly men, gathered in groups of three or four, equally spaced across the lobby. "That lady's like ice," he heard one of the men say.

When court resumed, Harlan Pierce took the stand. He had a full head of hair that was graying on the sides and he wore it in a rockabilly style, beeswax holding most of it in place, except for an unruly shock along his part. Tom noted that Pierce constantly moved his hand from his lap to his head, trying to press the hair into place.

Pierce, who operated a gas station just over the levee and sold nightcrawlers and other bait out the back door, testified he'd been on the river since he was just a boy. He had served as commander for the Taylor's Ferry river search team for the past 20 years or so. "We'll drag for a body just about every summer when people get out and get careless," Pierce said. "You learn to respect that river."

"What were the conditions on Christmas Day when Mr. Blackburn and Dr. Webb reportedly went out hunting?" Wallace asked.

"There was a mean fog bank that rolled in that morning and lingered most of the day. Most mornings, you're going to find fog rolling in off that river. That day it was as thick and grey as pea soup."

"Anything else that was remarkable about that day?"

"Other than it being Christmas?"

"Yes, Mr. Pierce."

"Well, I know a big storm rolled in late morning. That wind came in strong. I walked over to the shop to check on a few things and walked along the levee. Looking out, I could see even from far off that there were whitecaps on that river. You don't see that every day."

"Would you have gone out on the river that day, Mr. Pierce?"

"No, sir." Pierce ran his hand over his hair once, then twice. He looked over at the jury. "And that's what confounds me. Dutch knew that river. He grew up here. Doesn't make sense that he'd go out knowing a storm was coming, especially in a jon boat. I still can't wrap my head around that."

Pierce then told the jury how he met the sheriff the next day at the boat ramp and they quickly organized a search and rescue effort. Two boats were put on the river and they went upriver and downriver for several miles, but there was no sign of the hunters or their missing boat, an aluminum 14-footer. The searchers then began a systematic process of dragging the river, while also continuing to search along the riverbanks for any signs of the hunters.

"And, at this point, did you believe you would locate either Dr. Webb or Mr. Blackburn?"

Pierce looked at the coroner with no expression. "At that point, we knew we were looking for bodies."

There was a slight murmur from the gallery and the judge struck his gavel, asking for quiet in the court room. Tom glanced over at the crowd and watched as Thaddeus Lincoln entered through the double rear doors and quietly found a seat near the back row. The tall man was alone and placed his hat in his lap. Tom also noticed that Malachi Blackburn had also seen Lincoln enter and the boy stared at him for a few seconds before turning his attention back to the front where Pierce continued to testify.

"What did you find during your search, Mr. Pierce?" Wallace asked.

Pierce looked over at Sheriff Sturgill, who had seated himself at the desk beside the coroner after his earlier testimony. Sturgill stood and then carried over a large box to the witness stand. Many in the gallery, including Tom, inched forward in their seats to get a look as the sheriff began to pull items enclosed in plastic bags marked evidence.

"We ended up finding just about everything from the boat," Pierce said, as he held high the items that were passed to him by the sheriff and then given to the members of the jury to examine. There was a gas tank, a life preserver seat cushion, two oars, a pair of hip boots and automobile keys attached to a piece of cork.

"And those keys?"

"The sheriff took them over to Dutch's truck and it started right up," Pierce said.

"Did you ever recover the boat?"

"No, sir."

"And, neither —"

"Body. No, sir. We didn't find Dutch nor Dr. Webb." Pierce looked out at Virginia Webb, whose attention remained focused on her lap. "And we're mighty sorry about that. People need closure and we were hoping we could provide that."

Wallace asked, "How long did you and your volunteers search, Mr. Pierce?"

"We were out there every day. In that cold wind out on that water. Nearly six days looking."

"And when did you stop searching?"

"New Year's Eve. There was another storm coming and me and the sheriff agreed that it wouldn't be wise to put those good men who were volunteering their time in any more danger. It was the right choice."

Mr. Wallace turned and walked back to the table where Sturgill was sitting. The two spoke quietly for a minute and then Wallace walked back to the witness stand.

"With your many years of experience on the Ohio River, Mr. Pierce, not only in leading the search team, but also in just being a fisherman and boater, what do you believe happened to Dr. Webb and Mr. Blackburn?"

Pierce looked down and then raised his head. "As a boy, my daddy taught me, just like his daddy taught him, that you have respect for that river. There are hidden eddies, whirlpools, that'll grab you and hold you, wear you out if you try to swim out of them. And that current? That's the killer. There are some places down off Wabash Island where you can be in water not up to your knees and then you take two more steps, hit a deep pocket and that current will reach up and pull you down with it.

"I think that morning, Dutch and Dr. Webb got caught up in something they weren't ready for. That storm rolled in fast and with that fog thick, maybe they didn't see it until it was too late. We found most of those items down around Bell Island, about a mile downstream from the boat ramp. That's probably about where they realized the weather had turned bad and they needed to get shelter. I don't know why they didn't try to get over to Bell Island and wait out the storm. Or why not head to either shore?

"My guess is that they thought they could outrun the storm, so they tried to turn upriver and head back and a wave caught that boat. All it takes is just one big wave and your boat being broadside and that boat's going to flip, especially if it's a little boat like they were in that day. That boat flipped and they were tossed in that water."

Pierce paused and ran his hand through his hair.

"That cocksureness can get a man killed. I think they thought they'd make it back and that lack of respect for the river cost them their lives. Water was around 40 degrees or so and those two being weighted down in their heavy clothes, that current running fast and strong. They probably struggled for a bit and tried to swim to shore, but you weren't beating the river that day."

Wallace looked at the jury and then back to the man seated in the witness box. "And, Mr. Pierce, your opinion is?"

Pierce coughed once, cleared his throat, and said, "Those two men drowned in the Ohio River on Christmas Day. Dr. Webb and Mr. Blackburn are dead. And that's a shame."

There was a shuffle in the gallery and Tom glanced to his right in time to see Virginia Webb rise from her seat, smooth her skirt, then turn and stride with purpose toward the rear doors — eyes fixed forward. The eyes of Malachi Blackburn, Thaddeus Lincoln and nearly every other person in the gallery followed her until she disappeared behind the swinging doors.

The judge struck his gavel, declaring a recess for lunch. Harlan Pierce got up from the witness stand and walked over to the table where Sturgill greeted him with a handshake and Wallace patted his shoulder. The items found at the river had been placed back in the box near the sheriff's foot.

After lunch, two more witnesses were called and then the jury withdrew for deliberations. Tom was seated in the court room, reviewing his notes when he felt someone slide in beside him.

"Need company, Mr. Crutchfield?" JC asked.

Tom frowned, unsure of his boss's intent. Had JC lost confidence in his abilities? Was he hear to come in and take over the story. Tom held up his notepad. "Just going over the testimony. Jury's still out."

"And your expectation?"

"If you go by only what we've heard, then you have to think those two men drowned. But, I just have a feeling in my gut that there's more to it."

Tom turned and looked at the gallery. Thaddeus Lincoln had returned after lunch, as had Malachi Blackburn, but Virginia Webb was not seen. The judge entered the court room and the jury followed. It had been less than an hour since they'd left for deliberations.

The jury foreman said the six had reached a unanimous verdict: Dr. Wesley Webb and James Blackburn were deceased due to a drowning on the Ohio River on Dec. 25, 1964. The judge struck his gavel and thanked the members of the jury for their service and declared the inquest complete.

❧

Tom shook his head as those in the gallery started to leave.

"Doesn't seem right, how everybody is just willing to accept what others tell them," Tom said. "Blind belief in another person's words."

JC cupped his chin in his hand. "Sometimes, Mr. Crutchfield, things are that simple. Sometimes we create complications and conspiracies when there are simply none. Perhaps the question we need to be asking ourself is why do we not accept and believe in what others tell us?"

Tom grimaced. "Apologies, Mr. Wheeler, but that's a load of horse shit."

He pushed up from his seat and quickly made his way to the railing that separated the gallery from the tables usually occupied by the prosecution and defendants.

Sammy Dale Wallace was placing papers in a briefcase when Tom approached. Wallace glanced up and saw the notebook in Tom's hand and turned his attention back to stuffing the papers inside his briefcase.

"Mr. Wallace, a few questions?"

Wallace didn't look up, but continued to place the papers in his briefcase. "You're that reporter with the *Register,* right?"

"Yes, sir."

"Why is Junious not here?"

"Sir?"

Wallace looked up and regarded Tom.

"Well, I would believe with complicated and important matters such as the things discussed here today, Junious would want to be the one covering this story, with his knowledge and experience in the court room and such." Wallace smiled. "No offense, Mr....?"

"Crutchfield, sir. Tom Crutchfield."

Wallace snapped the latches on his brief case and was preparing to depart when JC walked to the railing to stand beside Tom.

"Ah, Junious, as I expected. So good to see you," Wallace said with a smile and nod. "As you may have heard, the matter is settled. Jurors heard reliable testimony and made their decision. Now, if the two of you will excuse me, I've been away from my trade the entire day and really must get back."

Wallace turned and took three steps toward the back of the court room.

"Have you considered that foul play could have been involved?" Tom asked in a louder voice than normal. JC went to raise his hand and place it on Tom's arm, but paused when the coroner stopped halfway outside the railing. Wallace turned to JC.

"Junious, will you please explain to your junior employee there was no other evidence presented other than this was a horrible tragedy. Two well-known, community-minded men lost their lives in an unfortunate accident. It's as simple as that."

Tom asked, "Did you know the relationship between Mr. Blackburn and Dr. Webb?"

Sammy Dale continued to look at JC. "I was aware they were hunting partners."

Tom asked, "And did you know of their push for the wildlife preserve on the old Camp Winchester land? And the fact that several former owners of that land, including some very influential people in this county, were not at all pleased with their intentions?"

The coroner sighed. "It's unfortunate, Junious. Everything points to an accidental drowning. Nothing more than that. I really need to go now."

As Wallace turned and walked up the aisle, Tom spoke again, raising his voice. "And what of the relationship between Mr. Blackburn and Mrs. Webb? Did you consider that, Mr. Wallace?"

JC dropped his head and leaned over to whisper, "I'm not certain this is the time nor the place."

But the coroner stopped, briefcase in hand, and turned. There was a sneer to his lip and he took two steps toward Tom and leaned in close.

"That's amateur hour, Crutchfield."

Tom stood his ground. "I've heard talk."

"Gossip. Pure unfounded speculation."

JC placed his hand on Tom's arm. "Mr. Wallace. We appreciate your time."

"I'm not finished," Tom said.

"Yes, you are," said a deep baritone voice. Tom looked up to see Sheriff Sturgill had joined them. The coroner's eyes remained locked on Tom and there was an angry twitch to his cheek.

"Sammy Dale," the sheriff said as he placed a hand on the shoulder of the coroner. "It's been a long day. Why don't you head on home?"

Wallace's stare remained on Tom. "The case is closed. If you were more of an experienced reporter, you'd realize that."

JC stepped between the two of them. "That's enough, Sammy Dale. We've all had our say."

Wallace shook his head and turned and walked out the door. Tom closed his notebook and began to follow him out of the court room, but was stopped when Sturgill's arm blocked his path.

"How much longer you going to stay here?" the sheriff asked Tom.

"Sheriff," JC said, "We were just —"

Sturgill raised his hand.

"What are you getting at?" Tom asked

"I'm just saying that all you're doing is stirring up a lot of trouble."

"I'm just trying to find out the truth."

"That so?" Sturgill crossed his arms. "Isn't it time to head back to Valley Station?"

"Cullen," JC said. "This really necessary?"

Tom's eyes widened. "How do you know about that?"

"I do my homework."

Tom shook his head. "That's really none of your business."

"Oh, but you see it is," Sturgill said. "It has resulted in bringing you to my county with your foolish accusations and questions. Why don't you just go home, son?"

Tom's right hand gripped the notebook and he felt his other hand clench. "I'll stay here until the job is done."

Sturgill chuckled and looked out over the empty court-room. The rear doors opened and Stick stuck his head inside. Seeing Tom and JC, he paused for a second and then said, "Sheriff, a minute, if you could?"

Sturgill nodded. "Thank you, deputy."

He turned back to JC. "Junious, remind your reporter these are people's lives. And while we may not seem much to those fancy folks of his up there in the Golden Triangle, we are good people. And I'll not have him upsetting the balance."

JC straightened and eyed the sheriff. "Cullen, my reporter

here is just searching for the truth and that is what these good people of Newton County deserve. The unvarnished, cleansing truth."

Sturgill slowly shook his head. He reached down and picked up the box of evidence. With his free hand, he patted JC on the shoulder.

"Aren't we all, Junious? Aren't we all?"

And he left and the two newspapermen were all alone.

CHAPTER 20

THE AFTERNOON LIGHT was fading as Tom and JC came out of the courthouse and stood at the top of six rows of steps.

"Well, that was certainly entertaining," JC said, straightening his back and buttoning the two buttons of his coat. "What's next, Mr. Crutchfield? Are we taking on the Ladies Auxiliary? Perhaps they have been funneling money to Castro with their bake sales in the basement of the Methodist church?"

Tom ignored JC's barb.

"I think the sheriff knows more than he's telling."

Tom's eyes followed Sturgill, who walked over to his parked cruiser and placed the box of evidence in his trunk. The sheriff then walked across the street to where Stick stood with Malachi Blackburn beneath a large elm, its limbs bare and reaching toward an overcast sky. The boy's arms and hands moved in a frantic motion as he spoke with Stick, and the sheriff placed a large hand on the boy's shoulder to calm him.

"Well, that may be," JC said. "But we've still got a newspaper to produce. And I'll be needing your copy early in the morning. Don't dawdle, Mr. Crutchfield."

JC slapped Tom on the shoulder and walked fast down the steps, his white head lost in the crowd that remained on the courthouse square. As Tom turned, his body was jostled by a shoulder.

"Apologies, my… ," Thaddeus Lincoln said, pausing once he saw who he had collided with. He looked Tom up and down, taking note of the notepad in his hand. He reached up and buttoned the top button on his overcoat and adjusted his fedora. "Ah, yes. The reporter."

"Mr. Lincoln," Tom said.

"Good day," he said, adjusting his fedora.

"Have just a moment?" Tom asked.

Lincoln stole a glance around. Only the group of men he'd just left stood gathered at the top of the steps. He placed his hands in his coat pockets and cocked his head at Tom, waiting.

"What brought you to the inquest?"

"It's not every day you have something of this consequence in our little hamlet," Lincoln said. "I was curious, as were most of the others."

"Any surprise with the jury's ruling?"

Lincoln glanced at the notebook that remained in Tom's hand. "As I told you once before, it is numbers and facts that dictate my actions. Based upon the testimony I heard in that court room today, then I have no reason to believe that it was anything more than an unfortunate drowning."

Tom flipped open his notebook and pulled a pencil from his inside coat pocket. Lincoln took notice.

"I really must be on my way," he said.

Tom partly raised his hand, the pencil between his fingers. "What's the latest on the wildlife preserve?"

"I'm sure you'll know when I know. That's the typical course of action for governmental agencies. Alert the press, create fanfare and a swelling of support. I'm sure they'll tout it as a boon of economic development for our poor, malnourished county."

"I've heard hunters will come from near and far to hunt those lands," Tom said. "They'll need somewhere to camp, somewhere to eat, buy fuel."

"All at the expense of the rightful land owner?"

"So, you'll continue to fight this?"

Lincoln sighed. "There are others like me who will not rest until that land is rightfully returned, or some corresponding type of financial retribution is afforded us."

"Sounds like a long fight," Tom remarked, making a note in his pad.

"Unfortunately, that is often the case when one takes on the federal government."

Tom looked up at him. "So, you'll not let anyone stand in your way?"

Lincoln stared at him, eyes as dark as coal mined from the ground below them. "Some may say I'm a rather sore loser. Thing is, I rarely am defeated."

Tom wrote his response and when he raised his head to follow with another question, Lincoln was making his way down the sidewalk headed toward the Bank of Newton. Tom glanced at his watch and saw that it was nearly 5 p.m. so he started back to the newspaper office.

He was on the sidewalk, past the diner, when he heard steps behind him. When he turned, he saw Malachi Blackburn. The boy came up fast and beneath his breath, he muttered, "Follow me. Up to the left, down the alley." And the boy continued on.

Tom looked behind him and watched as a man held the door for a woman as she stepped inside the diner. Across the street, the furniture store owner was sweeping the walkway in front of his doors. When he turned back to the sidewalk ahead of him, the boy had disappeared.

As directed, Tom slipped down the narrow, darkening alleyway, which opened into a small enclosure. Beneath a large cherry tree sat a concrete bench, screened from view by a thick stand of yews. Opposite the yews, across the court yard, there was a blue door in the back of the brick structure nearest Tom. Leaning against the brick wall, not five feet away, was Malachi.

"Why all the spy games?" Tom asked, his gaze taking in the boy's camouflage jacket and worn jeans.

"Best if people not seeing us talking."

Tom nodded. He remembered seeing the boy speaking with the sheriff outside the courthouse.

"Is that what Sturgill suggested?" Tom asked.

"He said it was best if any talk about my brother came from him."

Tom gritted his teeth. "Sounds like something he'd say."

"I thought what you wrote about Dutch was spot-on. I appreciate it."

Tom nodded. After his visit to Blackburn's cabin the day after new year's, he'd incorporated what Malachi had said about his missing brother in that week's update. There had been headshots of Dr. Webb and Dutch and file photos of the dentist shown in front of his office and one of Dutch with young anglers at a fishing derby. He'd quoted Malachi often in the story.

"My brother was a good man," Malachi said.

Tom looked the boy over. He appeared thinner, with dark circles beneath his eyes.

"How you been doing?"

"It's quiet out in the woods."

"I've been meaning to stop by and check on you."

Malachi nodded.

"I saw you speaking to the sheriff," Tom said.

"I'm not sure if he's telling me everything."

"Today had to be rough. Sorry you had to hear all that."

Malachi's gaze was on the green bank of yew. Through the alley, Tom could hear the noise of engines as business owners began to close up shop and cars began to move. Pretty soon, the downtown streets would be deserted.

"Mr. Pierce was right," Malachi said. "Dutch was familiar with that part of the river. We've been on it plenty of times, hunting ducks, fishing for big catfish."

"Accidents happen."

"But my brother wouldn't have made a stupid mistake like that. Just doesn't make sense."

Tom thought of his conversation with JC in the court room. "People do stupid things. Mistakes are made. Sometimes, it's as simple as that. Painful as it may be."

Malachi looked off and Tom was unsure if he was being heard.

"Maybe the question we need to be asking is why we don't accept and believe what others tell us."

Malachi stared hard at him. "That's some bullshit right there."

Tom smiled. He figured the boy was still grieving. And realizing he was now all alone in this world. Tom could relate.

"That blonde lady," Malachi said. "That's Dr. Webb's wife?"

Tom nodded, watching as Malachi started to say something, but then stopped. The boy kicked at the sparse bit of gravel sprinkled on the court yard.

"That day I came to see you. I visited her earlier that morning," Tom said. "She said your brother and her husband spent a lot of time together. They shared a love of hunting and were both pushing for the wildlife area — for the government to get the land."

The boy spit at the gravel and used the toe of the boot to grind it into the ground.

"She's a different kind of woman," Tom said.

"I heard somebody call her the ice queen."

"She's not a typical grieving widow," Tom paused, rubbing his chin. "Your brother ever say anything about Virginia Webb?"

"He never said her name." Malachi paused again. And then looked directly at Tom. "The things I say to you. You not gonna write up everything I tell you?"

Tom shook his head. "No, Malachi. We can speak off the record and the things you tell me will be strictly for my use as background material. I'll not put you at any risk or harm."

"My brother was a good man."

"I know. You've told me that."

Malachi pushed off from the brick wall and walked to the yew line. He peered through the greenery and looked up at the brick walls surrounding him. He turned and walked halfway down the alley, where he paused before he came back and stood near Tom.

"I've seen her before."

"Virginia Webb?"

The boy nodded.

"One day last October."

"Where at?"

"You know where you parked at the gate, by the path leading to the cabin?"

Tom nodded. "She was alone?"

"No."

Tom waited. Malachi shifted in his stance and then leaned back against the brick wall. He took a deep breath.

"Dutch had been talking about that big buck and it was the first day of bow season. He thought I'd gone to school like I was supposed to. But, damn, you know. I wanted to get that buck. Can you imagine if it was me who killed that monster? And with a bow?"

Malachi smiled. "So, yeah, I played hooky. Went hunting instead. Even knowing Dutch would be pissed off if he found out, but I thought the reward was worth the risk, right?"

Tom stayed quiet and let the boy speak.

"Anyhow, I'd been up in my stand in that tree line that runs along the fence near the front gate all afternoon. And I didn't see a damn thing. Just a few squirrels is all. Dutch had told me he was going to be over in Henderson County most of the day and probably wouldn't be back till late in the night so I was surprised when I was walking back and saw his truck parked near the gate. Thinking he'd see me with my bow and know that I skipped school, I jumped behind a thicket and got real still. That's when I heard another car pull up."

"Did you recognize it?"

"Nah. We don't get a lot of visitors. Anyhow, I heard the car stop and then the door open and Dutch's voice. I was peeking through the thicket and saw him walk around the front of the car and then come around to the driver's side door. I watched him stick his head inside for a few seconds and he pulled away laughing. My brother's got a great laugh."

"I'm sure."

"He had turned and was heading toward the gate, when I heard a woman's voice. She said, 'That's your goodbye?' And my brother stopped at the gate and turned around. And that door opened and that's when that blonde lady that I saw at court today. That's when I saw her."

Tom took a deep breath. "What happened?"

"She took a couple steps and they were all over each other. Know what I mean?"

"Kissing?"

Malachi nodded.

"Didn't appear to be the first time they'd made out. He put her up against that gate and I turned my eyes. I can still hear the way that gate squeaked."

"What'd you do?"

"I backtracked and went back to my stand and sat there for a bit. When it was later, I walked the trail and went back to the cabin. Dutch was there and we had ham sandwiches and pork 'n beans."

"You ever ask him about her?"

"There's a couple of times I was close. But I don't know. Just the way they were kind of sneaking around, out in the woods. Seemed like they didn't want people knowing they were together. I figured Dutch would tell me when he was ready to tell me."

"And so today?"

"Yeah, it was a pretty big surprise."

"You're sure that was the same lady you saw with Dutch."

Malachi nodded. "You've seen her, Tom. A woman like that you're going to remember."

The two of them stood in the courtyard in the approaching dark. There came a whiff of cooking meat from the diner nearby and Tom heard a rumble from Malachi's stomach. He reached into his pocket and pulled out a $5 bill. "Why don't you get something from the diner?"

"I told you... "

Tom said, "It's not charity. It's one friend looking out for another."

Malachi paused for a bit, but then took the money.

Tom said, "You find yourself in a bind—"

"I know."

"You mentioned an aunt and uncle?"

"Yeah. And the sheriff said with today's ruling that should free up the life insurance money."

"Life insurance?"

"Yeah. Being a job with the state, Dutch would have some. That's what Sturgill said. Figured I'd be the one to get it."

Tom hadn't thought about the life insurance as the companies would have to have a death certificate signed by a coroner before they'd pay out. He wondered if Dr. Webb also carried a policy and how much Virginia Webb would stand to make on that. Had Virginia Webb pushed for the inquest rather than waiting for the bodies to surface? Tom wrote himself a note.

Malachi saw him writing. "What I told you?"

"Don't worry," Tom said. "It stays between us."

Malachi nodded and turned to make his way down the alley. Tom suddenly remembered a part of their conversation from before at the cabin.

"Back on new year's, when I asked you about Dutch

having a girlfriend. You kind of avoided the subject, but said you believed he probably did. Why not tell me then it was some blonde?"

Malachi looked at him with a strange look. "It wasn't a blonde."

"What do you mean?"

"Well, I figured he was back with his girl again."

"His girl?" Tom asked.

"Yeah. Mary Diane."

Tom's mouth got dry. "Mary Diane?"

"Oh yeah. Brown-headed girl. Why do you think Dutch was down in Taylor's Ferry all the time?"

Tom dropped his head.

"Mary Diane was his girl, Tom. Everybody knew that."

Malachi turned and disappeared down the alley. Tom, meanwhile, was left with the approaching darkness.

CHAPTER 21

TOM SAT BEHIND the steering wheel of the Ford Fairlane and peered out at the front door of the Rainbow Tavern. He could hear the ticking of his engine as the eight cylinders cooled in the early evening air of mid-February. The steady tick-tick-tick nearly kept pace with his heartbeat.

You're a fool. Everybody keeping secrets and you just blindly believing what they tell you. You've been played again, Tommy. Just a damn fool.

After hearing Malachi's revelation about Dutch's longtime girlfriend, Tom had walked quickly to the newspaper office and the bell clanged when he charged in the front door. JC was pecking away at the keys of his typewriter, beside him a yellow pad covered with scrawled handwriting. He glanced up, but continued to type.

Tom grunted and opened the top drawer of his desk. He scrounged through the papers, tossing them this way and that, searching for a new notebook. Not finding one, he slammed the drawer and opened the second, fingers again flinging papers and envelopes, some taking momentary flight before landing on the floor. He slammed the second drawer and when it didn't close due to a roll of papers jammed topside, Tom kicked at it until it shut with a loud screech.

"That desk didn't cause you no harm," JC said, his fingers hovering over the keys, eyes up and looking across at Tom.

"A damn sham is all it is," Tom said. He ran his fingers through his hair and then searched through scattered papers on his desk. He muttered to himself, looking under a phone book, through stacks of photo prints. JC turned in his chair and pulled a new notebook from the corner of his desk. He turned back and held it out for Tom.

"Care to elaborate?"

Tom grabbed the notebook and stuffed it in the back pocket of his slacks. "Nobody wants you to ask the hard questions. It's like everybody's got their own little secrets and nobody's willing to call them out on it."

"That's why we're here, Mr. Crutchfield."

Tom pulled his car keys from his pocket. "I don't really know if what we're doing makes a difference at all."

"Somebody else beside the sheriff ruffle your feathers?"

"Who hasn't?"

"Told you it's one of the hazards of the profession. Not everybody is going to be always happy to talk with you."

"I just need to get out of here."

JC shook his head slowly. "Mind you don't burn down the town. I'll need that copy early in the morning."

Tom didn't reply. Instead, he had hopped in the Fairlane and turned it west toward Taylor's Ferry. He'd pushed the engine hard, passing three cars on the flat straightaways and now he sat in the parking lot of the Rainbow. Malachi's words lingered.

"Mary Diane was his girl, Tom. Everybody knew that."

Tom got out of the car and slammed the door shut. Four

long strides and he was at the front of the Rainbow. Just before he grabbed the door handle, it swung open and a uniform and badge filled his vision.

"Whoa, whoa, whoa," said the voice.

Tom paused and it was Stick before him. The deputy pulled the door shut and looked Tom up and down. "What burr has got under your saddle, Tom?"

Tom just shook his head and went to open the door. The deputy placed his hand on Tom's chest, stopping him. Tom went to swat away the hand, but paused when Stick's face came into focus. The deputy looked straight into Tom's eyes.

"Easy, Tom," he said in a low voice, his hand still on his chest.

"Why don't we have a seat over there," Stick said, motioning toward a table wedged between the parking lot and a stand of willows, its branches draped over the front half of the deputy's police car.

"Did you know?" Tom asked.

"What's that?"

"About her and Dutch?"

Stick sighed. "That's what's in your craw?"

"That and plenty more."

"What were you going to do, Tom?"

"Get some answers."

Stick shook his head. "Only thing they're serving up in the Rainbow is a cold Strohs. And if you haven't come here for a beer, then there's no reason to be here."

The deputy walked to the table and sat down. Tom stood for a moment, looking at the door, hearing voices from inside and the twang of a sorrowful country song playing on the jukebox. A part of him wanted to walk in there and hold Mary close, feel her body against his. But there was another that wanted to tear the place apart.

He kicked at the gravel and slowly walked over to the table before sitting opposite Stick.

"I've seen plenty of fellows with that same look on their face that you arrived here with tonight. Most of those fellows end up spending some time in the county jail."

"Dutch. Is he the boy's daddy?"

Stick slowly rubbed his palms together. "Now, you're asking questions I don't know the answer to. You and I have had this conversation."

"Why didn't you tell me the two of them had a relationship? I thought we had an agreement."

Stick frowned. "I'm not really sure what you're talking about, reporter."

Tom pointed his finger at Stick. "You're just like everybody else in this town."

The deputy's hands paused and he gave a hard look. "Maybe best you head on home."

"I'm here to see Mary."

"Don't think she's ready to see you, Tom. Especially in this worked-up state you've got yourself."

Fog was starting to drift in off the river and another song began to play on the jukebox.

Tom thought of the day before. The Healing Springs. Mary's body tucked against his, the smell of mint in her hair, the fullness of her lips. She may have been Dutch's girl in the past, but now, damn it, she was his.

"I'm just tired of being the last to know," Tom said. "Seems like everybody thinks they know what's best for me rather than letting me make that determination. I think I have a right to know."

Stick nodded. "In some matters, maybe."

"Why didn't she tell me about Dutch?"

"I'm sure Mary's got her reasons."

"Why didn't you?"

"Didn't seem pertinent."

Tom scoffed. "There you go again. Deciding what's best for me."

The deputy tapped his fingers on the table. "Best thing for you tonight is get back in that fine vehicle and drive back to Morgan's Gap and let that hurt cool a bit. You walk in there, asking questions, embarrassing Mary. Well, my friend, that won't end well. And I really have no desire to lock you up tonight."

Tom pushed away from the table. "Eventually, she's going to have to give me some answers."

Stick shrugged. "Don't understand why you can't let the past be the past."

∽

The fog continued to roll in and soon Tom was surrounded by the gray tendrils that left wet streams on his windshield. He had left the Rainbow and driven just a short bit before he'd pulled off to the side of the road, not far from the canebrake where he and Mary had walked just the day before.

There was nothing but the fog and quiet.

And Tom felt like life was closing in. Nothing as clear as he wanted it to be.

Had he been wrong about Mary? He'd exposed part of his

heart to her, more each day. But she'd not told him of Dutch. Nor anything of her past. And now, that hurt squeezed on his heart and there was a tightening in his chest.

He'd come searching for one who'd given up on him. And he was nowhere closer to answering that question than the first day he'd arrived in Taylor's Ferry. Every question left unanswered.

Was his daddy right? Was his rightful place there in Valley Station, at Crutchfield Construction, Sunday dinners at the long table just off the grand room? Momma's dumplings. Cash in his pocket. And the future mapped out and waiting for him.

Others making choices for him.

The betrayal of his parents not telling him of his true mother. The betrayal of Mary not telling him of Dutch. If they had lied about those things, what was left for him to believe in?

The fog grew thicker and the silence remained. He glanced at his watch and the hour was growing late. There was a story still to write and a deadline that loomed closer with each passing minute.

That was the only certainty now.

And so Tom snapped on his headlights, his hand reaching to turn on the engine and he stopped.

There again. Before him. No more than 10 feet away.

Creeping Jenny.

She was atop the mule, thin legs pressed against the hide. Her head cocked to the side, looking at him through the windshield. The mule stomped its foot and started a slow walk toward Tom.

Clop. Clop. Clop.

He slowly rolled down his window.

Clop. Clop. Clop.

The mule stopped and her body leaned down and her face

appeared in the windshield. Deep, worn lines of worry radiated from the sides of her sunken blue eyes. She wet her lips and in voice, raspy with little use, spoke to Tom.

"Storm coming," she said.

And she straightened and the mule began to walk.

Clop. Clop. Clop.

And they disappeared into the fog as suddenly as they appeared.

CHAPTER 22

On Tuesday, Tom wrote his story, as well as headlines and photo captions, laid out a few pages and helped JC make that night's deliveries. The day, as all deadline days do, passed quickly and Tom had little time to think and ponder.

But the next day, Tom silently stewed at his desk. JC had left a stack of notes from the county correspondents and he edited the copy with a flourish. He had little use for the unnecessary and he took relish in slashing through the handwritten words with his red pen. He hammered at the typewriter keys with a fury, fingers striking hard and fast, his hand swiping the return at the end of each line of copy.

Tom worked hard and he didn't notice the snow that was falling outside. There were a few flakes when he'd arrived that morning, but by noon, the temperature dropped and a strong wind blew from the north. The snow fell in near-horizontal sheets and drifted along the sidewalks and streets.

But Tom, deep in his thoughts, failed to notice, even when Doris shouted out from the front that she was going home for the day. He'd not replied. Instead, he yanked a sheet of copy from the typewriter and reeled another in.

It was only when JC came in and shed his coat, the snow

that clung to the thick wool fabric spilling onto Tom's desk, the flakes melting quick and leaving wet splotches on his fresh copy, that Tom looked up.

"They're saying it's a winter storm," JC said, rubbing his hands together. His cheeks were red from the wind. "They were lined up down at Frog's Grocery. Never seen anything like it. Man's not going to be able to find any milk or bread anytime soon."

Tom looked out the window and it was like looking through a snow globe. One that'd been shaken hard. A mailman passed by the front window, his head bent forward into the wind, the mail sack slung over his back. Other than that, there was little movement outside.

JC looked at the stack of completed copy Tom had left on his desk.

"Hard at it today."

"Finishing up the final one. All the news from Taylor's Ferry." The words stuck in his throat and Mary's face flashed before him. As well as Dutch Blackburn's. "It won't take me long."

JC peered out at the snow. "No reason to keep the office open. Nobody's going to be out in this mess."

He looked over at Tom. "Why not finish that up and head home?"

Tom hammered at the keys and with a flourish, he pulled the finished copy off the roll. "Done."

He handed the copy to JC, who glanced at it and added it to the pile. "I'm thinking this storm is going to cancel the high school dance Friday night and probably the chamber of commerce banquet Saturday night."

Tom rose from his desk and grabbed his coat from the chair.

"Make sure you got film for your camera," JC said. "Spend the morning walking the streets and snap some pictures. Readers love storm photos. This should be one of our top-selling issues."

JC smiled. "I love when Mother Nature drops a front-page package in our lap."

The snow had started to drift, but Tom's Fairlane was able to make the mile to Mrs. Tyner's garage apartment, minus a minor spin when he turned on Waller Street. He'd just started to climb the steps to his apartment, when Mrs. Tyner called out. "Thomas, Thomas!"

The snow was lost in the white of Mrs. Tyner's hair as she held a firm grip on the door against the wind that was increasing in intensity. When he stepped inside, she handed him a covered pot. "Warm vegetable soup," she said. "We'll not be dining tonight. Stay warm, Thomas."

That night, Tom sat wrapped in a blanket and sipped on the soup. The local radio station played Marty Robbins records and the disc jockey read reports from the Weather Bureau. Tom thumbed through the old high school yearbooks Mrs. Tyner had given him. He looked at each photo of each girl, but none made an impression. The shutters on the front window near the door knocked against the wood paneling as the wind increased and the temperatures dropped into the teens.

"This is a major storm, folks," said the disc jockey. "Please take upmost caution and stay indoors with your loved ones."

Tom pulled the blanket up and around his shoulders and picked up another yearbook and started his search again. When sleep came, he was left with no answers and he lay beneath his covers, listening as the wind continued to blow.

꿎

Thursday morning came and the sun appeared, its light nearly blinding as it bounced off the frozen, white landscape left behind by the storm. The firs in Mrs. Tyner's yard were heavy and white and the disc jockey reported that nearly a foot of snow had fallen during the night. Tom heard a scrape and glanced out his window to see Mrs. Tyner with a shovel in her hand, trying to pick away at a snow drift that ran across her back porch.

He pulled on a sweater and jeans, as well as his boots, jacket and gloves. He nearly fell on the slick steps of the stairs and walked across the back yard to where his landlady continued to dig.

"Mrs. Tyner, what are you doing?"

Silver hair dripped from the confines of her sock cap and her breath was caught frozen in the morning air. She wiped a gloved hand under her nose and looked up at him. "Thomas. Things to do. I'll be needing to get to the post office and LouEllen is expecting me this afternoon at the beauty shop."

Tom looked around at the snow that covered the back-yard and driveway. The only things moving were two squirrels that jumped from tree to tree in the yard across the street. Mrs. Tyner once again began to shovel at the snow, grunting from the weight of it, her thin arms straining. Tom reached out.

"Mrs. Tyner, please."

She stopped and placed her hands on her hips. She also looked at the snow, including a high bank, blown against the garage during the night.

"Tell you what," he said. "You make me some French toast,

I'll clear a path to the garage and then work on that driveway."
He held out his hand. "Deal?"

"You know I'm more than capable."

"Yes, ma'am."

"I've done just fine on my own all these years."

"I know that."

She looked again at the wave of white that covered her
back yard and glanced down at the snow that nearly reached
her knees.

"You don't have to take it on all by your lonesome," Tom
said. "Let me help."

"French toast?"

"French toast."

Mrs. Tyner handed him the shovel, stomped her boots at
the back door and went inside. Tom began to work. He flexed
his legs and dug into the snow, pulling out great chunks and
tossing them to the side. He felt a slight burn in his thighs and
shoulders and there was a thin line of sweat along his forehead
as he cleared the path to the garage. The exercise felt good and
burned away at some of the anger that lingered. The air was
crisp and cleared his lungs with each deep breath.

He had begun on the driveway when Mrs. Tyner yelled
out from the back door that his breakfast was ready. They sat
at her kitchen table and drank coffee with their French toast.
She pointed at him as she finished off the last bit of her toast.

"You'll make someone a fine husband, Thomas."

He laughed.

"I'm not joking," she said. "You're a hard worker. Intelligent
with an appreciation for the arts. A fine catch."

Tom shook his head. "There are many who wouldn't
think so."

"Well, they're fools then."

"I need to finish this up. Mr. Wheeler wants me shooting photos this morning."

"I can finish."

"No, ma'am. You do what you need to do in here. It won't take me much longer to get that drive clear."

When he was nearly halfway down the drive, a city truck outfitted with a plow passed by, a wave of snow before it and patches of black roadway left in its wake. The sun continued to shine, the temperature began to rise, and Tom loosened the first two buttons of his jacket as he continued to shovel. When he was nearly at the end of the drive, Tom felt a slight tug along his lower back and he straightened, the shovel resting on the snow bank beside him.

It was when he stretched that he first noticed the red jacket that stretched nearly to her knees. And then the shock of blonde hair that bounced on her shoulders as she walked along the street towards him. Tom wet his lips and they felt chapped from the wind and sun. She made steady progress toward him, her hands in her pockets, eyes hidden behind a pair of round black sunglasses. They were the only two people on the street.

"Morning," he said.

Virginia Webb stopped and cocked her head. "Tommy?"

"What's got you out on a morning like this?"

"I needed to get out of the house. So stuffy in there. Figured a brisk walk would clear my head." She walked over and glanced up at the cleared driveway. "I could use you around my house."

"I'm pretty sure it's not my new career," Tom said, glancing down at the shovel in his hands. "It's a pretty good bet my arms and shoulders are going to be sore after this. Not to mention my lower back feels like somebody's beating on it with a hammer."

"And here I thought you were young and virile."

Tom leaned his weight against the shovel. "Why do you do that?"

She made a smirk. "Do what?"

"Flirt."

"That was flirting?"

"It was."

"Wasn't meant to be."

Tom absently scraped at the snow at the edge of the street. "Why didn't you stay for the second part of the inquest the other day?"

Up the street, a car door screeched open and she looked that way. She pushed her glasses farther up her nose and turned back toward him. "Always with the questions."

Tom shrugged. "It's kind of what I do."

"Well, it can be annoying."

"So, you're a flirt and I ask too many damn questions."

"Quite the pairing, don't you think?"

Tom dug at a chunk of snow and tossed it to the side. Some of the snow drifted on to her black boots. He dug and tossed another shovel full and the snow landed not far from where she stood at the edge of the street.

"Did you push for the inquest?" Tom asked, his breath short with the exertion. He kept his eyes on the last remaining drifts of snow that blocked the driveway.

"I'm just a poor widow, Tommy. Nobody's listening to me."

Tom shoveled another clump and straightened. He looked at Virginia as he caught his breath. She remained before him, hands in her pockets, one foot crossed over another. Her eyes hidden behind the sunglasses. In some ways, she reminded him of a little girl teasing a kitten with a ball of string. The closer you got, the quicker she pulled the string out of reach. Tom was tired of being played with.

"How much do you stand to gain with the jury's verdict?"

"That's really none of your business."

"Being a dentist with a successful practice," Tom rubbed his chin. "I'm guessing he would have a life insurance policy of a half million dollars. Add in his estate and the dental practice and you being the only heir? That's quite a chunk of change."

Virginia stared at him, her lips taut. Neither of them spoke. Behind him, Tom heard a door open and close and the steady shuffle of rubber boots on the driveway. Virginia's face changed in an instant and her lips curled into a smile.

"Mrs. Tyner!"

Tom glanced over as his landlady appeared at his side, her brow furrowed and her glasses partly fogged with condensation, apparently unsure of the woman before her. Virginia pushed her sunglasses atop her head, revealing her face. "Mrs. Tyner, it's me, Virginia Coats!"

Mrs. Tyner pressed her hand to her chest and her fingers stayed there, fluttering against her coat. "Oh, Virginia. I'm sorry I didn't recognize you dear. How are you?"

Virginia glanced down at her feet and Mrs. Tyner, the memory coming back to her of Virginia Coats becoming Virginia Webb, raised her hand to her mouth. "Oh, dear. I'm so sorry. So rude of me. Of course you're not well."

Virginia raised her eyes and there were tears. "No, ma'am. I'm not."

Tom stood in silence, his hands still on the snow shovel, partly amazed at the transformation of Virginia Webb from femme fatale to grieving widow in mere seconds. Mrs. Tyner reached over and patted his arm.

"Virginia was one of my better students, Thomas. So precise with her language. Her elocution and command of the English dictionary were so impressive. She was a star on the debate team. Her ability to sway an undecided to join her side. A master of persuasion."

Virginia glanced at Tom and smiled. "Mrs. Tyner is too kind. She remains one of my favorite teachers."

"How long has it been?"

"Nearly 20 years now, Mrs. Tyner." Virginia reached her gloved hand out and Mrs. Tyner took it. "In some ways, it seems as if it was just yesterday. It was sophomore and junior English. Your room on the second floor, in the corner near the staircase."

"That's right. So many students. So many memories." Mrs. Tyner paused. "What year did you graduate, dear?"

"I was the class of '44. Oh, now it seems so long ago once you put numbers to it." Virginia giggled as though she was again a teenage girl walking the halls at Morgan's Gap High School.

"44," Mrs Tyner said, then exchanged a glance with Tom. As soon as she did, Tom knew what was crossing her mind and, even worse, he knew that Virginia had noticed the look between them. Virginia smiled as she withdrew her hand and looked at the cleared drive.

"I was just telling your help here how I could use someone to shovel my driveway."

Mrs. Tyner patted Thomas on the shoulder. "Thomas has been a godsend."

"I have no doubt," she said. "How do you know each other?"

"Thomas stays in the apartment above my garage."

Virginia bit her lower lip. "How convenient." She turned and pointed down the street from which she came. "And with my house just around the corner and a driveway full of snow. I had no idea you had a nephew, Mrs. Tyner."

"Oh, no. Tom is just a tenant. I'm sure you've seen his name in the *Register*. He's doing a fine job." Mrs. Tyner made a motion with her hand. "And, dear, with your love of language, I'm sure you would have an appreciation of his skills. We've had fascinating discussions over dinner."

Virginia cocked her head as she looked at Tom. "He not only shovels the driveway, but provides good conversation and pays his rent on time? I'm most impressed."

Tom glared at her. "I stay busy."

Mrs. Tyner touched his arm. "It's true. With all the reporting work at the *Register* and the search for his birth mother, I rarely see or hear him."

Tom winced. Mrs. Tyner's slip about his mother had not gone unnoticed. Virginia's head remain cocked and there was a slight uptick at the corner of her lips as she weighed this nugget of information. Tom could almost see her mind doing the math.

"Birth mother?" Virginia asked.

Mrs. Tyner started to speak, but then paused. She looked at Tom as though she was a little girl who'd been caught drawing stick figures with her crayons on a clean white wall, but then there was a quick wink meant only for him. She patted his arm and turned back to Virginia.

"Thomas received a most unexpected surprise this holiday season. There was an envelope postmarked Morgan's Gap and inside a card. The person who signed the card claimed to be his birth mother."

"Oh," said Virginia, her mouth open in surprise. "Is it true?"

Tom glanced at her. "My parents confirmed it. I was adopted when I was just a few days old."

Virginia's mouth remained partly open and she turned to Mrs. Tyner. "And you think?"

"I don't know, dear. I shouldn't have said anything."

Virginia was silent and Tom figured she was going through the list of her female classmates just as he'd been the night before as he searched the yearbooks. He could see her deep in concentration.

"I shouldn't have said anything, Virginia. It was not my place to tell. Please keep this to yourself."

Virginia smiled at her and pulled her sunglasses down from atop her head and covered her eyes.

"Of course, Mrs. Tyner. I'll keep Tommy's secret," she said with a glance toward him. "We all live with secrets and I would never divulge something such as that."

"Thank you, dear."

"Of course, Mrs. Tyner. I'd love to join you and Thomas for good conversation sometime. Make a date."

Thomas and Mrs. Tyner watched her turn and walk down the street. There was a bounce to her step.

"I'm sorry, Thomas," Mrs. Tyner said.

Tom shrugged. "It's Ok. People were bound to find out sooner or later."

Mrs. Tyner nodded toward Virginia, who glanced back and waved as she turned the corner. "She's a clever one." Mrs. Tyner smiled and gave a wave in return. "Once she sets her mind to whatever it is she hopes to achieve, she'll do whatever it takes, no matter the cost."

As the two of them walked back up the driveway and toward the garage, Mrs. Tyner told him of a debate competition years ago and how Virginia Coats verbally eviscerated the argument of the poor girl who stood in her way.

"She took it apart sentence by sentence by sentence, made the girl look quite foolish. Virginia could have simply summed up her argument and let it go at that. But it seemed as though she reveled in the satisfaction of the destruction of that poor girl."

Mrs. Tyner shook her head as they walked toward the garage. "It reminds me of a day last fall in my garden when I watched a spider wrap a moth in silk, tighter and tighter until that poor bug was compressed to maybe a hundredth of its original size. Then, at the end, that spider sucked whatever liquid was left from that tiny package. Virginia Coats is that spider."

Mrs. Tyner opened the garage door and Tom handed her the shovel. She placed it on a peg and then closed the door behind her.

"Later that day, after the debate, I found the poor girl crumpled in a corner of the ladies' room, eyes swollen from tears and a lap full of tissues. Any confidence she had prior to that debate now forever gone. And when I came out that door? Well, there sat Virginia Coats on a wooden bench by her lonesome, taking great delight in a vanilla ice cream cone."

Mrs. Tyner looked up at Tom. "It's best to have Virginia on your side."

"So, your little slip-up wasn't really..."

Mrs. Tyner smiled. "Call it a bit of bait. Did you see the hunger in those eyes when I let that little nugget about your birth mother slip?"

"Clever," Tom said, looking at his landlady in a whole new light.

"School mates often know more about each other than a

teacher would. Virginia has always been very inquisitive and if there was a girl in school who'd gotten pregnant, then she'd likely have known. Just like that spider, Virginia will set her web and once someone falls into it, she's going to wind them so tight that they'll eventually spill their guts. Then, she'll dangle that prize in front of you and it will be up to you to decide if her asking price will be worth the knowing."

CHAPTER 23

FRIDAY MORNING, TOM was at his desk at the *Register*. JC was out of the office, calling on advertisers, while Tom was finishing up a story from the snow that fell Wednesday and was preparing to head to the dark room to develop his film.

"Reporter," said the voice and Tom recognized it as Slick. "You might want to head down to the boat ramp across from Old Shawnee."

"Why is that?"

"Just go," he said.

"I've got a full day here."

"You're going to want to be there."

Tom looked at the half-finished page perched in his type-writer and his stomach grumbled as he'd not eaten breakfast.

"Stick —"

"Shush! No names. And remember, anybody asks, we didn't talk."

Then he hung up. Tom had not seen the deputy since they'd spoken outside the Rainbow five days earlier. Stick had yet to steer him wrong and if he was telling him to come to the river, that could likely mean one thing. Tom pushed back from his desk, grabbed a notebook and his camera bag and headed for the door.

❧

The boat ramp sat about three miles downriver from Taylor's Ferry. To get to it, one had to turn and head downhill off the state road that eventually led to Illinois. The state highway was elevated so that it would not flood when the Ohio River left its banks. Once you descended down the steep bank, you were then riding on a gravel road that'd been gutted with potholes from the heavy farm equipment that used the road to work the land located on either side. It was usually corn and soybeans that were planted each spring in the flat fields known as the river bottoms.

The steady melt from Wednesday's snow filled the potholes with water and heavy mud was piled just off the gravel road's edges, so Tom's Fairlane was streaked with brown dirt covering most of the green paint. The parking lot above the boat ramp was bordered by a thick stand of canebrake and a grove of tall sycamores with their mottled, gray trunks. Tom saw two Newton County Sheriff's Office cars, the Taylor's Ferry Search and Rescue truck and an empty boat trailer. He looked out toward the river and saw the rescue boat entering the main channel and guessed Harlan Pierce was at the wheel. There were also a couple of battered trucks parked nearby and two pockets of older men and one of the onlookers nodded as Tom walked past.

Tom snapped some photos of the rescue boat, which had headed downriver, and he followed a path through the canebrake. He hadn't gotten far when one of his loafers slipped on a patch of mud. Tom was able to get his hand down and catch himself before he fell on his butt, the camera swinging wildly from his neck. He brushed his muddy hand on his pants and continued to follow the track of footprints leading along the top of the river bank. When he had walked about a quarter mile downriver, Tom heard a buzz and thump as cars and trucks traveled over the towering, two-lane Old Shawnee bridge that connected Newton County to its neighbors to the north. Other than a ferry another 15 miles downriver, the toll bridge was the only link between Kentucky and Illinois from Paducah, Ky., to Evansville, Ind. And the road was busy as Tom had heard more than 2,000 cars and trucks passed over the bridge daily. He took a photo of the sun glinting off its steel structure and continued downriver.

He'd not gone much farther when he heard voices below him and Tom carefully made his way down the riverbank. And when he came through a thicket of briars, Tom saw the body. At least he thought that's what it was.

There was a camouflaged lump halfway draped over a massive piece of driftwood. Tom could make out a jacket and shirt and noticed there were no pants on the body as only a pair of brown underwear remained. He could see the harsh white flesh of thighs and calves floating in the river water. It was then that the wind shifted and he smelled the dead body and Tom's empty stomach lurched. He gagged and doubled over, turning away from the river. Tom didn't vomit, but he gagged again and felt a heavy sweat along his forehead.

When he turned around, he saw Sheriff Sturgill watching him, his hands on his hips, his jaw working as he chewed a peppermint. Stick stood behind the sheriff, rubbing his hand over his head, while the coroner Sammy Dale Wallace simply sneered at him.

"What are you doing here?" Sturgill asked.

Tom straightened and tried not to look at the body, especially the bloated legs with the grotesque, thick rope of purple veins that seemingly threatened to burst from the white flesh. He caught a breath of fresh air coming down off the river bank and used the back of his hand to wipe his mouth. Tom looked over at Sturgill.

"Seems the place be," he said.

Sturgill chewed on the peppermint, while Stick's attention was on the riverbank. The coroner simply shook his head as though Tom had stumbled up on a bunch of high school buddies just as Sammy Dale was about ready to deliver the punch line.

"Stay out of the way," Sturgill said.

The coroner sneered once more at Tom's intrusion, but eventually turned his focus back to the body.

"With that snow melt, river's going to rise and then fall back," Sammy Dale said. He cocked his head sideways and looked again at the body. "He probably rose several days ago and that's why you're seeing such a swelling and the smell of decomposition. Actually, he's pretty well preserved considering he's been in the river for a couple months."

Tom pulled his notebook from his back pocket and started writing.

"With the water temperature cold and him sunk pretty deep along the main channel, that's going to preserve the body some," Sammy Dale said. "I've had some drowners in the summer. That warm water. It doesn't take long for a body to fall apart. This one's actually in not bad shape, but…"

Sammy Dale bent down and peered at the flesh of the bare leg floating in the water. "There's still going to be predators picking at it. You can see that here."

Tom looked and he could see where bits of flesh hung loose and something had taken chunks off the thigh. Again, his stomach lurched and he took a deep breath.

"You think it's Dr. Webb or Dutch?" Tom asked.

Sturgill bent down and peered at the clothing. "We haven't turned him over yet. But it's probably a good bet considering we haven't had any report of any other missing persons."

"Who found him?" Tom asked as Sturgill straightened and cocked his head sideways, seemingly trying to figure out how the piece of driftwood had snared the body and held it in place.

"A couple of fishermen were working this part of the bank when they came up on him early this morning. They hightailed it across the river to Old Shawnee to the police department and, since it was on the Kentucky side, they called us. And here we are."

Tom glanced over at Stick, who gave him a quick look, and Tom figured the deputy had phoned him as soon as they'd gotten the call from the Old Shawnee Police Department. He owed the deputy a beer or two or three. Sturgill looked over and noticed Tom and Stick's interaction. His jaws flexed and he crunched down on the peppermint, but turned his attention back to the coroner.

"Flip him over, Sammy Dale."

The coroner grimaced and then walked to the water's edge and waded in. The water came up to his knees as he worked his way to the upper part of the torso. Sammy Dale turned his head and Tom wondered if he was trying to get a gulp of fresh air. The coroner looked skyward for a moment and then lifted and turned the body so that the dead man's face was exposed.

The smell of decay filled the air and Tom felt bile rise to the back of his throat. The body must have been floating face down for a good while as most of the flesh from his cheeks and forehead and neck had been stripped by catfish, turtles, gar and whatever other hungry carnivore had come upon the floating mass. One eye was gone, just a deep socket of black, while one remained, blood-shot red and a pupil black.

Tom turned his eyes away and he noticed that Sturgill flinched and Stick was looking anywhere but the body that was now facing upward. The coroner had pulled a rag from his pocket and covered his mouth and nose.

The stench was unbearable and Tom knew the face would haunt his nightmares for years to come. He was reminded of when he was about 8 years old and walking the woods behind his home when he came upon the half-decayed carcass of a possum. The animal's mouth had been frozen in a hideous grin as if he'd found death to be quite funny and that's what Tom saw when he looked again at the bloated body.

"Who is it?" Tom asked.

Sturgill glanced at the body and turned away. "Hard to say."

The coroner moved in the water and he peered at the swollen, disfigured head.

"There's some pretty heavy damage here along the upper hairline, but I can't say for certain if that was done before or after he'd been in the water," Sammy Dale said as he used the tip of a pencil to push aside a part of the scalp. "Could be he caught the edge of the boat when it capsized or the body was slammed up against some driftwood when it was drug by the current or maybe it caught on a pier or a propeller blade from a passing barge took a chunk of it. Hard to tell."

Sturgill looked over at the coroner.

"Possible an oar swung at the right amount of speed could do that amount of damage?"

Sammy Dale paused, considering the implication. "I'd say that could be possible."

The coroner stepped back and the river climbed higher on his thighs. He looked over the body from the head to the legs that still floated in the water.

"I'd estimate he's over 6-feet tall, a little over 200 pounds."

The sheriff nodded. "Dr. Webb and Dutch were about the same size."

Sammy Dale frowned. "I'd really rather not hazard a guess until we get the body back in my office and I can compare the dental records."

Stick took a step forward and pointed to a strip of leather that was sticking out of the top pocket of the camouflage coat. "What's that there?"

While holding the handkerchief over his nose and mouth, Sammy Dale leaned over the body and used his pencil to pull the leather strip from the pocket. Attached to the end of the leather rope was a wooden duck call. He held it up so that the sheriff could see the lettering on it.

"I'll be," Sturgill said, pointing to the gold Kentucky Department of Fish and Wildlife seal. "That's Dutch's. Damn if I don't think we're looking at Dutch Blackburn."

Tom looked away as did the others. There was something about assigning a name to a body. Made it personal. Minutes ago, their minds had been occupied by science and awful circumstances. Now, they had a name.

Tom thought of Malachi and wondered if the discovery of his brother's body would bring closure and if he'd remain in the cabin or if he'd go searching out his relatives in Illinois. And he also thought of Mary Diane and how she'd take the news about the fate of her boyfriend.

And then the newsman in Tom stirred and he realized he currently had the exclusive rights and access to what would be the top story in the county for the near future and a breaking news item that would soon go out across the region and the rest of the state. Tom pulled the camera up and started snapping photos.

Sturgill heard the click of the camera's shutter and glared at him. "Have some decency," he said.

"People have a right to know," Tom answered and snapped two more frames that showed the coroner in the water beside the body with the sheriff and his deputy looking on from the river's edge. "They're going to want to know where and how the body was found."

Sturgill motioned to Stick, who shrugged out of his jacket and handed it to the sheriff. Sturgill placed the deputy's jacket over the exposed part of the body. "Worse than a vulture," the sheriff said.

Tom took some more photos and was moving up the bank to get a wide-angle shot when he heard more footsteps coming up the path. A state trooper burst from the thicket. The highway patrolman, who Tom guessed wasn't much older than he, was apparently startled to see a reporter with a camera and he stopped.

"Who are you?" he asked, looking Tom over, noticing the mud that caked his loafers and was splotched over his pants.

He didn't give Tom a chance to reply. "Sheriff, you know this man? He's in the middle of our crime scene."

Sturgill looked up the bank. "Nice of you to join us, Jasper. Took you long enough."

The young trooper straightened his back. "I was over in another county. Got here as soon as I could."

He peered down at the river's edge and noticed the body. Tom watched the trooper recoil as his eyes took in the bare white flesh of the man's legs and the smell of decay was carried upwind. Sturgill and Stick began to walk up the bank, while Sammy Dale stepped out of the river, water running in streams from his wet pants.

"Jasper, I'm going to need you to call in your team," Sturgill said. "This is a little more than we usually take on."

The state trooper held one of his beefy forearms across his nose while his eyes remained on the body. Sturgill stepped in front of him. "Trooper. I'm needing you to call in the crime scene folks. Can you do that for me, Jasper?"

The trooper's round black hat atop his blonde crewcut shifted as he nodded and Jasper pulled a radio from his belt. As he stepped away, Sturgill turned to Tom. "Reporter, you're going to need to clear out of this area. He is right. This is a crime scene."

Tom pulled a pencil and notebook from his back pocket. "Crime scene?"

"All likelihood, it's an accident. But we'll need to be certain."

"Can you say for a certainty that is Dutch Blackburn?"

"Not at this moment." The sheriff looked down at the river. "You heard Sammy Dale. He's going to need to confirm with the dental records."

"Will you tell me when there's been a positive ID?"

"You're going to need to speak to the coroner about that."

Tom took a deep sigh.

"I don't know why you have to be so difficult."

Sturgill reached into his pocket and pulled out a peppermint. As he unwrapped it, he glanced over at Tom and then popped the candy into his mouth.

"I'd say you had pretty good access. I find it all pretty amazing how you just happened upon us."

Tom scribbled nonsense in his notebook. Sturgill nodded to his deputy. "Stick will walk you back. And show some decency with those photos. People don't need to see that. That down there is somebody's relative, reporter. I'm sure Junious will do the right thing."

Tom turned and Stick joined him as they walked along the path through the thicket and brush that led back to the parking lot at the boat ramp.

"You're always pushing, aren't you?" Stick asked as they skirted around a fallen log.

"All he is is a bully," Tom said, looking back at the deputy. "Why didn't he use his own jacket to cover the body if he was so worried about it? One of these days you're going to need to stand up to him."

Stick chuckled. "You don't stand up to the sheriff, Tom. I'd like to keep my job."

Tom took a step and his shoe sunk up to his ankle in a pocket of thick mud. When he lifted his foot, the shoe stayed in place. He tugged the shoe free from the mud and slapped the mud-coated loafer back on his foot.

"You're really out of your element, Tom."

"Maybe so. But I'm doing it my way."

"How's that working out for you?"

"Better than being an errand boy."

The two walked the rest of the way in silence. When they reached the boat ramp, Tom pulled his shoes off and scraped away the mud. Stick stood and watched. Word had apparently started to spread throughout Newton County about the discovery of a body and the parking lot now numbered close to 20 trucks. Men stood in groups and some were down at the river watching the rescue boat that worked its way back and forth across the river. Most of the men had turned and watched the deputy and reporter when they'd emerged from the cane break.

Tom placed his shoes back on his feet and held his arms out wide. "Anything else, deputy?"

Stick shook his head. "No reason to be an ass, Tom." The deputy walked over to his cruiser and pulled a tarp from the trunk and headed back into the woods. He didn't look back.

CHAPTER 24

TOM GOT IN his car and started back the way he'd come. As he drove downriver, close to where the body had been found, there were three more pickups pulled off to the side of the road and men were walking aross the open field toward the river's edge. He could see the faint outline of the state trooper with a roll of yellow police tape, wrapping it around trees as he marked off a perimeter. And there was the dark silhouette of Sheriff Sturgill, his hands on his hips as he stood atop the bank watching the goings-on.

At the edge of the field, just before a curve, stood five men beside a black Cadillac. It was easy to spot the lean figure of Thaddeus Lincoln, he in his fedora and black waist jacket at the center of the group. *Of course he would be here*, Tom thought as he pulled his car near the Cadillac and parked. In his hand he carried his camera and notebook.

Sensing a stranger, the men turned and, like worker bees protecting their queen, formed a barrier around Lincoln, who towered over them. They were the hired hands who did his field work. The men wore coveralls and hats advertising seed companies were pulled low, nearly shielding their eyes. The men were all thick chested with big bellies and big arms and big hands with thick, misshapen fingers. They were silent as Tom approached.

"Mr. Lincoln. Tom Crutchfield with the *Register.*"

Lincoln's attention had been focused on the river, where his gaze remained.

"Mr. Lincoln," Tom said a little louder, taking a step before he was stopped by one of the men, one large hand placed on his chest. Thaddeus Lincoln slowly turned and his gaze fell on Tom. Lincoln smirked and turned his attention back to the river.

"Imagine finding you here," Tom said. "A slow day at the bank?"

A truck passed on the gravel road and still Lincoln faced the river. Tom looked at the blank faces of the men who'd formed a pocket around their boss. If he'd been in New York City, he would have guessed Thaddeus Lincoln was the king pin of the mafia and these were his foot soldiers. Ready to do harm to whoever or whatever interfered with the boss's plans. He smiled at the man in front of him, but there was no response. Two men down to his left, one of the burly farm workers spit and a stream of tobacco juice splattered on the snow melt, not far from Tom's loafers. The man in front of him cracked a slight smile.

"They're thinking that could be Dutch Blackburn," Tom said, speaking over their heads in the direction of Lincoln. "But, of course, you already know that, don't you? Dutch being dead and all."

Tom pulled open his notebook and pretended to read from his notes. "Possible head injury. Almost as if somebody had whacked him upside the head."

Tom looked at the man's eyes in front of him and they retreated into tight slits.

He continued on. "Dutch being out of the way is, uh, really

going to put the brakes on that whole push for the wildlife preserve, don't you think? I mean, good for you, though, right?"

There was a long sigh and Lincoln turned and faced him again.

"What is it you want, Crutchfield?"

"Just curious."

"About what?"

"About how you always happen to be present when a man goes missing, he's declared dead or a body's found. I find it partly amazing that you don't carry a scythe in the trunk of that fine Cadillac. I mean you've already got the long black coat. The grim reaper comes calling."

"Your humor is juvenile and not worthy of a response."

"Wasn't meant to be humor."

"As I've told you before, I try to keep my finger on the pulse of this community."

"I wonder if it's more than that."

Lincoln adjusted his hat on the head, attempting to tilt the fedora to shade his face from the afternoon sky. "Who killed Kennedy, Crutchfield?"

Tom paused, slightly taken aback at the question. "I think we all know that, Mr. Lincoln. It was Lee Harvey Oswald."

Lincoln pulled his hat from his head and massaged the rim of it in his hands.

"No mystery shooter from beyond the grassy knoll?"

Tom didn't answer.

"Castro? The Russians?"

"What's your point?"

"Well, Crutchfield, to me it seems as if you go looking for a conspiracy where there simply is not one. And, in reality, your baseless verbal assaults are getting quite repetitive and tiresome. And some might even say libelous."

Lincoln smiled as he placed the fedora back atop his head and cocked it at an angle to block the sun.

"Crutchfield, I've grown quite bored with you."

And the lean banker turned and, joined by two of the men, started walking across the field toward the river bank. Tom started to follow, but the man in front of him who had stayed behind stopped him again by pressing his hand against Tom's chest.

"No, sir," the man said in a baritone that came from deep within his barrel chest. "This here is Mr. Lincoln's land and you're trespassing. I'll need you to step back to the road."

Tom considered slapping the man's hand and following it with a quick right cross to his meaty head, but as he sized up the two burly men who flanked him, he realized it would be a losing battle. And JC would probably have his ass. And the man was right. While the gravel road was a county public road, the mud he stood on was probably Lincoln's.

Tom retreated to the road and, in an act of defiance, he raised his camera and snapped three frames. In the foreground of the photo, the trio of men stood with their arms crossed and the thin figure of Lincoln could be seen on the horizon as he approached the sheriff.

Tom's attention was on the field before him so he didn't hear the sound of gravel being splayed.

"Whatcha doing, mister?" asked a boy, probably not quite yet a teenager. He was joined by another boy, this one much taller and thinner, and they rode bicycles, which they had stopped with a flourish, spraying gravel across the road and into a nearby ditch.

"What's it look like?" Tom asked, turning back to his camera and looking through the viewfinder.

"They found a body, didn't they?"

Tom turned back around and sized the boys up. He remembered where he'd seen the pair before — his first day in Newton County. The boys had been down at the boat ramp at Taylor's Ferry when the search began for the two missing hunters.

"They did find a body," Tom answered.

"Who was it?" asked the thicker and shorter of the two.

Tom considered his reply. Both were on the edge of their bike seats, waiting. He remembered the conversation with the boy and how Thaddeus Lincoln had ordered him over and the boy had responded like a puppy that had been trained with a whipping stick.

"You're Mr. Lincoln's son, aren't you?"

The boy shrugged. "Yeah. So?"

"Shug, right?"

"Yeah, that's right. And that's Robbie. Now, dang it, who did they find? Was it both of them? I told Robbie those bodies would float up when the snow melted."

"What's your daddy like?"

The boy frowned and his eyebrows scrunched together. "You ask a lot of questions."

"And you don't?"

Tom watched as the boy debated what bit of information to hand over in this game of give and take. He figured the boy was probably pretty good at it, learned in his dealings with his daddy.

Tom prodded. "Dr. Webb or Dutch ever come by your house?"

Shug lowered his head.

"That's really none of your business, mister," said the other boy.

Tom turned and considered the taller of the two, his arms already sporting lean muscles. In another year or two, he'd be as tall or taller than Tom. The boy's dark eyes stayed on Tom and didn't depart. Shug seemed to gather strength from his friend's support.

"That's right," Shug said. "That's none of your business, reporter."

Tom shook his head. "Go on. I'm sure your daddy will tell you what he wants you to know."

Shug spit on the ground and stood tall in his bike and the two of them pedaled fast and cleared the ditch, their wheels cutting into the snow melt and leaving behind a thin trail to the river's edge.

CHAPTER 25

WHEN TOM REACHED the main road, he turned left toward Taylor's Ferry rather than east toward Morgan's Gap and the newspaper office. He knew his news scoop would floor JC and he'd tell him to develop his film and start on his story, but there was somewhere Tom needed to stop first. He drove across the levee and turned near the Catholic church and saw the simple house across from the park.

Fergus was standing in the street in front of the house when Tom pulled up in the Fairlane and parked behind the pickup with the United Mine Workers of America sticker clinging to the back of a rusted bumper. The old man reached into the back of the pickup and pulled out two fishing rods. Tom nodded toward the man.

"Afternoon, Mr. Clanton."

Fergus stood with the fishing poles in his hands, glanced at Tom and then walked around the front of his pickup and into the yard. Joshua emerged from behind a tree when Tom shut his door.

"Tom!" Joshua yelled and came over to him. "Can we go for a ride?"

Tom bent and put his hand atop the boy's head. "Not today, Joshua. Sorry."

Joshua looked around him and back at the car. "It's dirty, Tom."

"Been down at the river."

Tom looked up and saw Fergus watching the two of them. The old man coughed. "Joshua, come get these poles and take them to the shed," he said.

"Aw, Pappy."

"Now, Joshua," Fergus said, his voice stern.

"Better do what's asked," Tom said to the boy. "I'll wash the Ford and we'll go for a ride soon."

Joshua smiled. "Really?"

"Promise. Now go do what your grandfather asked."

Joshua nodded and Fergus handed him the two rods. The boy took them and went around the corner of the house back to where an old garden shed stood in the back corner. Tom straightened and walked over to where Fergus stood, his hands in the back pockets of his jeans.

"Think it's wise to be making promises you can't keep?" the old man asked.

"Plan to keep them."

"Hmph."

"Good fishing?" Tom asked.

"They were biting."

"Mary Diane around?"

Fergus shifted his weight to his other foot. From his back pocket, he pulled a pack of cigarettes. He pulled one from the pack and stuck it in his mouth. From his front pocket, he pulled a box of matches. He struck one and lit the end of the cigarette. A thin line of blue smoke rose and his eyes followed it upward. He stayed silent.

"I think I have news she's going to want to hear."

Fergus dropped his eyes to Tom's face and he took a draw off the cigarette. He held the smoke in and when he exhaled, he pointed a thin, crooked finger at Tom. "My concern is with my daughter and that boy there."

"Yes, sir. I know that. I swear I'll never intentionally do anything to harm Mary Diane or Joshua."

"It's the unintentional I worry about."

Tom looked to his left and up the stairs to the front door of the home. The screen door had been left ajar and it swayed in the wind. Tom resisted an urge to climb the stairs and push the door shut. Instead, he looked back at Fergus, who continued to smoke, one hand still resting in his back pocket.

"I'd really like to speak to Mary Diane, Mr. Clanton. They found a body down at the river. I think she's going to want to know."

Fergus pulled the cigarette from his mouth and it was followed by a long, slow release of smoke from his pursed lips. Gray stubble was on his chin and under his nose and his stringy brown-grey hair reached past his ears and nearly to his thin shoulders. Fergus appeared to be a much older man than his actual years. He motioned with his head to the side of the house.

"She's around back."

Tom nodded and stepped around him and when he looked back, Fergus had brought the cigarette back to his lips and turned his eyes skyward again. What he was searching for, Tom was uncertain.

❧

In her hands, Mary held a bone-handled knife, its long, silver blade glinting when it caught the late afternoon sun. Blood was on the blade and it ran down the bone handle and curled around her fingers and down to her wrist and elbow, where it dripped and pooled on the clump of white snow that lingered beneath. She looked up when Tom came around the corner of the house and then went back to slicing open the catfish laid out on the wooden table before her.

"Fergus said they were biting," Tom said.

She didn't respond, but instead pressed down on the handle of the blade and the blade disappeared into the white underbelly of the fish. Tom saw a bowl beside her and inside it were fillets floating in the water. At her feet, the severed head of a catfish stared up at him, its eyes bulging and whiskers sprouting from its mouth.

"Another talent?" he asked.

She grunted and placed the blade on the table. With the fingers that she used to rub along the back of his hairline while they wrestled in the backseat of his Fairlane, she reached up into the underbelly of the dead fish and pulled free its stomach, heart and intestines in a long, slimy, messy clump that she flicked to the ground. Mary glanced up at him as her fingers went back into the fish's cavity searching for any of its insides that she may have missed.

"Where have you been city mouse?" she asked. "Stick said you stopped by the Rainbow on Monday night, but I never saw you. No phone call. No letters. Not like you to go quiet all of a sudden."

"I've been working through some things."

"That right?"

"That's right."

She shook her head and her fingers pressed deeper into the catfish.

"What do you want, Tom?"

"How are you?"

"Well, my hand's inside a dead catfish right now."

"I've been meaning to come see you."

"Well, here I am."

Mary pulled her hand free and splayed the catfish flat on the table. She picked up the blade and cut the fish down its middle and began to slice it into strips, the meat firm and white and it rippled as she cut in broad strokes.

"I've come from the river," Tom said. "They've found a body."

There was a momentary pause in her cutting and Tom saw her take a long breath. Then she began to filet the fish, tossing the clean meat into the bowl of water. Her eyes were on her fingers that moved in and around the sharp edge of the knife's silver blade.

"It's Dutch."

Her hands stopped. Overhead, Tom heard a squirrel as it leaped from one branch to another. Across the street, there was the metallic creak of a car door opening and the laughter of children. Farther down, he heard the scrape of a shovel as somebody worked at a last bit of stubborn ice.

"I'm sorry," Tom said.

"You're sure?"

Tom thought of the bloated body, the black hole where an eye had been, the pockmarked flesh. He looked again at the ground and the dead catfish still stared up at him.

"They'll need to confirm with dental records, but they

found in one of the pockets a duck call that the sheriff says belonged to Dutch…. I'm pretty certain it's him."

Mary Diane placed the blade on the table and rested her hands on the wood. A string of guts lie near her fingers. She had her head bowed and her eyes closed, but Tom did not see a tear on her cheek. Tom heard movement from the back corner near the shed and he watched as Joshua came running up to his mother. The boy must have sensed there was something unusual with his mother as he placed his arms around her thigh and hugged her. She touched his shoulder.

"Joshua, take this bowl into the kitchen for me. And then check on Pappy, please."

The boy took the bowl and did as his mother asked, the screen to the back door shutting behind him. She remained standing at the table.

"I mean we all expected it, with them being missing all this time," she said, looking out over the backyard. "Still, it's a shock."

She reached up to a strand of her dark hair that had fallen across her face and pulled it back behind her ear. "Dutch was a good guy. He really did care for me. That's why it hurts."

Tom felt the heat rise along the back of his neck and he toed the severed head.

"Should have told me about you two," he said.

Mary paused. "What?"

"Should have told me about him being your boyfriend."

Tom looked up at her and he saw a dark flash of anger cross her face.

"What are you getting at, Tom?"

"Just seems that it might have been nice to let me in on what apparently everybody else knew — the girl I was making out with in the back seat of my car was the girlfriend of Dutch Blackburn. That would have been the kind thing to do."

"Oh, and you are being kind right now?"

"I'm just tired of being the last one to know everything. I look like a fool."

She stuck out her lower lip. "Poor Tom. No worries there. You are a fool."

Tom felt his anger rise. "You should have told me, Mary."

"It wasn't any of your business."

"You're my business, Mary."

She scoffed. "Oh, that's rich."

"If we're going to move forward with what we've got, which is what I thought you wanted, I need to know things."

Mary picked up the knife and scraped the last of the fish guts off the table with a flourish.

"And just what do you want to know, Tom?"

"Is Dutch… is he Joshua's daddy?"

Mary pointed the knife at him. "Back off."

Tom took a step toward her.

"You know why I'm here. You know what my parents hid from me. You know how that hurts me. I'm telling you. That boy needs to know who his daddy is."

Mary stabbed the knife into the table. "Leave it, Tom!"

"I won't!"

"Tom!"

"Dutch is down there floating in the river! I can't unsee what I saw. His body's all swollen, fish been eating at him, the smell. Damn, that smell. I'm telling you. Dutch ain't coming back. He's deader than dead, Mary. He's dead!"

There was the scraping sound of the screen door opening

and Tom looked over to see Joshua standing there, his lower lip quivering, eyes already wet with tears.

"Momma, is what Tom says… is that right?"

Mary shot Tom a hard look and bent down, reaching for Joshua, who began to shake his head and tears began to fall. "Is Dutch really… Momma…. is what Tom said… is Dutch dead?" The boy's voice broke and he began to sob harder, his shoulders shaking.

Tom stood there, near the door, hands at his sides. "I didn't know he was…"

Mary glared at him. "There's plenty you don't know, Tom!"

"I'm sorry."

She put Joshua's hands in hers. "Come here, baby."

"Mary, I didn't… "

She didn't look at Tom, but pulled Joshua in close to her. "I think it's best if you leave us, Tom. I don't want you around."

"Mary…"

"I said, leave Tom! Now!"

Joshua began to cry even harder and Mary wrapped her arms around him and carried her son inside, the door slamming shut behind her. The force snapped an icicle off the gutter and it smacked the bare dirt near Tom's shoes, scattering into fragments.

And the dead, severed head remained, its black eyes locked on Tom.

CHAPTER 26

JC WAS ALONE in the *Register* when Tom arrived, the editor's feet propped up on his desk, hands laced behind his head.

Mary was on Tom's mind. During the drive back to Morgan's Gap, he replayed their conversation, over and over. Each time it ended the same way, with her shutting the door and telling him to go away and leave her alone.

"It's Dutch, right?" JC asked.

Tom paused as he stood before his desk. "What?"

"The body. Down at the river. It's Dutch, right?"

Tom shook his head. "Yeah, yeah. Of course."

"And?"

"And?"

"Did you get notes? Photos?"

"Yeah."

JC paused. He looked Tom up and down. "You alright? I mean seeing a dead body can stay with somebody."

Tom ran his hand through his hair. "Yeah. No. Yeah, I'm good. It's not that."

JC looked up at the clock situated over the layout table. It was near 5.

"Want to get drunk?" JC asked.

Tom shook his head.

"Well, you are certainly lacking in conversation."

Tom stared hard at him.

"You contradict me?"

Tom turned and shook his head. He placed his notebook and camera bag on his desk. Instead of taking off his coat, he turned and made his way for the front door.

"Think I might take off early."

"Whatever it is, you need to get that shit figured out."

Tom reached for the door, but JC's words stopped him.

"I'm serious, Mr. Crutchfield. You're no good to me if your future work is going to be a carbon copy of that half-assed effort you turned in this week. Your copy was uninspired. The captions were lacking and those headline busts were just sloppy. And you've been no joy to be around. And now you come in here moping around like a boy who lost his best dog. You're better than that, Mr. Crutchfield."

"You're right."

"You're damn straight I'm right. Now, what is it?"

Tom turned and came back to his desk. He pulled out his chair and sat, but didn't remove his coat.

"I've been seeing someone."

"That girl down at the Rainbow?"

"Yeah, Mary."

"So?"

"Well, we had a fight and she said she didn't want to see me anymore."

JC let out a long breath.

"How old are you, Mr. Crutchfield?"

"Twenty-one. You know that."

JC had a smirk on his face. "There's going to be a long list of Marys in your future, Mr. Crutchfield. This is just a bump in the road."

Tom shook his head and looked back out at the dark street. He didn't plan to admit it to JC, but he'd been thinking about a future with Mary.

Two weeks earlier, he'd been at his desk, reading over that past week's edition and his eyes came across the real estate listings. Tom gave a quick search for a two-bedroom place, a little "starter home," where he, Mary and Joshua could live. They'd marry, he'd take Joshua on as his own, and, in a few years, they'd have their own child, maybe a little sister for Joshua. Tom would join the Lions Club and Mary would sell Mary Kay in her spare time when she wasn't taking Joshua to baseball practice or the little girl to dance. He'd continue to learn as a reporter under JC and one day the old man would retire and sell him the newspaper. He and Mary would grow old and they'd have grandchildren. They'd die within a few days of each other and be buried in adjoining plots at the old cemetery near the city limits.

"We didn't even last two months," he said.

JC glanced over at him. "You sure you don't want to get drunk?"

"Not tonight."

JC leaned toward Tom. "What was it about?"

"What?"

"What was the fight about?"

Tom thought back again to the two of them in the backyard, Mary cutting up the fish, Joshua in tears, the slamming of the back door.

"She didn't like my questions."

"What'd you ask?"

"About her son. And his daddy."

JC flinched as if a bee had landed upon his bare cheek and shook his head. "What'd she say?"

"Basically that it wasn't my business."

"What do you think about that?"

"I thought I had a right to know." Tom paused. "Especially if we're going to have a future together."

"You tell her that?"

"Not in those exact words. Anyhow, the conversation kind of went off-track."

JC was quiet for a moment. "So, she's not aware that you were hoping for a future with her?"

"Well, I think she knows I like her."

"Oh, Mr. Crutchfield. Let me offer you some advice for any future relationships that you may somehow stumble upon. A woman needs to feel secure, Mr. Crutchfield. She wants to know that she's loved and protected. From what you've told me, I'm believing the only thing she was feeling in that moment was a big heap of insecurity. You have no ties here. In her mind, she's thinking, 'What's keeping you from up and leaving as soon as another adventure appears?'"

Tom shook his head. "I'm not like that."

"Well, you're going to have to show her. That's if you truly want to make a go of it here, Mr. Crutchfield."

Classes at the university had started a month earlier. Still, Tom knew that he could hop in his Fairlane the very next morning, turn east and be back on campus in about five hours. A quick trip to the admissions office, some proper begging before some professors, and that afternoon he'd be back at the *Kernel*, writing copy and finishing up his degree. On the second Saturday in May, he'd walk the graduation line and on the following

Monday, he'd be at his desk at Crutchfield Construction. That's what awaited him.

But, at this moment, 40 years at Crutchfield Construction, many of them spent working under his daddy's direction, was not what he wanted. Plus, he also had plenty of loose strings to tie up in Newton County. And those things gnawed at him.

"Even with the coroner's inquest and Dutch surfacing today, this story doesn't feel like it's over," Tom said. "There just seems to be more to it than a simple drowning."

JC fumbled in the bottom drawer of his desk and pulled out a bottle of Early Times bourbon. He peered into his coffee cup, wiped it clean with the hem of his shirt and poured a healthy shot into the glass. He looked up at Tom.

"My watch says five o'clock."

Tom sighed and handed over his own coffee cup. The two of them sat in their chairs, feet on their desks, and drank. The bourbon was harsh as it lingered at the back of his throat and Tom swallowed, feeling its warmth spread through his chest. He took another sip and this time the bourbon didn't burn as bad on his tongue.

"You forget about them," JC said.

"Who's that?"

"The stories. The disappointments." JC took another drink. "You move on. You have to. If you sit there and wallow in it, then most of your days are going to resemble the kind of piss-poor effort you gave this week."

"So you just wipe them from your memory?"

"Oh, no, Mr. Crutchfield. They'll always be there, taking up space in your mind. What we do is we learn from them. The good, the bad. And then the next time the next big story...."

or the next good woman comes along… then we'll be much better prepared for it."

Tom thought back to those first days when he met JC and the cot in the back of the office. Since the new year, JC had been sleeping at home. The cot had been folded up and there were now empty boxes in the storage room.

"Is that what you're doing?" Tom asked. "Waiting for the next good woman."

JC stared out into the darkness of Morgan's Gap and its nearly deserted streets.

"No, Mr. Crutchfield. I've had my good woman," JC said. He drained the last of his bourbon, grimaced and placed the cup on his desk. "I'm just living day to day. Week to week. Paper to paper. I think that's what Carol would want me to do. It's like her ghost will haunt me if I miss a deadline."

Tom removed his feet from his desk and held the cup between his legs.

"What if Mary is my one? Like Mrs. Wheeler was yours?"

JC looked over at him.

"You know I didn't go looking for Carol. We found each other."

He told Tom how he had walked into a book store down on Bardstown Road one Saturday morning in the spring of 1935. A hangover lingered from a rough night before as he'd gotten drunk after turning in his news copy.

That night he'd written a story about a boy who'd been struck by a hit-and-run driver in one of Louisville's toughest neighborhoods. Hours later, still fresh in his mind was the image of the boy, one of his shoes lying 30 feet down the street from his lifeless body. JC could still smell oil and gas and hear the screams of the dead boy's mother. The story had run on an inside page of the Local section. He had woke that Saturday needing something else. And so JC had come to the book store hoping for a bit of levity by reading something by James Thurber.

JC was standing over a table where he had picked up a copy of John Steinbeck's "Tortilla Flat." He was on the fourth page of the first chapter, when he caught a whiff of gardenia. Across from him, she stood, in her hands a worn copy of Thomas Wolfe's "You Can't Go Home Again." Their looks lingered, both of them seeing the literature in their hands, and they exchanged smiles.

"I'm Junious," he said.

"Carol," she replied.

And they slipped away to a coffee shop down Bardstown Road. For many afternoons after, they lay naked in bed as he read Steinbeck to her and she read Wolfe to him. He talked of a future, she brought him to Morgan's Gap, and they never left.

"I don't think you go in search of love, Mr. Crutchfield," JC said. "Just like a good story, love will find and rescue you. Have faith in that."

Tom thought of the first night he met Mary. The way her gaze stayed on him for a second longer than needed. The way the moonlight fell upon her as they stood close behind the Rainbow. The smell of her when she leaned in to fix the buttons on his coat.

"How do you know?"

"Know?"

"That she is the one."

"I think your heart will tell you, Mr. Crutchfield. Don't let a bruised ego stand in your way."

JC stood and placed a hand on Tom's shoulder. "If you

truly do have strong feelings for this girl, and think she's one you can have a future with, then I suggest you give strong consideration to appearing on her doorstep in the morning with your hat in your hand. If not, then that bottle of Early Times will be plenty of company."

He patted Tom on his back and headed for the front door.

"Remember what Cervantes wrote in *Don Quixote*, Mr. Crutchfield. The brave man carves out his fortune, and every man is the son of his own works."

And the door shut behind him and Tom was left alone with his thoughts.

CHAPTER 27

TWO NEWTON COUNTY Sheriff's Office cars were parked in front of Fergus Clanton's home when Tom arrived in Taylor's Ferry Saturday morning. The blue lights were slowly turning, but no sirens, and Tom pulled to the side of the street and leaped from his car, the engine left running.

He jogged to the front yard, but was stopped by the bulk of Sheriff Sturgill, who suddenly appeared between the two vehicles. There was concern on Sturgill's face and Tom noticed he did not chew on a peppermint this morning.

"Reporter," he said.

"Sheriff, what is it? What's happened? Is everyone alright? Is it Fergus? Something happened?"

Sturgill tilted his hat back and Tom noticed the gray forming at his temples and the deep lines of worry that radiated from weary eyes.

"What's your business here?" the sheriff asked.

"My business?"

"I don't have time this morning for your nonsense."

Off to his right, there was a sudden shuffling of feet across dead leaves and Tom saw Mary bundled in a blanket, coming from the back yard, walking with her head down. Stick was beside her, the deputy's arm across her back and he seemed to be offering words of comfort.

"Mary!" Tom shouted.

She raised her head and Tom saw the redness in her eyes, her hair tangled and falling across her forehead. She frowned and shook her head and continued to walk with Stick, who led her up the front steps and into the house.

"I don't understand," Tom said. "What's happened?"

Sturgill, who had watched the interaction, turned to Tom. "You and Miss Clanton know each other?"

"We've been seeing each other."

The sheriff nodded his head, then scratched at his jaw.

"How's the state of that relationship?"

"What do you mean?"

"I don't know, reporter, but it didn't appear that Miss Clanton was overjoyed to see you."

Tom narrowed his eyes and looked back to his car, the door open and the engine running.

"We had a bit of a disagreement yesterday," he said.

Sturgill raised an eyebrow. "That so?"

"I don't see how this is any of your business."

Sturgill chuckled. "Bit ironic, don't you think? You saying that."

"That's my job, sheriff."

"And this is my job, reporter. I've got a little boy missing and I'm trying to figure out if a disgruntled boyfriend would have anything to do with that?"

Tom's mouth opened. "Josh."

"That's right."

Tom felt the heat rise along his neckline. "You can't think —"

"I don't know what to think anymore, reporter. Seems as if every day I'm learning more and more about people. And rarely is it any good. So, you'll excuse me, if I ask you again. You have anything to do with the disappearance of this boy?"

Tom felt his fists clench, but he breathed in and then out. And he repeated the pattern. "I did not, sheriff. And I'm insulted that you'd think I would. Joshua means a great deal to me. Just like his mother. I care very deeply for both of them."

Sturgill's jaws flexed and Tom felt the sheriff weighing his words. The front door opened and Stick came down the stairs. He stopped alongside Sturgill and glanced over at Tom. The deputy pulled out a notebook and began to read.

"He's not around back and none of the neighbors reported seeing him or anything unusual during the night. Mary... uh, Miss Clanton, said when she woke this morning, he wasn't in his bed. Appears that it's been slept in, but there doesn't appear to be any signs of forced entry or a struggle of any type."

The sheriff continued to watch Tom, who listened as Stick continued to read.

"Fergus was on the night shift at the coal mine. They've called him. He should be here shortly."

"How's Mary?" Tom asked.

"She's pretty shook up... " Stick said, stopping when Sturgill turned to look at him.

"Anything else, deputy?" Sturgill asked.

Stick fidgeted, his pencil tapping the notebook. "She said Joshua was very emotional last night. He heard the news about Dutch and he took that hard. Apparently the two of them had formed a bond over the years. And then, according to Mary, uh, Miss Clanton, the boy overheard her and Mr. Crutchfield, here, having an argument. He cried most of the night and went to bed early. She checked on him near midnight and he was still in his room."

The deputy closed his notebook and looked down at the ground.

Sturgill kept his eyes on Tom. "Any ideas, reporter?"

Tom felt a void inside, as though part of him had been ripped out. He hadn't meant for Joshua to hear him. He hadn't meant those words he said to Mary. It had been pure jealousy and hurt that had fueled his fire.

"He was upset when I left. But I went back to the newspaper and did some work and then went on home. JC can vouch for me at the paper and Mrs. Tyner looked out her window when I was walking up the steps. I came here this morning to apologize to Mary."

The three of them stood there until there was a call on the sheriff's radio. Sturgill turned to Stick. "That's probably the state police. We'll get a search party organized. I'll stick around here for now."

The sheriff paused as a thought seemed to enter his mind and grimaced. He turned to Stick and said in a softer voice. "Probably best if you swing down by the river. I hope not, but we need to consider all possibilities."

The deputy nodded and Sturgill slid into his front seat. Stick began to walk to his cruiser and Tom had to hurry to catch up with him.

"Mary," Tom said, his hand on Stick's arm. "Can I see her?"

The deputy glanced over Tom's shoulder, back at the sheriff's car and shook his head. "Best not, Tom. I don't think she's in the mood to see you right now. The girl's in a world of hurt."

Stick pulled away and Tom was left standing in the street,

watching as the deputy's car made a swift U-turn and headed toward the river.

When he got back to his car, Tom sat there with the engine still running. Part of him wanted to run up those steps, fall on his knees before Mary and ask for her forgiveness. But, as Stick said, her mind was on her missing son, not her relationship with Tom.

Here he was again, thinking only of himself. He was plotting and thinking of the words he'd say to Mary, asking for her forgiveness. To get his life back. To begin anew. To begin a future with Mary.

And Joshua. A six-year-old boy out there somewhere, all alone.

He tried not to think of the river and the bodies it had claimed in just the short time he'd been in Newton County. He struggled to erase the bloated, disfigured image of Dutch from his mind.

He thought of being a boy. A child. One who has heard the most awful news and seen bad things.

And he sat there and the sun continued to rise and the last of the snow melted away.

Then Tom turned off the engine, got out from his car and began to walk.

The gravel road bordered by the canebrake was still wet and Tom slipped when he turned down the path that led up to the Healing Spring. When he pushed himself up from the muddy ground, Creeping Jenny was there at the edge of the brake. Atop her mule, she cocked her head and considered him.

The mule stomped its hoof one, then twice and mud splattered.

"A boy," Tom said.

Jenny looked at him, those blue eyes intent on his face. She didn't say anything, but turned her head toward the path and nodded. And Tom began to walk.

The path was even muddier, the snow melt running down-hill, and twice more, he slipped and fell. Each time he picked himself up, rubbing his muddy hands down the front of his trousers and continuing the uphill walk. When he reached the spring, he paused to catch his breath and saw his reflection in the water. His hair was matted with sweat, mud flung from his hands caked his cheek and there was a tear along the top of his coat where he had tangled with a thorn bush.

"Joshua!" he yelled.

And there was nothing but an echo that raced out and down below to Taylor's Ferry.

"Joshua!"

Again, nothing but his own voice over the valley. He looked out toward the river and its muddy waters ran strong. If there was a boy's jacket floating in the waters, Tom was certain he would fall to his knees and remain there for a very long time.

Again he yelled. "Joshua!"

Again, just an echo.

Tom looked at the rocks above him and he placed a hand atop the nearest one and began to climb. The surface was slick with the runoff and his grip slipped once and he banged his knee, the pain enough to stop his breath for a second. He looked upward and for the first time in a very long time he offered a prayer to God.

And then he lifted his hand and pulled and climbed and finally lifted himself onto the ledge where he and Joshua had sat just a week before. Tom straightened and then walked around the corner and pulled away the knot of cedar that blocked the cave entrance. The branches were heavy and wet, but the ground inside was dry.

And sitting there, his back to the stone wall, was one six-year-old boy who had heard the most awful news and seen a bad thing. And Tom silently offered thanks, breathed a sigh of relief and sat beside the boy.

♨

A toboggan was pulled down so low that only Joshua's eyes were visible. His chin was balanced on crossed arms and they rested atop his knees. His skin was pale and lips chapped and he was silent as Tom settled beside him.

"This is a good place," Tom said, patting the earth beneath him. "I imagine if I heard some words I didn't like and they hurt me and upset me, and there were things I couldn't under-stand, then this would be a place where I would want to come work things out."

Joshua remained quiet, his eyes gazing out toward the muddy river.

"Yes, sir. This is a very good place," Tom said.

The two of them stared out at the river and watched as

a barge headed south came around the bend. Tom cleared his throat.

"I'm sorry you heard what I said. It wasn't right for me to say those things to your mom and I'll have to make it right with her. And that's what I intend to do."

Tom turned and looked at him. "And I'm very sorry if my words upset you. I'm sorry you heard about Dutch that way. He seemed to really care about you and your mother."

Joshua turned his head. "He was my friend."

Tom nodded. "I know that. And I'm sorry you lost your friend."

Joshua rubbed a hand under his eye and turned back toward the river. Tom straightened his legs before him and picked at the mud that clung to his trousers. "You know, the two of us are a lot alike."

"How so?"

"Well, I think we're both trying to figure some things out and thinking we can do it on our own," Tom said, pausing to look upward and gather his thoughts. "But, truth is, there are quite a few people who care very deeply about us and are willing to help if we just ask."

Tom nodded toward the valley and Taylor's Ferry. "There are a lot people down there searching for you, Joshua. The sheriff. Stick. All your neighbors. A lot of people care about you. Most of all, your momma."

Joshua sniffled and shuffled his feet. "She OK?"

"She's mighty upset and scared. She wants to know that her son is safe and he's ready to come home." Tom placed his hand on Joshua's back. "We all do, buddy."

"I didn't mean to make her cry."

"She knows that, Josh. She just wants you back home."

Joshua looked at him and wiped at his chin. "I am mighty hungry."

Tom smiled as he rose from the ground. "Well, let's get down from here and I bet she'll have biscuits waiting. What do you say?"

The boy took Josh's offered hand and they made their way down the rocks. This time was much easier as the sun had dried the round edges and they landed with a thump near the Healing Spring. They both made their way over to the pool and looked into the water. Two dirty, tired faces stared back.

Joshua looked over at Tom. "I heard what you said about Dutch and him being my daddy."

Tom winced. "I'm sorry I said that. Sometimes I get angry and say things I shouldn't. And I shouldn't have said that about Dutch."

"Well, he ain't my daddy."

Tom's gut felt like it took a punch and he searched for a breath. In one way, it brought him relief that Dutch wasn't Joshua's daddy. But, in another, he'd started to make peace with the idea. And now, uncertainty and the unknown began to gnaw at the fringes of his mind.

Tom rubbed hard at the mud that had dug in deep to the fabric of his trousers. The harder he rubbed, the more dirt rose and covered his hands. He stopped rubbing and kneeled, gathering the water from the Healing Spring and washed his hands clean. Josh knelt beside him and did the same.

"You know, I'm looking for my momma and daddy, too," Tom said.

Joshua cocked his head. "But I thought you already had a momma and daddy. That's what momma said. That they lived far away, but they cared very much for you."

"I do. You're right. I just…"

"Well, I think you'd be a good daddy."

Tom stared into the spring water. "You really think so?"

"Uh huh."

Tom brought the cool water to his face and washed away the grime and dirt. He thought of JC and how each person's actions and choices define them more than their origins or background. And when he looked into the spring again, it was a new man who appeared.

"Tom?"

"Yes, Josh."

"I'm really hungry. Can we go get them biscuits?"

And so the two of them left the spring and walked down the path and emerged from the canebrake. And there, still waiting, patient and trusting, was Creeping Jenny and her mule.

"Hi Jenny," Joshua said.

Hearing her name, the woman slid down from the mule and lowered her head. She glanced up at Tom and he smiled.

"I think Jenny wants to know if you want a ride?" Tom asked.

"Heck yeah," Joshua said.

So Tom lifted him up onto the back of the mule, who remained straight and calm, and Joshua got a grip on his mane. Jenny took the rope and the three of them began to walk beside the canebrake. Each of them in their own thoughts, accompanied by the steady clop-clop-clop of the mule.

Home just around the corner.

CHAPTER 28

Sturgill was in his car and appeared to be talking on his police radio when Tom saw the sheriff lift his eyes and watch as he and Creeping Jenny approached, the missing boy perched on the back of a very fine mule.

Sturgill pushed open his car door and stood, the radio mic still in his hand and the mule stopped in front of the Clanton home. The mule stomped its foot once, then again, and Jenny put a tighter grip on his lead. Sturgill spoke into his mic and then shut his door.

"Joshua!" yelled Mary as the screen door burst open and she jumped, clearing the bottom two steps. Tom and Jenny stood to the side as she ran to the mule and opened her arms to her son. Joshua slid down the mule and into her arms and she pulled him in close. Fergus came out and watched from the top step.

"Never, ever leave me, Joshua Clanton! My baby, baby boy," and she kissed his forehead and his chin and hugged him again. Sturgill walked over and stood beside Tom and Jenny.

Mary pulled back and looked into her son's eyes. "Where were you, Joshua? You had me worried sick. Don't ever, ever do that again."

Joshua's lower lip trembled. "I'm sorry, momma."

And she brought him close to hug again. Joshua looked over at Tom and Jenny.

"It was Tom who found me, momma," Joshua said. "He knows our secret place."

Mary looked at Tom, her eyes softening. "The spring?"

Tom nodded yes.

"You remembered?" she asked.

He nodded again.

Sturgill looked at Tom and then Joshua. "Are you hurt, son?"

"No sir," Joshua said. "Just hungry. Tom said there would be biscuits."

Mary smiled. "Is that right?"

Tom looked at her. "I told him there were a great many people, including his momma, who were worried about him and cared for him. The biscuits were the icing on the cake."

"Pappy!" Joshua yelled and ran to his grandfather, who opened his arms and hugged the boy close. They watched as the two embraced, Fergus Clanton with tears in his eyes, running his hand over the boy's head and kissing his forehead.

Mary stood and reached for Tom's hand. "You'll stay?"

Tom nodded. "I'd like that."

She squeezed his hand and turned to the sheriff. "Looks like I have biscuits to make. Thank you, sheriff."

"Miss Clanton," Sturgill said, with a curt nod of his head. He and Tom watched as she joined Fergus and Joshua and they climbed the stairs and went inside the home. The sheriff turned to Tom.

"The Healing Spring?"

"Yeah. We'd been up there about a week ago. He'd found a

cave up above the spring. Once I sat and gave it some thought, that cave seemed as good a place as any. Wasn't all me, though."

He turned and it was then that Tom noticed that Jenny and the mule were no longer there. She and the mule had slid away amidst the joyful reunion. "It was Jenny who showed me the path and who was there when we walked back down. Funny how she's always there to point me in the right direction."

The sheriff considered Tom's words as he reached into his coat pocket and pulled out a peppermint. He tossed the candy into his mouth, sucked on it for a short moment and then bit into it with a loud crunch.

"Reporter."

"Yes, sheriff."

Sturgill reached into his pocket and pulled another peppermint. He handed it to Tom. "Good work."

And the sheriff turned and got into his car and soon Tom was left alone in front of the Clanton home.

After having biscuits smothered in honey and strawberry jam, and sitting with Fergus and Joshua until the two of them fell asleep on the couch together, Tom and Mary walked across the street to the park.

They sat on a bench and let the sun warm their faces and they unbuttoned their coats. And when Tom reached for Mary's hand, she did not pull away. Instead, their fingers entwined and became one.

"I'm sorry for what I said," Tom started. "None of it was right. It was my stupid ego and jealousy and I was wrong in so many ways..."

"Shhhhh," Mary said. "Let's just sit here and enjoy this moment."

And so they sat there in the sun and closed their eyes.

"I've always done it on my own," she said.

Tom opened his eyes and looked at her. "I know. And you've done great."

She frowned, her eyes still closed. "I've done my best. But, it's certainly not where I thought I'd be in life. Twenty-six years old. Living with my daddy. Working at the Rainbow and raising a son on my own."

"I'd like to help."

She sighed. "I've heard that before, Tom."

Tom squeezed her hand and her eyes opened and turned to him. "I'm serious, Mary. I've been giving it a lot of thought. I think we could have a future together. All of us. Me, you and Joshua."

Her eyes stayed on his. Tom leaned closer.

"I came this morning to apologize for my terrible actions on Friday. And then, to see the police cars, the fear and hurt on your face. And with Joshua disappearing? And knowing that I played a part in all that. My words. My actions. It tore me to my soul, Mary. My heart and every part of me was in pain. And I knew I had to make it right."

He raised her hand and kissed it. "For all of us."

Mary turned away and he noticed tears.

"I want that life together, Mary. And I think you do, too."

Mary shook her head. "I wish it was that easy."

"It can be."

"There's things in my —"

Tom stopped her with his fingers to her lips. "The past is the past. A wise man told me last night that a person's actions and choices define them more than their background. A family is more than one based on blood. It's one built on love. And I do believe I love you Mary Clanton."

And he leaned forward and they kissed and Tom carried that weight that had been on Mary's shoulders. And he felt safe and loved. And after they kissed again, Mary leaned forward and stared out at the playground where Joshua spent many hours on the swings, his head back and legs kicking in the sky.

She touched Tom's hand. "Despite what people say, Tom, there was nothing more than a friendship between me and Dutch. I should have told you that first weekend when you came into the Rainbow when I realized you were covering the story. But I really liked you and thought if you found out about my past you'd go running."

Tom nodded and squeezed her hand. "Your past is your past, Mary. You don't have to explain."

"But I do. You seem to think my relationship with Dutch was something more than what it was. We did date for a while. It was several years ago. We'd been friends for a good bit before that and we tried to make a go of it. And, you know, I think Dutch wanted more, but in the end he was just a good friend. In some ways, he was like my guardian angel."

"As if you need a guardian angel." Tom said with a shake of his head. "Joshua told me this morning. Up at the Healing Spring. He knows Dutch isn't his daddy."

Tom held her hand tighter and she slid closer and leaned her head against his shoulder.

"Dutch cared for us. He really did. He wanted to make sure we were taken care of. He'd offer to help with groceries. He'd stop by the Rainbow and hand me an envelope with cash and tell me to go buy Joshua something nice, a toy or something. I told him I didn't need his money. I just needed his friendship."

She lifted her head and looked into Tom's eyes. "He was like you. The questions about Joshua's daddy. The only time I ever saw him lose his temper was when he'd talk about how low it was for a man to not support his child. That really bothered him. I think it had to do with him and Malachi and the fact they lost their parents so young.

"He'd say, 'Here's a man who knows he has a son and refuses to take responsibility.' I'd tell him that me and Joshua were doing just fine with Daddy and we didn't need the man in our life. But, Tom, I swear there were times when I thought Dutch was capable of beating the man to death. And that scared me and that's why I saw less and less of Dutch."

Tom looked out over the park and squeezed Mary's hand. "I'm sorry."

Mary nodded. "Dutch just wouldn't stop with the questions. I finally told him last fall, about a month before the accident."

Tom looked at her. "Will you tell me?"

"I fear what you will think of me."

Tom leaned into her. "You have to know that I love you, Mary. And what you tell me will not change that. My life's been torn apart from a secret that my parents hid for 21 years. And my biggest fear is this weight, this burden you carry, stops us before we start. But I know the fear you have as well. When you want to tell me, I'll be here to listen."

Mary took a deep breath.

"He denied it. He said Joshua wasn't his."

"But, you…"

Mary's eyes narrowed and her grip tightened around his hand. "I know my son's daddy."

CHAPTER 29

TOM SAT IN the Fairlane and looked at the two-story house situated on the corner lot. Late afternoon shadows crept across the lawn and darkness lay across the back end of the royal blue Cadillac that sat parked alone in the driveway, its color a contrast to the stark concrete.

Tom had driven here after leaving Mary and he wasn't really sure why. The sheriff and Stick had pulled Dutch's body from the waters the day before. He was uncertain if they'd been here to deliver the news through the proper channels. Was it best that way?

He listened to the slow metallic tick of the engine as it cooled and his fingers traced the rough edges of the reporter's notebook lodged in the seat beside him. He'd gone through about three of the notebooks so far and this one had plenty of clean white pages, but he wasn't certain if there'd be anything to write and he was even more unsure of the questions he'd ask.

"You chase the story, that's what you do," JC had advised him those first days along the river. And that's what Tom told himself he was doing as he sat outside the home of Dr. Wesley and Virginia Webb. He opened his car door and put the notebook in his back pocket and made his way to the back door.

The Christmas tree he'd dragged, along with its silver string of tassels, was long gone from the curb, where he'd left it alongside his pile of vomit. And in the back yard, where a worn rope hung from an oak tree's branch, Tom wondered if a tire had once hung there, pushed only by a strong breeze from the northwest. He figured the rope, much like the Webbs' marriage, had frayed over the years, snapping finally to leave the strands unconnected and blowing in the wind.

Tom knocked on the door and waited. He noticed the shift of a curtain and it wasn't much longer until Virginia opened the door. Her face was flushed and Tom noticed the redness extended along her neck and across her chest, the two top buttons of her blue silk shirt untethered and the skin exposed. There was the scent of pine and lime and Tom wondered if it had been her second or third martini she'd drained just before opening the door.

"Well, Tommy," she said. "Aren't you always a surprise."

Tom gave a half-smile and Virginia opened the door wider and extended her arm. He paused and looked to the ground.

"Oh," she said, "so, this is not pleasure?"

Tom shook his head. He looked behind him and there was no one on the street. The last thing he needed while trying to patch things up with Mary would be talk around Newton County that his car had been spotted in the evening, parked outside the widow Webb's home.

Virginia leaned against the door frame. She raised an eyebrow.

"Well, I have news," she said.

Tom's brow furrowed.

"I'm sure Mrs. Tyner told you I was never one to dawdle. She'd give us an assignment for the next week and, the very next day, I'm standing before her with my paper, all T's crossed, all I's dotted. The old biddy would be left speechless. That was reward enough."

"I don't know what you're —"

She smiled wide and her green eyes danced.

"Your special problem, Tommy. Come now. You haven't forgotten have you?"

Tom's jaw's tightened and he held his eyes on hers.

"Mommy."

"Stop it."

"Mommy."

Tom took a step closer and his body filled the door frame. Virginia held her ground and looked up at him. She ran her tongue across her lips and he thought of a snake and the way it would slither through the grass and you'd be unsure whether its bite was harmless or potent enough to lose a limb or a life.

"Dying to know aren't you?" she asked.

He'd seen women like Virginia Webb before — the way they lurked in the shadows of the nightspots not far from campus. Youth had left most of the women and what they bartered with were their flirtations, a hand that lingered on an arm or the way a body pressed close to whisper words that they damn well knew the meaning of. What you didn't know precisely was what they sought. And that was the dangerous part.

Even though her looks and figure were still holding true, Tom guessed Virginia was nearing 40. The perfume she wore was popular five years earlier and the loose threads that hung from her sleeve were a hint of things coming apart. The flirtatious banter was just part of her foreplay and Tom had grown weary of it after two months in Newton County.

He leaned in close and whispered, "They found a body, Virginia."

There was the briefest bit of satisfaction as Tom watched the smile fade, her lips now a bloodless, straight line. He held her gaze.

"Who?" she asked.

He paused, relishing that which he held over her. How the game had turned. It was reward enough for the moment.

"Dutch."

There was a deep sigh and she turned away from him. Virginia moved to the kitchen table and ran her hands over the bare surface. She walked to the sink, ran the faucet and picked up a dish towel, on the fabric a bounty of red rose petals, and she wiped her hands in one quick continuous motion.

"A couple of fishermen found the body washed up on a piece of driftwood, down on the Kentucky side, not far from the Old Shawnee bridge."

Virginia said nothing but opened a side cabinet where she pulled a half-empty bottle of gin and another smaller bottle of vermouth and placed them on the kitchen table. She pulled a spotted glass from the sink, as well as half a lime and knife, and brought them to the table. There was a slight shake to her hand as she made the cut and the blade nicked her skin.

Tom watched as she brought the bloodied finger to her mouth and, with her other hand, poured two shots of gin into the glass. She dropped her hand and drank the gin in one smooth gulp. She picked up the knife and cut another slice of lime, this time the cut straight and true. She poured more gin and vermouth and sat at the table.

Tom entered the kitchen and shut the door behind him. He pulled a chair and sat across from her.

"A cause of death?"

He thought of Dutch's bloated corpse and grimaced.

"Hard to tell. He'd been in the water for a good while. Fish and turtles, you know."

Virginia took a long drink. Tom glanced around the kitchen, noticing the orderliness of it. There was a large wooden buffet that dominated one wall, dishes stacked in rows of four, cups hanging above and each saucer in its appropriate slot. A stack of cloth napkins neatly folded and poised for use stood next to a basket full of fresh lemons and limes.

"Anything of Wesley?"

Tom shook his head.

Virginia turned her head, looking through the window over the sink and out towards the back yard. Tom noticed there was a slight breeze and the frayed rope swayed.

"I never would have chosen roses," she said.

Tom waited. She nodded toward the buffet and he noticed the pattern of white roses and green garland that lined the cream-colored plates and saucers.

"The dishes. They were Helen's. Wesley surprised her with them as a wedding gift. He absolutely refused to get rid of them."

She eyed Tom and took a long drink, draining the rest of the martini. She used the back of her hand to wipe her mouth and Tom noticed the paleness of her naked lips.

"Ever eaten your dinner on a dead woman's dishes, Tommy? It's no fucking delight."

Tom coughed and pulled his reporter's notebook from his pocket and placed it on the table. Virginia shook her head.

"You're not getting anything from me."

"How well did you know, Dutch?"

She said nothing as both hands curled around the empty glass.

"Were you having an affair with Dutch?"

Her fingers tightened around the glass and Tom noticed the slice along the edge of her finger and the red inside as the cut opened with the pressure.

"I've got a good source who spotted the two of you together about a month before he and your husband went duck hunting. And from what they saw it was certainly more than two friends together. More like lovers."

She raised her eyes to meet his.

"Who?"

"Not at liberty to say."

"People are going to spread rumors."

"I believe this person's story. They'd have no reason to lie."

"You have no idea what some people will do to hide the truth."

Tom nodded his head.

"The longer I'm here in Newton County, the more I'm learning that's true."

Virginia smiled. The banter seemed to revive her.

"You haven't found her, have you?"

Tom picked up his pen and asked, "Did Dr. Webb find out about you and Dutch?"

"Would it matter?"

"I'd say it would matter a great deal if he found out his wife was having an affair, especially with someone who he considered a friend, a hunting buddy."

"You are so naive, Tommy."

"I prefer Tom."

"Oh, so grown up now."

The two of them stared at each other across the table. From another room came the sudden chimes of a clock and they listened to the count of six. Tom shifted in his chair.

"Did Dr. Webb know about Dutch?"

"You know. She's in Taylor's Ferry."

Tom paused, his pen in mid-air and his mind went to Mary.

"Who?" he asked cautiously.

"Well, who is it you've been looking for all this time, Tommy?"

"We're talking about you."

"Are we?"

Tom flipped opened the notebook with a flourish. A blank page was before him.

He'd been assigned a test story early in his days at the *Kernel*. "Let's see what you got, kid, " said the editor, a senior from Litchfield, who told him a fencing club had started and was seeking some publicity. Who better than the sophomore cub reporter to write the feature? He'd gone in with low expectations, but came away fascinated by the skills of each competitor. Tom had been drawn in by how their expressions were hidden behind masks, the way their muscled torsos lunged forward and fell back, the foil extended, always searching for an opening, scoring only when they struck the target that lay near the heart. His feature had run on page one — and was one of his better stories.

Now, sitting across from him, Virginia Webb was every bit as skilled as those fencers with their sabers. She pushed her chair back and walked to the counter where she filled her glass with more gin and vermouth. She stirred her drink with her finger, either not noticing or caring about the bite of the alcohol and the open cut.

"I mean isn't that what brought you here in the first place?" she asked, settling once more into her chair. "If you don't come looking for mommy, then we never sit here at this table to engage — to have this conversation."

She stirred the glass and her eyes watched the green of the lime as it circled the rim.

"Do you believe in fate, Tom?"

His pen drew a straight line across the open white of the page and ended with an open circle. He raised his eyes.

"Is that what you're saying brought Dutch and Dr. Webb together on the river that morning?"

"Oh, I'm not saying that at all."

She took a drink from her glass and set it down. She rose again from her chair and went to the buffet, yanked open the top left drawer and pulled out a pack of cigarettes and a tab of matches. She pulled one free, lit it, then slid the pack of big size Kents across the table to Tom. He ignored her offer. Instead, he increased the pressure.

"Maybe you hoodwinked Dutch. Told him of how things would be so much better if your husband was no longer around. No more need to sneak away to the woods. And just imagine the life insurance money if Dr. Webb suddenly passed? The two of you could do whatever and go wherever you pleased."

She took a draw off the cigarette and slowly let the smoke fall from her wet mouth before she spoke.

"Always with the active imagination."

Tom rapped his knuckles against the table.

"And then when both men disappear and the coroner rules them dead and the life insurance money arrives? Oh, even better for Virginia Webb. Two dead men. Nothing to hold you back then."

"Who's to say my husband is not alive? Have you considered that?"

"We both know the man you married is 30-feet below and probably down past Golconda by now."

"Do we?"

Tom knew until Dr. Webb's body surfaced, if it ever did, the question would go unanswered. She took another draw off the cigarette and flicked an ash into the half-empty glass.

"What I can't figure out is which one you were hoping was coming off that river that morning? Dutch or your husband?"

Virginia eyed him across the table.

"My husband never told me he was going hunting that morning. Dutch just showed up. It was just like I told the sheriff. I was expecting him home later that evening and when I awoke and discovered he still hadn't returned, then I called the police and told them he was missing."

"Did Dutch kill your husband out of love or was it just lust between you two?"

She took another long draw and then snubbed the rest of her cigarette in the pool of gin.

"I'm bored of this." Virginia leaned forward and said, "Time for a new game."

"I'm not done—"

She smiled and then in a sing-song voice said, "I've got a secret."

Tom sat quiet. Again she taunted, "I've got a secret."

"Sometimes you're really like a child."

Her shoulders moved and her head rocked. "I've got a secret. I've got a secret. I've got a secret."

Tom reached for the pack of Kent's and pulled one free.

"Come on, Tommy. Play."

He struck a match and lit the end. He watched the red embers form and then took a deep drag, the smoke filling his lungs with a warm embrace. The nicotine left a pleasant feeling and he stayed with the escape as long as he could.

"What's your secret?"

"I know your mommy."

"How do you know?"

"Wasn't hard to figure out. Just do the math and remember which of my classmates all of a sudden went away for a year and wasn't seen until the following fall. It's not rocket science."

Tom took another draw and then released the smoke, watching the grey tendrils as they climbed toward the ceiling.

"Could be anyone," he said.

She reached over and poked his free hand with a tangerine-splashed fingernail. "But it's not."

He took a long glance at her. The smug look on her face. The color back in her cheeks, the flash in her eyes. He pulled her glass of gin close and flicked the spent end of his ash into the cup, the white-and-black flakes sitting on the surface.

"I'll play," he said, slowly raising his eyes to meet hers. "I've got a secret."

Her fingers lingered on his hand, but it wasn't her touch or the way she softly bit at her lower lip that stirred Tom. He raised his cigarette and pointed across the table.

"Perhaps it wasn't you who Dutch killed for. Have you considered that? I believe it was somebody else. Another woman's heart he hoped to gain by making the doctor pay for what he'd done."

Virginia pulled her hand away and sat back in her chair. She coughed and it was followed by another, this one deeper in her chest. It was the hacking cough of a smoker and one who'd been practicing the habit for nearly 20 years. She wiped her mouth with the back of her hand and, for a brief second, Tom felt sorrow for Virginia.

The teasing school girl was gone. Tom took in another long draw and then dropped the rest of his cigarette in the glass of gin where it was doused with a quick fizzle. He slowly released the smoke through his nose and kept his eyes on her through the haze, the taste of tobacco on the tip of his tongue. Her eyes darted to the window above the sink and then over his shoulder to the closed door. The mouse was cornered, looking for a way out.

Tom flipped through the blank pages of his notebook, seemingly in search of a missing fact, but he knew full well what he intended to ask. In the growing darkness, he heard the sharp bark of a dog and the laughter of a child. In the kitchen, a drop of water fell from the faucet and another minute clicked past six.

"Now," Tom said, "how long ago was it when Dr. Webb told you about his baby boy in Taylor's Ferry?"

CHAPTER 30

When Mary told him Dr. Webb was the father of Joshua, Tom's first instinct was to react much like he believed Dutch likely would have. The anger surfaced, but then subsided as he looked at Mary's face and realized the trust she was placing with him.

"Again, maybe I should have told you," Mary said. "It was nice being with someone who didn't know my history. Or felt like he had to immediately protect or provide for me. I've done well enough on my own for these past years."

Tom looked at Mary, her eyes on him. She'd been alone for most of her life. When her mother died, Mary was only 8 years old. Fergus coped by going underground and working double shifts at the Hamilton mine. Mary made her own dinner and ate alone.

Men had been letting Mary down for a while now. Tom did not want to join that list. He leaned back and watched the untethered clouds run across the sky. Dusk neared and another day would end and another begin. Time marched on.

Mary told him of how she'd graduated from Newton County High School and was planning to attend Henderson Community College that fall. A school counselor had encouraged her, saying she had the learning and willpower to succeed. Mary thought of becoming a dental hygienist and she'd jumped at the chance to start work that summer for Dr. Webb, answering the phone, scheduling appointments and greeting patients.

"He seemed nice," Mary said.

Dr. Webb seemed to take a genuine interest in her and would let her watch as he'd fill a cavity or repair a broken crown. He gave her a book on dentistry.

"Maybe I was a fool, but I'd never really had anybody sit and listen to what I had to say," Mary said.

As the summer stretched into July and early August, Dr. Webb increased her hours and pay. More and more often, she found herself staying after the last patient had left. She'd help with the cleanup and go over the following day's schedule with Dr. Webb.

"He was more than happy to sit and talk with me at the end of the day. It's funny, but during those times, he made me feel like I was the most important person in his little part of the world."

She told him of how she'd lost her mother at a young age. He asked her if she had a steady boyfriend. He had smiled when she said no boy in Newton County interested her and she didn't want to be be just a wife to a coal miner or farmer. Dr. Webb rarely mentioned his second wife, Virginia, only to say that she had an affinity for large purses and the cash that went inside them.

"At times, he seemed a lonely man," Mary said. "I was left feeling that he was in search of something that he'd lost. And I was a pretty face willing to listen to him."

So, when Dr. Webb placed his hand on her shoulder that one Friday evening in early August and his hand lingered, she'd not balked. He told her how pretty she was and how she was much better than anything Newton County had to offer. He kissed her and she'd not turned away.

Tom lowered his head and closed his eyes. He gripped the bench, the wood still wet from the storm days earlier and how the wood shredded in his hands. He listened as Mary told him how Dr. Webb had lifted her onto the desk.

"Did you try to stop him?"

"It was just… quick."

Tom shook his head, not wanting to hear more.

"It was rushed. So fast."

Mary stopped to wipe a tear from her cheek.

"Things changed after that."

The following week, Dr. Webb said he'd not need her to stay late anymore. Conversations became clipped and Mary's hours decreased once her college classes began after Labor Day. The first week of October, she missed classes after waking that morning with an awful sickness. The morning sickness lingered and a pregnancy test a week later confirmed Mary's worst fears.

The following Monday, she lingered in the office after the last patient left for the day. Dr. Webb was surprised to see her seated in the waiting area.

"Mary, you're not needed," he said. "Everything's well in hand here."

He nodded to the bag of golf clubs in the corner. "I was hoping to get in 18 with the boys at the country club, you know. So…."

"We need to talk," she said.

Dr. Webb crossed his arms as Mary told him of the morning sickness and the pregnancy test.

"You're the father," she said.

"That's impossible."

Anger rose in her voice. "There was no other."

"I'm sorry, Mary. But the child is not mine. And, frankly, I'm disappointed in you. I'd have never thought you'd resort to this kind of back-handed, hillbilly shakedown."

"I can't believe you'd say that."

Dr. Webb looked at his watch and shrugged.

"Maybe it's best, Mary, if you didn't work here any longer. Since you've started school, I've noticed you've been late a few times, not as quick to catch the calls. I'm sorry, but I really need someone a bit more reliable.

"And in light of this," he said, nodding toward her belly with a doubtful look. "It's really for the best that we go our different ways."

He cocked his head to the side.

"I'm going to be late, Mary, And that's not like me. So, if you'd please."

He had escorted her out of the office and locked the door behind him. He'd nodded as he jumped in his truck and backed out of the driveway. Mary stood, alone, and realized how life had changed.

"It happened so fast," she said, turning toward Tom. "Maybe I could have looked at adoption, but I couldn't ever do that. Part of what was growing inside me was my blood, my flesh. I grew up knowing what it is to be alone. And I vowed my child would not grow up without knowing my love."

"Momma," Joshua called out as he opened the front door of the house.

"Here hon'," Mary said, lifting her hand.

Tom watched the boy jump from two stairs up, run across

the street and wrap his arms around her legs. He saw a look of worry come across the boy's face as he looked up at his mother.

"What's wrong?" Joshua asked.

"Just a sad story is all," Mary said, her lips forcing a smile.

"I don't like when you're sad."

"I know, baby."

Joshua looked at the two of them together and grabbed their hands.

"Will you push me on the swings?" he asked.

"You get started and we'll join you," Tom said, watching as Joshua turned and ran for the swings.

Mary's words hung heavy on Tom. He thought of his own mother, wondering what had compelled her to hand him over to strangers just days after his birth. How long had she held him? Was he pulled away as she kicked or screamed? Or had she simply turned and walked away?

"What are you thinking?" Mary asked.

"Lots."

"Do you understand now why I was reluctant to tell you about my past? It's not a fairy tale."

He looked over at her and nodded.

"And then, when you told me how you were searching for your mother and how you'd been adopted. It just hit really close my heart."

Tom sighed. "I wonder why she couldn't have been more like you. Not wanting to give up so fast. Willing to fight, to do whatever it took to keep her baby."

"Each woman is different. Every situation unique."

Mary reached over and held Tom's hand. They could hear Joshua's voice, his happiness as it filled the air.

"I can't imagine my life without him," she said.

Tom sat in Virginia Webb's kitchen, she across the table from him.

"Now, how long ago was it when Dr. Webb told you about his baby boy in Taylor's Ferry?"

There was a flash of scarlet across Virginia Webb's skin, the heat of anger quick to come to the surface.

"You're bluffing," she snapped.

He shrugged.

"Who?" Virginia asked.

"Mary Clanton."

There was quiet in the kitchen as Tom watched Virginia and he thought of her mind going back to seven years earlier and the cute, young woman who had shown up at her husband's practice one day begging for a job.

"That's a lie."

"I'm sure that's what he told you."

Virginia pushed her chair away from the table and stood up.

"Dutch never mentioned it?" Tom asked. "You do realize his only interest in you was in getting back at Dr. Webb, right? Payback for what your husband did to Mary. What better way, than to steal the affections of a man's wife. Dutch never had any love for you."

Virginia began to pace. "I think you need to leave."

Tom rapped his knuckles on the table. "I'm guessing Dr. Webb had quite the story when he suddenly sent Mary on her way, didn't he?"

Virginia shook her head. "That girl was looking for a payout. Blackmail. The baby wasn't his. Couldn't have been."

Tom held her gaze.

"That's not the way I see it, Virginia. I see it as an older man taking advantage of a much younger woman. Hell, his own employee. And then not owning up to his responsibility. A low-down coward and worthless piece of shit is what I see."

Virginia Webb held his stare. "Just leave. Now."

Tom rose from the table, closed his notebook and placed it in his pocket. He opened the door and paused. Virginia stood at the table, her hands gripping the top of a chair. Her body, her gaze, her expression — all unsteady. The creases at the corner of her eyes deepened.

"I'm sorry you had to find out like this."

"Get out."

"Secrets are the worst kind —"

"Get out, now!"

And Virginia's scream was muffled as he pulled the door behind him. He'd gone three, maybe four, steps when he heard the sound of a glass smashing against the kitchen wall.

CHAPTER 31

IT WAS A Wednesday morning when they buried Dutch Blackburn. Two days before, a cold front had stalled and a day-long
drizzle fell. Tuesday, the cemetery caretaker had dug the hole
8-feet long, three-feet wide and six-feet deep and now the dirt
lay piled, a brown heap, beside the grave and atop an open
slab of brown grass that Tom guessed would one day cover the
remains of Malachi.

The cemetery was small, some 50 headstones. Some of the
stone markers were slanted — the older the grave, the more
severe the angle. Weather had grayed some of the stones, their
words and remembrances harder to decipher. Many of the dead
had been members of the Little Bethel Baptist Church, its
white-washed walls and dark-green shingled roof a short walk
away.

Preacher man Jarrod Speece spent most of his week filling
sacks at the grain and feed store in Morgan's Gap. This morning, he stood at the foot of the grave, in his hand a dog-eared
King James Bible, and he spoke of the Blackburn family and
their love for Jesus and one another.

Dutch would lie in eternity beside his mother, Hazel,
while his father, James II, rested on her right. Tom wondered

if Malachi had any reservations about where he'd be placed. Had it been Malachi who decided Dutch would lie beside his momma or had it been the caretaker who placed his shovel in the ground, pushed down and chose the path of least resistance? Tom guessed it was the call of the caretaker, who he noticed lingered at the edge of the tree line, his bald head turned upward, wary of dark clouds that could bring trouble before he'd get the grave filled.

The small crowd gathered and, led by Preacher Speece, they sang the Carter family's "Will You Miss Me When I'm Gone." Most of the 20 or so who gathered around the grave knew the haunting words and their voices filled the valley. However, Malachi stood silent.

Though 18, he looked more a boy than a man this day as he stood beside the simple wooden casket. His blue jeans had been pressed and the robin's egg blue button-down looked borrowed, the shirt loose on his shoulders. A step behind stood a woman clutching a pearl-handled purse tight against her bosom and beside her a slick-haired fellow, his black felt hat pressed against his chest. The man seemed not to know what to do with his free hand as he went to his pocket and, for a moment, appeared as though he'd reach out to touch Malachi's shoulder, only to retrieve his fingers in a hasty retreat.

Tom recalled Dutch's obituary and figured the couple were the Blackburn boys' aunt and uncle from across the river over near Equality. Hazel's kin. The only known relatives. Malachi's closest link to family was being put in the ground much earlier than any of them had counted on.

Mary stood beside Tom, one of her hands in his and the other on the shoulder of Joshua, who stared quietly at the coffin hovering over the open grave.

"I ask that we look to the book of Psalms, 121, verse 1 as we bow our heads in prayer," Brother Speece said in a voice that rose in timbre as his long, thin fingers traced the scripture he read. *"I lift up my eyes unto the hills, from whence cometh my help? My help cometh from the Lord, which made heaven and earth.*

"He will not suffer thy foot to be moved: he that keepeth thee will not slumber.

"Behold, he that keepeth Israel shall neither slumber nor sleep. The Lord is thy keeper: the Lord is thy shade upon thy right hand. The sun shall not smite thee by day, nor the moon by night."

Tom watched Malachi, who remained still, his eyes to the ground.

"The Lord shall preserve thee from all evil: he shall preserve thy soul. The Lord shall preserve thy going out and thy coming in from this time forth, and even for evermore."

Brother Speece paused and then looked skyward as he closed the good book. "Farewell and rest in peace, Brother Blackburn. Amen."

Malachi took the offered hand of Brother Speece, who whispered some words and then made his way to the aunt and uncle. A man wearing a Kentucky Department of Fish and Wildlife uniform approached, then two boys who wore purple and gold letter jackets from Newton County High School. A brown-haired girl in a green dress came close and kissed Malachi on the cheek. She was followed by Sheriff Sturgill, who stood talking with Malachi for a few minutes before he moved on, the sheriff giving a long look back at Tom before he joined Stick, who stood near their cruisers at the edge of the graveyard.

Mary squeezed his hand and then she and Joshua made their way to Malachi. She gave him a brief hug and Joshua shook his hand, his eyes darting once more to the coffin, before he hugged his momma close and the two of them walked toward the church.

Tom remained and stared down into the waiting grave.

"Sheriff said it was a drowning," Malachi said from across the grave. "He said, 'It's a terrible accident, son.' Told me not to linger on that, but rather remember the good times I shared with my brother. And to get on with my life. Told me that's what Dutch would want me to do."

Tom raised his eyes and met Malachi's, who were rubbed red. He was trying to put on a brave face, but the pain and uncertainty remained. The boy's aunt was now kneeling before her sister's grave, pulling at the high grass at the back of the tombstone. Nearby, her husband stood, eyes down, hat still pressed against his chest.

Tom shrugged. He'd not known a loss such as one Malachi had suffered. What advice could he offer?

"That girl," he said.

There was a hint of a smile from Malachi.

"She's a friend."

Tom nodded. He looked down into the open grave again and then to the tree line where the caretaker had begun to stir. A cloud passed overhead and the cool air felt good against the back of Tom's neck.

"You given any thought as to what's next?"

Malachi tugged at his shirt collar.

"I'll finish school this spring. One of my shop teachers says I'd make a good welder and he knows some barge operators that are always looking for a good worker. He said they pay a decent wage and I'd get the chance to see some of the country, traveling up and down that river. He said he'd put my name up."

Tom nodded over at Malachi's aunt and uncle, who had

finished tending the grave and were slowly walking towards the parking lot. "They seem nice enough."

"I reckon'." Malachi reached out and swept a wayward white dogwood blossom off the coffin. The two of them watched the white petals spin in space as the flowers tumbled into the dark of the waiting grave. "Aunt Rose says they've got a spare room that she uses for her sewing and it'd be no trouble to make over. I'd be more than welcome. But... "

He stared at the coffin. "We never really knew them though. You know? It was just me and Dutch for the longest time. I know we share the same blood, but Aunt Rose and Uncle Bill, they just seem more like strangers than family. Feel like I'd be an inconvenience."

Tom nodded. "Blood kin's not everything."

Aunt Rose called out from the parking lot, "Malachi."

He looked over the grave at Tom and shrugged and turned to make his way towards his aunt and uncle, who were standing beside an old red Ford, one of the back passenger doors open and waiting.

"Hey!" Tom yelled out.

Malachi turned.

"That monster buck."

Malachi nodded.

"You think he's still roaming those hills near your cabin?"

Malachi smiled. "I'd be lying if I didn't say I didn't think it was true."

"That'd be a shame for someone not named Blackburn to make that kill."

"A damn shame."

"Awfully hard to track him when you're in the bottom of a barge somewhere down the Ohio."

"That's true."

Tom looked around at the woods that bordered where the dead slept. The high hills that flanked the valley were waiting for the green of spring. He could hear squirrels rustling in the back brush and nearby lingered the boastful call of a small wren, its song lifted above the stand of cottonwoods that lined the creek still full of rainwater. The ground of Newton County teemed with life and promise.

"Home is where you make it, Malachi," Tom said. "If that's the one thing you take from all this, try to remember that."

The boy nodded and made his way to the car where Rose and Bill waited. Malachi turned and raised a hand in farewell just before he pulled the door shut and the red Ford coughed and sputtered, headed, no doubt, on its way to Equality.

❧

Tom turned and made his way toward Mary and Joshua. They'd been joined by JC, who was kneeling and had pulled a string from his pocket and wrapped it around his fingers. In one instance, the old man's hands formed a cup and saucer. Then a cat's cradle and, finally, Jacob's ladder. Joshua clapped his hands and asked for more.

JC straightened and handed over the string. "Ah, you show me, young Joshua. Show this tired old man what you can do."

The three of them stood and watched as Joshua ran the string through his fingers, over and over again, in search of what JC had showed him.

JC looked out over the cemetery where the caretakers had moved forward and were beginning to lower Dutch's coffin into the ground.

"Appears that this puts a cap on this story," he said.

"Maybe," Tom said.

⋅⋅⋅

On Monday, Tom had written the front-page story and taken the photographs that detailed the discovery of Dutch Black-burn's body. When he had finished with the story, Tom filled his cup of coffee and paced back and forth as JC read over the finished copy. Tom had watched as the editor's eyebrows rose and fell, a red pen ready and twitching in his hand. He grimaced when he saw JC make a red slash through the third paragraph. But there were few marks of red and, when done, JC had leaned back in his chair and placed his hands behind his head.

"Mr. Crutchfield," JC said.

"You didn't like it?"

"Did I say that?"

"No, but I did see you making plenty of marks."

JC chuckled. "Even the best bleed a bit from the edi-tor's pen."

"So?"

"You look as anxious as a boy sweating honey on his first bear hunt. Relax, son."

Tom sat down at his desk.

"Mr. Crutchfield, do you recall the first day we met at the river?"

Though coming up on three months, Tom remembered as though it was only the week before. He had a roll of film and a tale about two missing hunters. Since then, there'd been city council and school board meetings, winter revivals and high school basketball games. He'd reported on how to store your potatoes for winter and the best corn and soybean yields. He'd covered a coroner's inquest and saw his first dead body. He'd found a friend, maybe two, and made a few enemies, maybe more.

"Are all your facts correct?" JC had asked.

"I've spoken with the coroner. And the sheriff."

JC had sighed and looked upward toward the plastered ceiling above their desks.

"At first, I didn't know what to make of you, Mr. Crutchfield. Actually, I didn't know if you'd last a week, much less a month. That kid I met at the river seemed to not know who he was or where he was headed or whatever the hell it was he was looking for.

"And your first attempts at news stories reflected that. Your words were tentative and mainly made up of assumptions and not facts. That's why your copy was covered in red, Mr. Crutchfield."

JC had then leaned forward and held up the three pages of copy that Tom had handed him earlier.

"This," he said, "this is fine writing, Mr. Crutchfield. You've done quite well in setting a scene and letting the facts drive the narrative. The quotes move the story along and also engage the reader in a way that is both informative and entertaining. It does everything a news story should do. I see no reason why this won't be our centerpiece on the front page."

JC had stood up and walked over to Tom's desk where he placed the pages before him.

"Not bad, Mr. Crutchfield. Not bad. Now, clean up that copy and get it to the typesetter in 15 minutes. We've got a newspaper to print."

◉

And so the story had run on the front page of Tuesday's edition of the *Register* and, on Wednesday, they had gathered to pay their final respects to Dutch Blackburn. The sun was climbing higher in the sky and Mary and Joshua, still with the string in his hands, walked along the headstones, she taking her son to see where his grandmother lay buried.

Tom and JC watched them, her hand in his as they matched the pace of the clouds shadowing the tombstones.

"I still find it hard to believe the sheriff didn't push the coroner for a more thorough investigation," Tom said. "That head wound —"

"Could have been the result of any myriad of consequences," JC said.

Tom had told his editor of his conversation with Virginia Webb, as well as Mary's revelation.

"I still got the feeling that one, or both of those men, showed up at the boat ramp Christmas morning with evil intentions in mind," Tom said. "Dutch angry with Dr. Webb for betraying Mary. Or maybe it was Dr. Webb who found out about Dutch and Virginia. Plenty of motives."

"And plenty of speculation," JC said. "In the end, we print verified facts, Mr. Crutchfield. That is our duty."

Tom kicked at the brown grass. "This happens on a summer day, we've got tons of witnesses. Plenty of people able to see and verify whatever happened on that river."

"Wishful thinking, Mr. Crutchfield."

Tom looked out at the parking lot. Sheriff Sturgill and Stick were in conversation with a middle-aged man who kept reaching up to keep his well-coiffed black-and-white hair from falling across his forehead.

"Well, damn," Tom said. "There was one witness that day and, damn it, if I'd completely forgot all about him."

"Mr. Crutchfield?" JC asked.

Tom gripped his editor's arms. "I've got one more card to play, Mr. Wheeler. This story's not done."

∽

Harlan Pierce had just finished speaking with the sheriff and his deputy and was nearly to his truck, when Tom reached him out of breath, having run across the cemetery and parking lot.

"Mr. Pierce… uh… Tom…Tom Crutchfield with the *Register*," he said.

Pierce looked him up and down and nodded. "Yes. Yes, Mr. Crutchfield. I'm aware of who you are."

"I'm sorry, sir. Sorry to rush up like this, but I'm just trying to put a wrap on this story."

"Horrible, horrible tragedy."

"Yes, sir. I agree."

"Well, good day. Mr. Crutchfield."

Pierce opened the door to his truck, the seal of the Newton County Search and Rescue squad just below the handle. He hopped in and there was a quick glance in the mirror and he reached up to smooth back part of his pompadour. Tom knocked on his window. Pierce grimaced and unrolled the window.

"Just a few questions about Christmas morning, down at the river."

"Mr. Crutchfield, I believe you were at the inquest. I told them everything I know."

"You said you went out that morning, right?"

"Yes, yes. That storm rolled in early and brought with it a lot of wind. I walked over to my bait shop to check on a few things. Make sure my sign was still hanging. It was a nasty morning."

"And you looked out over the river?"

"Yes. Just like I said at the inquest. I was walking along the levee."

"And you didn't see anybody out on the river?"

"It was hard to see much. That weather went bad quick. It was spitting snow and freezing rain. I didn't stay out long. There wasn't anything nor anyone out on the water. Not even barges."

Harlan Pierce ran his hand once more through his hair. "I'm sorry, Mr. Crutchfield. I'm needing to get back to my shop."

Tom raised his hand. *What was he missing? What thought kept pecking at his brain? There was something there. Something.*

Pierce began to roll up his window, but stopped when Tom's hand reached in and gripped the frame. "Mr. Pierce. One last question. Please."

Pierce waited.

"You said you looked out on the water and nobody else was on the river that morning. But, what about the levee? Were you all alone that morning or was there anyone else?"

Pierce squinted and was quiet for a few seconds. And then a smile formed on his lips.

"That's right. That's right. Only me and Creeping Jenny and that stubborn mule. The only fools to be out in that kind of weather."

CHAPTER 32

"I JUST NEED to try and chase down this last lead," Tom had said minutes earlier as he sat parked in front of Fergus' home. "I shouldn't be long."

Mary had nodded, grasped his hand and kissed his cheek. "You are a persistent one, Tom Crutchfield. I'll be here."

Following Mary's handwritten directions, Tom drove down the street, made a turn, then another and parked in front of a simple house. Two concrete steps led to a covered porch and at one end hung a swing, white paint peeling from its wooden slats.

He stepped from the car and noticed a wooden post that had begun to lean to the south, atop it a dented mailbox with the word Flowers stenciled in black. The mailbox door was partly open and Tom glanced inside to see two letters. He lifted the door and shut it, holding the door firm to make sure it remained closed.

To his right, on the other side of a gravel drive, a foot stomped and a cloud of brown dirt rose. Tom smiled and made his way to the fence. The mule lowered his head and came forward. Tom reached over the wooden plank and rubbed his hand along the mule's long face, brushing against his muzzle and the patch of white centered in his forehead.

"Imagine finding you here," he said and the mule's large ears twitched.

"He's fond of you," a voice called out and Tom turned and watched as an older woman descended the front steps. There was a slip in her gait and in her hand a worn, wooden cane and she slowly made her way to where Tom stood by the mule.

"He's normally not friendly to strangers. Not many of us are."

The mule snorted and placed his head over the top rail as the woman came forward and offered her hand. Tom ran his hands along the smooth muscled withers.

"He's a fine mule," he said.

The woman eyed him and Tom noticed there was a droop to one side of her face, but her eyes were clear and alert. Her dress went to her ankles and she wore shoes dusted with dirt. The cane dangled from a leather loop around her thin arm as she patted the mule along its massive neck.

"You could say he's a fine mule, but Job tends to break free when he sets his mind to it." She shook her head. "He'll wander the streets all night long. Still, he usually finds his way back home."

Tom stepped away from the fence and held out his hand. "My name's Tom Crutchfield. I'm with the *Register.*"

She took his hand in both of hers and Tom felt warmth. "I know that, Tom." She patted the top of his hand and her fingers lingered. "I'm Cora."

"Cora."

"Yes."

"You know Job here was the first one to welcome me to Taylor's Ferry."

"That so?"

"Came upon him the day after Christmas while I was chasing police sirens."

"That so?"

"It is."

The two of them stood and looked at the mule. His tail swished like the pendulum of a clock.

"I was hoping I could talk to Jenny."

Cora nodded and tilted her head toward the back of the house. "She's out in the barn."

"Ok if I go back to see her?"

"I think she'd like that."

The mule snorted and then stamped his large hoof and, again, a cloud of dirt rose. Tom noticed the mule matched his stride as he walked toward a small barn at the back of the property. Beyond it, a bank rose, some 50 feet high. The earthen wall was part of the levee that held back the Ohio River's flood waters and kept this little wooden house and its occupants and the hundreds of others like it in Taylor's Ferry dry and safe.

The mule snorted again and flopped his head once, twice and a third time.

"Shush mule," Jenny said, appearing in the barn opening. Her legs were in jeans and she wore her red-and-black tartan coat. Long wisps of hair were tucked beneath a wide-brimmed hat. A pair of gloves stretched nearly to her pointed elbows.

Tom watched as her blue eyes drifted toward his. Jenny glanced at him and then went back into the barn. Tom turned to Cora, who had walked up behind him.

"We've been waiting for you," she said.

Tom looked at her quizically. "Who told you I was coming?"

"I figured you'd eventually find us. You're a smart boy."

Tom shook his head. "I'm just wanting to ask her a few questions about Christmas morning. Whether she saw Dr. Webb or Dutch down at the river."

Cora cocked her head. "That so?"

"You think she'll answer?"

Cora shrugged. "No harm in asking."

Tom walked into the barn and waited for his eyes to adjust to the darkness. Jenny was shoveling a pile of manure out of a stall that he guessed served as a home for Job.

"Can I help?" he asked.

She looked at him and he noticed the rusty freckles that ran across the bridge of her nose.

"All right," she said, then went back to shoveling.

Tom found a stack of hay and he bent down and lifted a bale and carried it over to the stall. The smell of hay was heavy in the air and there was a cloud of dust when he dropped the bale. He smacked his hands together to shed the dirt and looked over at her.

"Jenny, I want to ask you some questions. About Christmas morning. You remember that day, don't you?"

Jenny continued to shovel, the manure filling a nearby bucket.

"I was wondering if you saw anyone else out that morning? Maybe Dr. Webb? Or Dutch Blackburn?"

Jenny stopped, the shovel in her hand. She gave a quick glance. "All right."

"All right? All right, like yes, I did see somebody? Or all right that I ask questions? I don't understand, Jenny."

Her eyes danced and her lips moved silently as though there

were a great many things she knew and wanted to say, but there was no way to say them. Tom stepped closer.

"Did you see them at the boat ramp that morning? Was there an argument? Did you see them on the water, Jenny? Did Dr. Webb do something to Dutch? Did he swing a paddle at him? Did Dutch try to fire his gun and the boat overturned? What was it? What did you see, Jenny? Tell me, please."

Jenny threw the shovel to the ground and her hands began to flap and she bounced back and forth on her feet.

"What was it? What happened, Jenny? Tell me. Tell me!" Tom yelled as he reached for her.

Jenny jerked and lurched away from him, fleeing to the farthest corner of the stall, where she turned her back. And slowly whispered, "All right. All right. All right. All right."

Tom felt a thickness in his throat and he lowered his head in shame.

"Tom," Cora said, her feet shuffling close to where he stood. "You're not going to get the answers you're searching for."

"I know that now. I was just hoping that maybe she'd be able to tell me what I wanted to know."

Tom raised his head and looked at Jenny, who remained in the corner, whispering words of comfort. "I shouldn't have pushed her. It was wrong. I'm sorry, Jenny."

He turned to Cora. "Do you think she'll forgive me?"

Cora's face softened. "Why did you come here, Tom?"

"I told you. The river. Christmas morning. I don't ..."

Cora was silent. Jenny still in the corner. The two of them. Waiting for Tom.

They'd been waiting for him.

Jenny turned and he saw her. The hair with its tint of sand brown, straight and falling to her broad shoulders. Her chin coming to a point, her skin tanned and tight across high cheekbones. It was a face Tom had seen before. One he'd seen staring back at him in the pool at the Healing Spring.

Tom's eyes widened, his breath caught in his chest and he stumbled, reaching for the stable post. Adrenaline rushed through his body and Tom doubled over with the weight of it all falling down upon him and then sliding off with the realization. He straightened and opened his eyes, tears wetting his freckled cheeks.

"No," he said.

"Yes," Cora said, placing her hand on his back, her eyes looking into his.

Tom looked at Jenny and she brushed a glove across her nose and he noticed a smudge of dirt remained behind. He slowly approached her in the corner and reached into his pocket to pull a handkerchief free. He leaned forward and looked into her eyes. In his hand, he held the handkerchief.

"Ok?" he asked.

She bit her lower lip and her eyes darted to the left and right. He waited until they stopped and focused on him.

"Ok?" he asked again.

"All right," she said.

And Tom wet the handkerchief with his mouth and wiped the dirt from his mother's face.

She smiled and nodded.

"Ok?"

"Ok."

"I'm Tom," he said.

She nodded as she tilted her head, her eyes searching. Tom followed her gaze, smiled and reached over and handed her a rake.

"Tom," she said.

He stepped back and watched as Jenny began to spread hay across the barn floor, to make a comfortable home for Job.

"It was you, wasn't it?" Tom asked.

"Took some doing," Cora said.

"How?"

"It's hard for people to deny an old woman's wish."

"Why?"

Cora sighed and shifted her weight, the tip of her cane digging into the dirt.

"Blame it on a mother feeling guilty over something she shouldn't have ever done."

She turned and shuffled outside to a hand pump and motioned for Tom, who followed. As Cora pumped the handle, Tom cupped his hands under the spout and splashed cold water on his face.

"I don't understand."

"Sit with me," Cora said and she walked to where a wooden swing hung from the large branch of an oak.

CHAPTER 33

"YOURS WAS A difficult birth," Cora said as she looked out toward the barn. "I nearly lost my girl that night."

It was a Thursday in 1943. Cora had spent the biggest part of her work day washing linens. The maids always washed linens on Thursday and the hotel was expecting a big crowd for the Fourth of July that next day. So, it had been late when Cora arrived home. Curtis was working nights at the mine then. She'd gone to the stove to brew herself a tea when she heard a sharp cry from behind the bedroom door.

And when she'd opened the door, she found her daughter curled in a heap on her bed, her grandmother's quilt tossed to the floor, a patch of blood staining the bed sheet. Jenny's skin wet and hot to the touch and she kept saying, "it hurts bad, momma." It was "too early, way too early."

"She'd hid you for most of that spring and summer. Her daddy in the mines. Me working at the hotel six days a week. We were just trying to get by, like most folks were. And we'd never had troubles with Jenny. She's a good girl. Always quiet that one."

It had been mid-June when Cora noticed the bump, the afternoons turning hot and Jenny no longer able to withstand the heavy cloth of the long dresses she'd been wearing for most of that spring and early summer. Cora had come upon Jenny looking at herself in the mirror one morning, her hands beneath her belly. "Oh, child. What have you done?" she asked.

Cora had thought nothing of it that previous November when Jenny said two of her schoolmates had invited her along for a dance at the new Army camp that'd been built near Morgan's Gap. She said, "There'd be soldiers, yes, momma, but there were plenty of chaperones and the girls came in on a bus and left on a bus. What harm could come of it?

"Like I said, she was a good girl. Top of her class. Never no trouble. She'd never asked for much and, maybe I thought, meeting others and seeing there were things more than Newton County, maybe it'd be good for her."

There were plenty of dances that winter and Jenny would blush when Cora asked if there was any dancing partner she preferred over another. She said there was a boy with the brownest eyes, an Italian from New Jersey, and Jenny would giggle when she tried to mimic his words and accent. Some of the maids at the hotel said some of the local girls were meeting the soldier boys in town — they'd see them at the drug store counter or at the movies. Raised eyebrows hinted at other activities, but Cora never suspected Jenny. Her daughter was smarter than that. Plus, she was just 17 years old.

But the harsh winter winds came, as did the soldiers' orders, and basic training and whirlwind romances withered, only to renew with spring and another class of recruits. But when Friday and Saturday came and other girls boarded the buses for the dances at the Army base, Jenny remained home. She'd walk to the top of the levee and stare out past the Ohio and its waters. She mailed letters. Cora guessed they were to the Italian foot soldier, but no letters arrived in the Flowers mailbox and the nights remained long and cold.

"I should have known," Cora said. "She'd been more quiet than normal. I mean we never talked much, but a mother should know when there's something weighing on her child. And I failed her. I failed miserably at that."

So, when she came home that July night and found her daughter short of breath and blood from her womb, Cora was determined not to fail her again. She ran two blocks down and banged on the door of her in-laws, waking them. She told her father-in-law to drive to the mines and get Curtis quick and bring the doctor. She and her mother-in-law gathered towels and basins and pitchers and they rushed back to Jenny.

"That night was the longest of my life. I learned how much of a fighter she was," Cora said. She reached over and patted the top of Tom's hand. "She fought so hard for the both of you that night."

The doctor came and Cora held her daughter's hand and whispered hymns, hoping to silence the screams of anguish and hurt of a way-too-early birth. The sun had just risen, its first rays barely breaking over the eastern stand of evergreens, when the baby was born. And Cora gathered the boy from the doctor, wiped his pinched, red face and wrapped him in a robin's blue blanket.

She found Curtis on his knees in the front room, coal dust on his face and neck, his miner's hat still atop his head. The white beads of a rosary were wound through his dark fingers and he said, "Thank you, Lord Jesus," when he saw the boy in Cora's arms. She placed the baby in her husband's hands and that's when her mother-in-law said, "Cora, come quick!"

When she came back into her daughter's room, the doctor

was straddling Jenny, his hands pressing fast and hard against her chest. "She's not breathing," he said. "Help me woman! Help me now!" Cora went to her daughter and placed her mouth over her chapped lips and tried to breathe life into her lungs. More compressions. More breaths. Again. And again. And Cora fought for her daughter, just as Jenny had fought for her baby boy. And after a long time and when Cora nearly felt she had no more breath to give, Jenny's eyelids fluttered.

"But it wasn't the same Jenny. She lost a lot of herself that night and that spirit never returned."

Jenny and the baby were rushed to the hospital in Morgan's Gap and tests were done. The boy was healthy, despite his premature birth. Jenny, however, wasn't responding and more tests were done. The doctor said while her body appeared healthy, her brain had been without oxygen and there'd be damage. Maybe with her speech. Her thought processes. Her social skills.

"Can she care for a baby?" Cora had asked.

"Not in her present condition," the doctor replied and walked away, leaving Cora alone.

She tried, oh she tried. But Jenny turned her head when Cora lifted the boy from his crib and held him out to her. So, instead, Cora returned the boy to a nurse and spoon-fed her daughter, the apple sauce spilling from her lips and staining the hospital gown. Jenny said nothing and it was only the twitch of her fingers that kept time with Cora's voice as she read aloud the story of Jonah and his escape from the great whale.

The next night, a man in a dark blue suit carrying a tortoise-shell briefcase knocked on the hospital door. He inquired about "the young Miss Flowers" and shook his head as he stood looking at Jenny in the bed. He noticed the small baby Cora held in her arms and walked over, smiling a thin grin as he looked down upon the infant wrapped in blue.

"A healthy lad," he said, extending a bony finger, which the baby boy grasped and held onto.

"A fine, fine boy," he said and the baby cried out. Cora pulled him close and away from the man, a hushed hymn on her lips.

"And the father?" the man asked.

Curtis had shook his head.

The man said he was an attorney, acting on behalf of two fine folks who had for years been hoping for a baby of their own. But science had proved unable to help achieve their wish and they'd left it up to God to provide.

"And I believe God has brought me to this room," the man said. "They are fine Christian folks who have had much success in their life. The boy would be loved and he'd not want for a thing. I know it's not a decision to make in haste, but they'd provide for the child and also make it worth your while."

He looked again at Jenny in her bed, a mute near-skeleton with tubes running out from her arm, her pale face lit by the monitors that surrounded her. Again, he shook his head.

"Often times, we get caught up in the now and forget the needs of the future," the man said as he slowly shook his head, both hands clasped around the handle of the briefcase. "I can only surmise as to the cost, both financially and emotionally, this toll has taken upon your family. You have my condolences."

Taking a pen and white card from a pocket within his suit, he wrote a number on the square and placed it upon the table. He nodded once and then gently closed the door behind him. His appearance had been as quiet as a whisper, but carried with it a sledgehammer's worth of weight.

Curtis and Cora gathered at their daughter's bedside. They placed the baby boy beside his mother and he squirmed and cried out. Jenny stared out the window to the blackness outside, her eyes with neither life nor joy.

It was much later that same night when Curtis walked to the lobby where the man sat sipping from a cup of coffee, his fourth. The man rose, opened the briefcase and handed Curtis his pen.

The next day, Cora and Curtis brought the baby to the parking lot of the Baptist church and they handed him to a woman dressed in a white sweater. She brought the little boy close and kissed his forehead and said, "Thomas." The couple got back into their sleek, silver four-door sedan and pulled away. The man in the dark suit with the briefcase handed the Flowers an envelope and bid farewell. Curtis and Cora stood there alone — in Curtis' hand a five-figure check, and in her heart already, a world of hurt and regret. Still they were hardy country folk so they turned and went about trying to rebuild their lives, as well as their daughter's.

"We truly had the best intentions for you," Cora said, "and for Jenny. You have to remember, she was still just a child, not yet 18. Younger than the man sitting beside me today."

Jenny tried to return to high school, but she was unable to keep up with the other students and Cora kept her home after just a few days of torture. Doctors said she was healthy physically, but damage had been done to her brain and she'd always need a simple life. And that's what Cora provided. Curtis died in December of '61 due to black lung and it had been just the two of them since.

❦

"She's never driven a car. All she knows is this little patch of Taylor's Ferry." Cora paused, using the back of her hand to wipe at a tear on her cheek. "I don't know if I've done her more harm than good. I truly don't."

Tom reached into his pocket and pulled out the handkerchief that he'd used to wipe the dirt from his mother's face. He handed it to Cora. She wiped at her tears and took a deep sigh.

"My time's short. I had a fall last spring, over there by the well. Doctors said it was a slight stroke. They told me Jenny found me, went to my neighbors and they got me to the hospital. Come full turn, didn't we, she saving my life?"

Tom turned toward the creak of the stable door and watched Jenny emerge from the barn. She glanced at the two of them and walked over to where Job stood. She climbed the fence, pulled a stiff brush from her back pocket and began to scrub the mule's flank, dust rising from his hide. Cora shifted in her seat and crossed her legs while she watched her daughter.

"Figured I owed it to her to find you. I called the attorney who handled the transaction. He's much older now. And I'd say he's a little more sympathetic to a broken-down widow's request. He gave me your parents' address. And, yes, it was me who signed and sent the card. Maybe it's selfish of me to intrude on your life like that. But I figured you deserved to know your history."

Cora handed the handkerchief back to Tom and he held onto it before placing it back in his pocket.

"I'm sorry if I caused you hurt," she said. "That was never my intention."

Tom looked out at Jenny and watched her hands glide over the mule's coat, the dirt falling off, replaced with a dark shine. He saw the way Job's ears were alert and twitched while her fingers untangled the knots in his mane and how he glanced back when Jenny lifted his hoof and picked free a pebble that had been lodged there.

"Do you think she knows me? That I'm her son?"

Cora slowly shook her head. "I wish I knew all that was in her head. It's a lot of goodness, I have to believe. Maybe it's like a fog and you're making your way through it and you can see just shadows of someone or something that once was."

Cora reached over and held onto his hand.

"A mother will always care for her child. Whether it's gone off on its own or been taken away, she'll always be comfort and home for that child. Seems to me Jenny is stuck in that fog in her mind and I believe she's drawn to one of those shadows and she searches and reaches out, but can never get a firm grip on who or just exactly what it is. It's all a big scramble, you know? And maybe that's all she'll ever get, but I got to hope Tom, that it's enough."

"What about my daddy?"

Cora shook her head.

"I wish I had answers for you. But I don't. Jenny never mentioned his name. She'd written him before you were born. I think he was stationed somewhere in Africa. I don't know if he ever received the letters or knew she was with child or if he's even alive today. And, of course, with the complications from the birth… "

Tom watched as Jenny brought a rusty steel bucket to the well and hammered the pump, the water coming out in spurts. She filled the bucket and some of the water sloshed over the rim as she carried the pail back to the mule. She stood and placed her hand on her hip as she watched the mule drink.

"Thank you," he said, with a squeeze of Cora's hand. He

stood and walked over to the fence. Job raised his head to acknowledge him and water dripped from his muzzle. Tom reached over and rubbed the white mark on his forehead and the mule lowered his head, drinking more from the bucket.

"You take good care of him," he said.

"Yes," Jenny said.

"He's lucky."

"Yes."

"I'd like to visit some more."

"Yes."

"Would you like that?"

"All right."

Tom slowly reached up and placed his hand on his mother's shoulder. She flinched for a second and then relaxed. They stood there and watched the mule drink until the sun dropped near the top of the levee.

"I have to go, but I'll be back," he said.

"Yes."

Tom squeezed her shoulder softly and turned to leave. He walked four steps along the fence, his eyes on the path before him, when he heard his mother's voice.

"Tom," she said.

When he turned, he saw her standing still beside the fence. The sun's light, its late afternoon magic, fell softly on her shoulders and Jenny raised her hand.

"Tom," she said.

And he raised his hand and said, "Mom."

And he turned and walked and tears blurred his vision. All Tom saw were shadows, and he followed them.

CHAPTER 34

As the Fairlane picked up speed, Tom glanced in his rearview mirror and smiled.

Jenny's eyes were closed, her head outside the open window, the sun warming her face and the spring wind leaving her hair in a sandy brown halo. Cora winked at him from her seat opposite Jenny and placed her hand on Joshua's head. The boy sat between them, his stubby fingers on Jenny's leg and he asked for Tom to turn the radio louder.

Tom did so and his hand reached across the seat for Mary's and they shared a glance and he wanted to pull over and kiss her right then. But instead, he pressed down on the accelerator and they sang as the Fairlane growled and the miles between Taylor's Ferry and Morgan's Gap evaporated.

Mrs. Tyner had not balked when Tom had asked if it was OK for him to invite some friends over that Saturday. In fact, she told him to gather the grill and charcoal from the garage and announced they'd dine under the clouds. She'd then gone into her den in search of Johnny Mathis records.

"A bit of Mathis is a proper appetizer to a picnic," she said, her back to Tom as her fingers thumbed through her EPs.

So, when Tom pulled the Fairlane into Mrs. Tyner's drive

and shut off the engine, he was not surprised to hear Mathis singing of "Chances Are." He breathed in the spring air and it filled his lungs. The first buds had begun to appear on the maples and Easter flowers shot green stems up from the black dirt, seeking the sunlight.

He took Jenny's hand in his.

"Ok?" he asked.

"All right," she said.

Mary and Joshua went before them, while Cora followed behind as they made their way to the backyard. They turned the corner and Tom saw Stick tending the grill. The deputy, who was not in uniform, was watching the briquets turn white, when Mrs. Tyner walked out with a plate of hamburger meat smashed into a dozen patties. She peered over Stick's shoulder, eyed the coals and patted him on the shoulder.

"That will do," she said, handing him the plate and a spatula. Tom noticed Mrs. Tyner had changed into a yellow floral print dress that went just to her knees and a red band held back her carefully brushed hair. He thought he even detected a smudge of peach color on her lips. Tom chuckled to himself, remembering the morning a few months earlier when she'd stood in the backyard in her tattered nightgown, a spent shotgun half-cocked in her arms and a flock of starlings filling the gray sky.

"You know, it's not the king and queen of England dining with us," Tom said with a loud voice.

Mrs. Tyner looked up and clapped her hands. "Oh, Thomas. You devil you."

She opened her arms. "Everyone, everyone welcome."

Tom had stepped forward to make the introductions when

there was a sudden opening of the back door and JC stepped out, an open glass in one hand and an empty pitcher in another.

"Elizabeth, I'm not finding that lemon you speak of…" He stopped when he noticed the crowd before him. He smiled a deep grin.

"Mr. Crutchfield."

"Mr. Wheeler."

Tom looked at Mrs. Tyner and there was a slight blush along her neckline.

"Junious," she said. "I told you there was a bowl full in the bottom of the refrigerator."

Joshua stepped forward. "I like lemonade."

JC nodded. "Well, young squire, how about if you and I go in search of lemons, then?" He bowed again. "Ladies, if you'll excuse us."

Tom then made introductions. And when he came to Jenny, he said, "Mrs. Tyner. This is my mother, Jenny."

And Mrs. Tyner clasped her hands together and brought them to her lips. And there were tears in her eyes.

"Jennifer Flowers. Such a talented, talented student you were. You are a treasure, Miss Flowers, and I am very, very happy to have you here at my home." Mrs. Tyner reached out and took Cora's hand in hers. "You and your dear mother are always welcome here."

As Mrs. Tyner showed them the forsythia in their yellow bloom, Tom and Mary joined Stick at the grill.

"You look comfortable with a spatula in your hand," Tom said. "Sheriff know about that?"

Stick grinned. "Wait till you see what I'm doing with the potatoes and peppers. A felony of fine cuisine, reporter."

The deputy leaned closer and lowered his voice. "The other

day, I stuck a can of Stroh's inside a chicken and put in on the grill for 30 minutes."

Mary and Tom looked at each other. "Up the chicken's rear?" Tom asked.

"Fiiinnnneeee eating, Tom. Damn fine eating."

All three of them laughed and watched as Joshua and JC exited the house, the boy holding the pitcher of lemonade. Mrs. Tyner and Jenny and Cora joined them and they stood together and talked of the warming weather, Joshua's learning of addition and subtraction, and Cora telling them of how Tom had fixed some loose planks of fence and now Job didn't wander off as often.

"He's a good son," Cora had said and Tom had smiled.

Suddenly, there was the sound of a motor stopping and the opening and shutting of car doors. Tom took a few steps down the driveway, saw who had arrived and turned back to those gathered.

"And now," he said. "My surprise."

Edna Crutchfield loved Johnny Mathis and Tom remembered watching her and his father dance in the great room while a fire burned in the hearth and snow fell outside. He'd been just a teenager then and had no idea of just how big and complicated the world was beyond Valley Station and that great room and the warm fireplace.

Now, as he greeted his mother and father outside Mrs. Tyner's home on this April day, Tom realized his life had changed a great deal in just three months.

He had a full-time job at the newspaper and a month earlier, not long after they buried Dutch Blackburn, he'd called his mother and told her he'd met a nice girl named Mary and they were good friends, maybe more. He said she was smart and kind and she called him city mouse. "She sounds nice," his mother had said. He told her that Mary had a 6-year-old son named Joshua who liked to climb things, take rides in Tom's car, and had a sudden fascination with dinosaurs.

And he had invited his mother and father to Morgan's Gap to meet his boss, his friends and the girl and little boy he'd fallen in love with. And so they stood.

His mother hugged him and kissed his cheek when he greeted her.

"You've gotten thin," she said, her hand brushing away a stray winged seed that fell from the maple.

His father gripped his hand and looked at the two-story before him. "Quite the home," he said.

Tom grinned. "That's Mrs. Tyner's. My place is around back. Above the garage."

"Of course."

Tom took his mother's hand. "Come on, let me introduce you to everyone."

Tom brought Mr. and Mrs. Crutchfield around the back and the conversation stopped. Tom stepped forward, his hand still in his mother's.

"Everybody, this is my mother and father, Edna and Owen Crutchfield. Mom and dad, this is everybody."

The three of them stood and there was near silence as the record changed. Suddenly, Jenny stepped forward and nodded at Mr. and Mrs. Crutchfield.

"All right," she said.

And there was a chuckle from JC, then Stick and Mary and soon everyone joined in.

Tom turned to his parents and they could see in his face what he meant to tell them.

"That's her?" his mother asked.

"That's Jenny," Tom said. "She found me first. She was there the entire time and I just couldn't see her."

Edna Crutchfield stepped to Jenny and offered her hands. Jenny bit at her lip, her eyes looking to Cora first and then Tom. He nodded. And she took Edna's hands.

"Dear, dear Jenny," Edna said. "You gave me the most wonderful gift and I'm forever grateful. We loved him as best we could. As any mother and father could."

She paused. "Can I hug you?"

Jenny nodded. "All right."

And Edna pulled Jenny close and they embraced and Owen Crutchfield placed his hand on his wife's shoulder and Tom would later swear that he saw his father brush away a tear.

Then Tom brought Mary and Joshua close and he introduced his mother and father to his future. Joshua told them of his secret place and how only Tom knew where it was. And Mary blushed when Tom said, "This is my Mary, Mom."

JC soon pulled Tom's father off to the side and told him of the need to build another bridge to Illinois and a four-lane highway similar to those parkways Crutchfield Construction was building in Appalachia. Cora and his mother sat in chairs and watched as Jenny tossed a ball with Joshua.

Mary came to him and his gaze lingered, appreciating the way the wind shifted the strands of her brown hair and how the tail of her white cotton blouse came untucked from her knee-length jeans when she moved to tuck the wayward locks back behind her ear.

"You look very nice," he said and took her hand. She smiled and her hand was warm in his.

Then, Mrs. Tyner brought out glasses of tea and they had burgers, fries, grilled peppers and a salad. Joshua told them of a salamander that he'd caught that morning while he and Fergus walked along the fence line.

"Did you keep it?" Mrs. Tyner asked in all seriousness.

"Of course he did," Mary said. And they all shared a laugh.

Mrs. Tyner brought out red jello and they spooned the dessert from bowls while they sat on the grass beneath a willow oak. Tom listened as Mary spoke of how she'd grown up in Taylor's Ferry and how, at one time, she thought she'd like to be a dentist. But things had happened and she was no longer certain if that was the right vocation for her. Still, she'd enrolled in classes at the community college this summer and Joshua was excited to be starting first grade that fall.

Mrs. Tyner brought out a framed, black-and-white photo of her husband, Nicholas. In his airman's suit, he stood with legs spaced apart and hands clasped together, behind him a P-51 Mustang fighter plane.

"Your husband flew that?" Joshua asked.

"He did. Many, many times."

"Did he ever take you flying?"

Mrs. Tyner patted Joshua's hand.

"Once. Right after he got his pilot's license. We went up and all I could see were wispas of white clouds above me. And when I glanced down, it was all just a patchwork of green woods, fields of yellow corn and that Ohio River, muddy and brown. I still can recall the way the sunlight reflected off the water and Nicholas reaching over to hold my hand."

She paused and looked at those gathered around her. "It was all so much. I felt as though I was flying with angels."

"I would have been scared," Joshua said.

Mrs. Tyner smiled and her hand went down to rub at the gold wedding band she still wore on her thin finger.

"I had Nicholas," she said. "He was with me the whole time. There was nothing to be afraid of."

Tom noticed Mathis was no longer playing through the open window. He watched as Joshua picked up a wooden stick and pressed it into the ground, its blunt point lifting the grass and exposing the brown dirt beneath.

"I bet you miss him," Joshua said.

Mrs. Tyner reached over and hugged the boy close.

"More so every day," she said. "More so every day."

Stick, with Joshua's help, covered the grill and Mary and Mrs. Tyner took the plates inside the kitchen. Tom walked his parents out to their car. He shook his father's hand and then held the door open for his mother.

Edna leaned in close and whispered, "She's a keeper, Thomas."

"I've come to realize that," he said.

"And that boy, he is something special."

"That he is."

She looked around her.

"You found what you were looking for?" his mother asked.

"I have, mom."

"And you're happy?"

"Very."

"That's all a mother can wish for," she said, leaning upward to kiss his cheek. Tom shut her door and leaned into the car window. "Thank you," he said.

"What's that?" asked his father.

"Thank you. For coming here today. For being you. For being mom and dad."

His mother patted his hand and his father nodded. Tom waved as his parents drove off and then turned to head back to the party. Jenny stood there in the shadows, eyes down, but still on him.

"All right?" she asked.

"All right," he said and took her hand.

CHAPTER 35

IT WAS NEAR dusk when Tom and Mary walked along the top of the levee.

Across the Ohio, they could see the Illinois farmlands where farmers had started breaking the ground. Tractors pulled plows along, trailing behind them a ribbon of rich, brown dirt. The farmers would disc the fields soon and then plant seed. Rain would fall and, if the river didn't rise, the corn and beans would grow until the summer sun turned the plants brown. And then the men and their machinery would return to reap the harvest, leaving the land to heal over the winter, to be reborn in the spring.

The ritual was the same as that of the many years before and the many years to come.

Tom and Mary walked down the slope of the levee, then along the gravel river road to the Taylor's Ferry boat ramp. The parking lot was nearly empty, nowhere as busy as that day after Christmas when he arrived. Nearby, a fisherman was at work, storing his rods in the back of his truck, water still dripping from the back of his trailer, the sides of his boat wet.

"Any luck?" Tom asked.

The man looked up at the two of them and shook his head.

"You're doing much better," he said.

Tom laughed and put his arm around Mary. They walked to the water's edge and the waves lapped at their shoes. Upriver, a barge stirred and they heard its air horn before they saw its white bulk as it came around the bend in the river.

"Do you think he'll ever surface?" Mary asked.

Tom shrugged.

"Does it change anything? Seems like most folks are moving on. It's like JC says, 'Mr Crutchfield, there will always be another week and another newspaper. Time marches on.'"

Mary pulled a flat, black piece of shale from the water's edge, weighed it in her hand, then flung it sidearmed — the two of them watching it skip across the calm waters two, three, four, five, six times until it sank.

Tom reached down and grabbed his own rock. He tossed it at the water and it sank after just one cross.

Mary laughed. "City mouse."

He grabbed her around the hips and pulled her close. The late afternoon light fell upon her face and he could hear the sound of frogs stirring in the backwaters.

"Oh, Mary. What will I do with you?"

"What will you?"

"Do we have to decide today?"

She cocked her head. "I've often heard my daddy say, "Either fish or cut bait.'"

He smiled. "Country mouse."

"You planning to go somewhere?"

Tom looked out at the river, the wake from the barge growing in size and nearing the shore.

"I've nowhere to be," he said. "I think I've found my home."

He reached down and pulled off his socks and shoes. Mary

watched and then did the same. And the two of them didn't run when the wake from the barge came and covered their bare feet. Instead, Tom pulled her closer, the river cool against their skin, and they watched the tow churn the waters till the sun sank below the western hills.

And Tom was content, knowing another day would come and the Ohio would still flow south to Ledbetter and Cairo and ports beyond, its current dragging along secrets and desires, while carrying hopes and dreams. Life, never a straight shot, but one made ready for each bend in the river.

Mailing List

Bend In The River is my first novel.

And there are more to come.

If you're not already, I'll hope you'll sign up for my author newsletter. You'll be the first to know of new releases and get access to occasional discounts, signed editions and even free stories.

I'll not share your email. I'm not that guy. And you can unsubscribe at any time.

Sign up at:
www.authormichaelbanks.com

Also, you can follow me via the various forms of social media. It's a good place to converse and keep up to date with what's going on in this writer's journey.

Thanks again for reading. Keep in touch.

REVIEW

I hope you enjoyed Bend In the River. Would you do me a favor?

Like all authors, I rely on online reviews to encourage future sales. Your opinion is invaluable. Would you take a few moments now to share your assessment of my book — even if it's just a few lines — at the review site of your choice? Your opinion will help the book marketplace become more transparent and useful to all.

Many thanks.

ACKNOWLEDGEMENTS

THIS IS A story inspired by the place I still call home.

Though I've been gone 25 years now, I treasure that part of Kentucky where its never-ending fields of corn and soybeans sprout over layers of coal. Woodlands and hills are bordered by the Ohio River to the north and west. Its people are as true and complicated and generous and wary as the winters are harsh and the summers humid.

Bend In The River is a complete work of fiction, but in writing this story I pulled from my mind bits and pieces from the places and people I know. I'm proud to say I'm a product of Western Kentucky. Most of my relatives still call it home and it's probably where my bones will eventually be buried. I hope this novel reflects the love and respect I have for that part of Kentucky and the people who live there.

It was 2019 when I turned to my wife and told her of a story that sat in my mind when dreams did not come. "I think I want to write a novel," I said. "Then, let's do it," she answered.

The path to publication was filled with starts, stops and plenty of pauses. There was Covid and a job layoff. There were good days and bad. And there were a great many people who helped along the way.

The talented folks at Charlotte Lit — Kathie Collins, Paul Reali, Megan Rich and Kim Wright — provided the guidance and encouragement as I began this writing journey. I'm forever thankful for the various instructors and my fellow Author's Lab members, who may have chuckled and silently groaned when reading my first attempts at dialogue while wading through the muddy middle.

I would be nowhere without my readers and fellow writers: Curtis Crockett, Axel Dahlberg, Betsy Dreier, Karen Garloch, Matt Myers, Gala Palmer, Dimpal Patel, Andrea Reimers and Regan Shaw. Special thanks to Jeremy Dreier, who has a shared appreciation for mules and disdain for intransitive verbs; and Joan Ruark, who can weave a love story much better than I and spot a flawed character arc from a mile away.

The writing journey is long and often requires hours at the keyboard — time that could be spent with family and friends. I'll always remember the sacrifice and encouragement shown by those named Banks, Robinson, Yoder, Phillips, Kerner, Law, Stowers, Smith and Gordon. Know that I'm grateful to call you all family.

To my sister, Stacie Banks, you keep doing you. You're dang smart, driven and can be quite funny given the right circumstance. It's nice to be known as "Stacie's older brother."

My mom, Linda Banks, drove me to Grove Center to the bookmobile where I checked out books about Davy Crockett and she later bought me my first typewriter. I do believe she's saved everything I've ever written. She's been my biggest cheerleader and the first one to tell me, "You've got a novel in you, son." Love you, momma.

And, finally, all my love to my wife, Danette. She's the one who supported us while I wrote this book, prodded me when I felt like taking a day off, and encouraged me when I thought it was nothing but garbage. She read, edited and re-read all 85,000 words. This story is as much her as it is me.

I know I'm a better writer and, more importantly, a better man because of her.

Christ is in me and I am enough.

— July 23, 2025

About the Author

Michael Banks is an award-winning journalist who spent 30 years working at newspapers in Kentucky, North Carolina and Mississippi. He is a regular contributor to *South Carolina Living* magazine and his work has been recognized by the Charlotte Writers Club and *Litmosphere*, the journal of the Charlotte Center for Literary Arts. This is his first novel. He and his wife, Danette, reside in Belmont, NC, with a pair of cats who have the misguided belief they rule the roost.